I0773535

The
Only Death
That Matters

a 509 Crime Story

by Colin Conway

The Only Death That Matters

Copyright © 2022 Colin Conway

All rights reserved. No portion of this book may be reproduced or used in any form without the prior written permission of the copyright owner(s), except for the use of brief quotations in a book review.

ISBN: 979-8-9859409-5-4

Cover Design by Zach McCain

Original Ink Press, an imprint of High Speed Creative, LLC
1521 N. Argonne Road, #C-205
Spokane Valley, WA 99212

This is a work of fiction. While real locations add authenticity to the story, all characters appearing in this book are fictitious. Any resemblance to actual persons, living or dead, is purely coincidental.

Visit the author's website at www.colinconway.com

What is the 509?

Separated by the Cascade Range, Washington State is divided into two distinctly different climates and cultures.

The western side of the Cascades is home to Seattle, its 34 inches of annual rainfall, and the incredibly weird and smelly Gum Wall. Most of the state's wealth and political power are concentrated in and around this enormous city. The residents of this area know the prosperity that has come from being the home of Microsoft, Amazon, Boeing, and Starbucks.

To the east of the Cascade Mountains lies nearly two-thirds of the entire state, a lot of which is used for agriculture. Washington State leads the nation in producing apples, it is the second-largest potato grower, and it's the fourth for providing wheat.

This eastern part of the state can enjoy more than 170 days of sunshine each year, which is important when there are more than 200 lakes nearby. However, the beautiful summers are offset by harsh winters, with average snowfall reaching 47 inches and the average high hovering around 37°.

While five telephone area codes provide service to the westside, only 509 covers everything east of the Cascades, a staggering twenty-one counties.

Of these, Spokane County is the largest with an estimated population of 506,000.

Even good men die screaming.

-        Kevin Smith

The Only Death That Matters

PART I

Chapter 1

When Ray Christy stepped into the office, he immediately stopped. Irene Herbison stood there with a look of concern frozen on her face.

"What's the matter?" Ray asked.

Irene pointed at a silver-haired man sitting behind the reception desk.

Vern Kuehn slouched awkwardly in the chair, which pressed his chin against his chest. Vern was a heavy-set man with a jowly face made worse by this position. His arms hung limply from his sides like two static pendulums.

"Is he dead?" Irene whispered.

Ray Christy frowned. "How should I know?"

"You're good at this kind of stuff."

The late afternoon sun beamed through the western windows and bathed the third-floor office in a yellowish haze. Particles of dust floated in the air.

Ray slowly moved around the desk. "He's probably sleeping."

They were in the lobby of Volunteer Services, a unit within the Spokane Police Department. Most of the SPD was in the neighboring Public Safety Building or the recently constructed Gardner Building. Only Volunteer Services and a couple of non-standard units remained in the privately-owned Monroe Court Building.

An hour before, the entire Volunteer Services office had walked over to the PSB to attend an award ceremony in the department's roll-call room. Just Vern stuck around to staff the Volunteer Services' office. Ray wanted that assignment, but Sergeant Newman insisted he go along.

The sergeant was concerned about appearances and decided Vern was better suited for staying behind.

After the ceremony, Irene returned immediately to the office with Ray a minute behind. He'd been slowed by a well-meaning chaplain.

Ray held the back of his hand directly above Vern's mouth.

"Should we call an ambulance?" Irene asked.

"No." Ray playfully punched Vern in the shoulder. "Wake up, deadbeat."

Irene walked around the desk to stand next to Ray. She was a petite woman and stood several inches shorter than him. "Maybe his hearing aids are off."

"At the front desk?"

She shrugged. "It could be what he does. I don't know him well enough."

Again, Ray punched Vern in the shoulder—harder this time. "Get up."

"Should you be hitting him? Maybe he's dead."

"He's not dead."

"Are you sure?"

Ray grabbed the chair and shook it. Vern slid sideways from his position. The sudden movement caused the man to snort and grunt. His head snapped back, and he popped upright to his feet. He lifted his hands into a boxer's stance, but no one stood in front of him. Then Vern looked to his left and saw Ray and Irene. His gaze continued down to Ray's hand still on the back of the chair. "Hey! What's the big idea?"

"You were asleep."

Vern's eyes widened, and he glanced to Irene. She nodded in agreement.

"Did anyone else see?"

"Just us," Irene said, "but everyone should be headed this way."

"The award ceremony is over?" Vern plopped into his chair. It groaned its displeasure. The man rubbed his face with both hands. "I guess I should say thank you."

"No need," Ray said. "You would have done it for us."

Now, Vern massaged his left shoulder. "Yeah. I guess I would have."

"Are you okay being on the desk? Can't have you catching forty winks if the sergeant walks in."

"Won't happen again."

"You sure?" Ray asked.

"I said it won't happen again." Vern angrily pulled himself in tight to the desk. He busied himself with some paperwork.

Ray eyed Irene then jerked his head—a signal for them to leave. They proceeded deeper into the office.

She said, "Vern doesn't seem to appreciate what we did for him."

"Doesn't matter."

"If the sergeant found him, he might have gotten dismissed from the program."

"I doubt it." Ray sat at his cubicle. "Others have done worse. Besides, it's not my problem."

Irene crossed her arms and leaned against the divider wall. "How's it not your problem, Ray? You're head of the program."

"I'm not the head."

"Unofficially."

He raised an eyebrow.

"Everyone looks to you as the leader. I know I do."

"Newman is the leader."

Irene waggled a manicured finger. "The sergeant is only making time until the next rotation."

"Marking time. He's *marking* time until the next rotation."

"That's what I said." Irene winked. "And Sergeant Newman doesn't care about this program. As far as he's concerned, this is some sort of punishment."

Ray pulled out the volunteer schedule. "I don't know what he thinks."

"Yes, you do." Irene leaned in close to whisper into his ear. "You know a lot about a lot, Ray Christy." He detected her perfume now. Unlike the other women in the program, she only wore a hint of fragrance, and it could only be smelled when very close. "Stop playing so hard to get."

He did his best not to make eye contact and concentrated intently on the calendar.

Her breath was warm in his ear. "And you know exactly what I'm talking about."

When she left, Irene dragged her hand along his shoulders. Ray was happy she was gone. The woman was too damn distracting. All the men in the program thought the same thing—even some of the younger ones.

More voices floated through the office now. The others were returning from the award ceremony.

"Hey, Christy."

Ray looked up as Sergeant Brandon Newman approached his desk. He crossed his arms and leaned against the cubicle. It was the same position that Irene had taken only moments before.

"Sir?"

"Why'd you take off so quick? Chief Dillon was asking about you. You guys know each other or something?"

Ray held up the scheduling calendar. "I wanted to make sure things are covered for the weekend."

Newman flicked the piece of paper with a finger. "Why print that off? Use the computer and save a tree."

"I like it better this way."

"But it's not up-to-date." The sergeant pointed at a name. "Mel canceled his weekend shifts. Something to do with a hernia, I think."

"Mel's got a hernia?"

Newman shrugged. "Or something."

"Who's covering his assignments?"

"No one. But it's not a big deal. Let it slide."

Mel Dolan was scheduled for two hours of vacation checks on Saturday and Sunday. Citizens could call into the department and request a drive-by of their homes while they were gone. It was a service that the Volunteer Services department provided. Mostly, it was Ray's group that did it since members of the Explorer and Co-Op programs were too busy playing with their phones, and the Reservists were too busy pretending that they were cops.

Ray grabbed a pen and lined through Mel's time slots on both days.

Sergeant Newman said, "Get one of the explorers to print a new calendar for you."

"I can print it for myself. I know how to use a computer."

"I didn't say you didn't. I was only suggesting." Newman looked up and smiled. "Cake's here." He absently patted Ray's shoulder. "Take it easy, Christy."

When the sergeant walked away, Ray muttered, "*You* take it easy."

Ray stood and looked around. The office teemed with the activity of a celebration. Several of the volunteers carried a large cake, bags of potato chips, and soda bottles. A few college-aged kids laughed and excitedly moved around. Thankfully, none of the high school kids were there—they were still in class.

He disliked it when the office got this way, especially when it was over something he didn't believe was deserved. He grabbed a set of keys from his top drawer and headed for the exit.

At the front desk, Ray asked Vern Kuehn, "Need anything delivered?"

The heavy-set man exaggeratedly searched his desk. "I don't think so."

"Then I'm going out for a bit."

Vern smiled. "Where to?"

"One of the shops."

"Which one?"

"Are we married?"

Vern's smile vanished, and his brow furrowed. "Huh?"

"If anyone asks, I'll be back in an hour."

Without waiting for Vern's reply, Ray slipped out of the Volunteer Services office.

***

A male voice called out in the parking lot, "Hey, Ray! Hold up."

Ray stopped and searched for the voice. He found its owner—Chief Liam Dillon—talking with a woman in a suit. Dillon lifted a finger for Ray to wait.

He slowly walked in the direction of the chief. Dillon was about twenty years younger and built like an aging linebacker. His bald head gleamed in the morning sun.

The chief broke away from his conversation and approached with a smile. "How you doing, my friend?" He extended his hand, and Ray shook it.

"I'm good, Chief."

"We've talked about this, Ray. Call me Liam. No one's around."

"You're in uniform, sir. It's old habit."

"Roger that." Dillon put his arm around Ray's

shoulder and smiled genuinely. "But when I'm out of uniform, it's Liam. I missed you after the award ceremony."

"I'm sorry about that. I had to leave to take care of some errands."

"Is that where you're headed now?"

Ray nodded. "Unless you need me to do something. I can put it on hold for a bit."

"No, no. Do what you've gotta do." Dillon removed his arm from Ray's shoulders. He kept his hand on Ray's upper arm, though. It was a friendly gesture, much the way Ray used to do with his father. "We haven't gotten coffee or lunch in a while, and I'd love to catch up. How's next week?"

"I'm free most days."

The chief pulled his phone from a back pocket and consulted it. "I can't do Monday." He looked up. "Let's do lunch on Tuesday. My treat."

Ray smiled. "That sounds fine."

"Then it's a date." The chief's fingers bounced over his phone's screen. "Swing by my office on Tuesday around noon. I'll drive."

"I'll be there."

"Maybe we can try that new barbecue joint downtown." Dillon patted Ray's upper arm. "Good to see you, pal. Until next week."

Ray watched him head into the Monroe Court Building.

Chapter 2

Ray Christy parked his car along the curb and climbed out. It took less than five minutes to get to the COPS West office. A brass bell tinkled when he walked into the building.

A woman sat behind the counter. Kay Wenzel lifted a hand as a smile of recognition spread across her lips. Frizzy hair peaked out from beneath a tattered Spokane Indians baseball hat. "Raymond Christy. What brings you to our humble abode?"

"Hi ya, Kay. Is Cliff in?"

"He's always in." She turned her head as if about to share a secret. "What he's up to is another story." Kay chuckled, then thumbed toward the back.

Ray stepped around the counter.

"Don't be a stranger."

He nodded but didn't respond. Instead, Ray headed into the back. He passed a couple of offices used by Department of Corrections officers. The lights were off, which meant the occupants were likely in the field. It was Friday, so perhaps the officers were attempting a last contact with some of their probationary clients before the weekend. Or maybe the C.O.s cut out early to get a jump on their days off.

In the back office, Clifford Beck stood in front of a large metal cabinet. A folder lay splayed out on an open drawer. He turned when Ray knocked on the door jamb.

"Buddy boy!" Cliff grinned, which widened his already broad face. He stood over six and a half feet tall and weighed close to three hundred pounds. "What are you up to?"

"Needed some space." Ray dropped into one of the leather and metal chairs that sat in front of Cliff's desk.

"Ol' Monkey Court was getting a bit crowded, huh?"

Ray never cared for Cliff's nickname of the Monroe Court Building. However, since Sergeant Newman took over the volunteer program, the term seemed more appropriate.

He absently fingered the identification card clipped to his left breast pocket. "There was an award ceremony today."

"Yeah?" Cliff shoved the manila folder back into place and closed the drawer. "Who got pinned?"

"Newman. They gave him a Life Saving Award."

"That pencil pusher? You're kidding. For what?"

"For that time he used the paddles on Wally."

Cliff settled into his chair. "Wally's heart attack? But he died."

"Not that day. And Newman's chain of command wanted to make a stink about it."

"It stinks all right. What was their reasoning behind the award?"

"Newman's quick thinking." Ray air-quoted his statement because Sergeant Newman's lieutenant had said those exact words. According to the administration, Newman's 'quick thinking and decisive action' resulted in saving Senior Volunteer Wallace Owens.

Cliff leaned back in his chair. "Newman deserves a Life Saving Award like he deserves a Medal of Merit."

"He's already got one of those."

"You're kidding." Cliff's chair fell forward. "That place is as bad as the government."

"It *is* the government."

"You know what I mean."

Ray nodded. "Yeah, I know what you mean."

"Did you come out here to raise my blood pressure, or

was there some other reason?"

"The whole office is celebrating Newman's award, so I figured I'd come over and lay low for a few minutes. If that's okay with you, that is."

"Of course, it's okay. You're always welcome here. Hell, you should quit that program and join us. We need men of your caliber."

Ray smiled. "I appreciate it, but I like it there."

"You're a glutton for punishment."

"Newman will be gone soon enough. There've been good people in charge before. I'll outlast that sycophantic bastard."

"What if they bring in someone worse?"

"Than Newman? It won't happen. Besides, you could always dump this shop and ride with me."

Cliff spread his arms wide. "And give up my kingdom? I'm the big boss around here."

"You answer to a director who answers to a board."

"We all answer to someone, Ray."

He crossed his legs. "Isn't that the truth?"

"Enough shop talk, buddy boy. What are your plans for the weekend?"

"I've got to cover a couple shifts this weekend. Nothing else, really."

"Plans for tonight?"

Ray rubbed his aching knee. "Dinner with Audrey."

Cliff's face slackened. "Yeah? How's she doing?"

"The same. Maybe we'll watch the game."

"Who's playing?"

"Shadle Park and Mead. They play it on that one channel."

"Friday night football. Good stuff." Cliff tapped his desk with a single finger. "Is your grandson playing?"

Ray nodded. "Starting safety. First year on varsity."

"That's fantastic. I mean it."

"What about you?" Ray asked. "Anything on the weekend docket?"

"June and I are staying home. She's got a bunch of honey-dos for me. Just how I like it." Cliff smiled, but it quickly dimmed.

Ray interlaced his fingers around his arthritic knee and tried to ignore the pain. "I'm happy for you, Cliff. Enjoy those chores while you can."

The two men chatted for a couple of minutes further, and then Ray checked his watch. "Listen, I should get back. The party is probably fading by now."

Cliff stood. "I understand. The grindstone waits for no man."

***

"Hey, Christy," Sergeant Newman called from his office.

Ray leaned back in his chair to look at the man. In the world of policing, Brandon Newman was a climber. The rumor was that he'd been promoted as fast as he could from patrol officer to detective and then to sergeant. He completely skipped the corporal rank.

As a retired Army first sergeant, Ray thought jumping over corporal was a horrible idea. Although the police department considered detective and corporal the same rank level, a detective did not provide an opportunity for leadership growth.

Detectives handled caseloads while corporals were essentially evidence specialists within the patrol ranks. However, a corporal would occasionally fill in for an absent sergeant and get necessary exposure to leading a group of officers.

Since the department didn't make corporal a required rank, that meant officers like Brandon Newman tested their way into leadership positions without previous management experience. That bothered Ray.

Hell, a lot of things bothered Ray these days.

"Come here," Newman ordered.

Ray entered the sergeant's office and waited. Sergeant Newman was in his mid-thirties. His short dark hair was combed in a businessman's style. His mustache was too long for Ray's liking. It made Newman appear smarmy, but Ray didn't care for facial hair. He thought any man who wore a beard or a mustache was trying to hide something. He'd read that in a magazine many years ago, and the concept struck a chord with him. He shaved off his mustache after reading it.

Sergeant Newman asked, "Is there a problem?"

"Sir?" He relished calling Newman 'sir.' That would have been an affront to any career non-commissioned officer, but Newman never seemed to mind. And why would he? Ray thought. The man would soon test his way into a lieutenant position.

The sergeant's eyes narrowed. "You didn't hang around for the celebration."

"I had a personal matter to attend to."

"Yeah?" Newman crossed his arms. "What?"

"It was personal."

Something white clung to the tip of Newman's mustache. Ray's gaze flicked to the trash can at the side of the sergeant's desk. A paper plate rested on top. It appeared to have the remnants of cake on it. Near Newman's elbow was yet another plate with a second piece of cake.

"Over at the award ceremony," Newman said, "it looked like you ate a lemon."

Ray thought he'd hidden his displeasure better than that.

Newman continued. "And you bolted out of there as

soon as it was over and came back to the office. Then you split from here when the celebration started. I didn't even see you take a piece of cake. You like cake, don't you?"

Ray wanted to say he'd never been much of a cake-eater, but he figured that Newman might be clever enough to pick up on the insult. Instead, Ray answered with a simple, "Sure."

"Then what's the deal?"

He shrugged. "Like I said, it was a personal matter."

"Was this related to your wife?"

"No."

Newman lifted his hands. "Relax. I'm just asking."

"I'll go have a piece of cake now."

"There's none left."

Ray eyed the uneaten piece of cake on the corner of Newman's desk.

"You sure you're doing okay, Christy?"

"I'm fine."

"If you say so. It's just that I'm worried about you."

The words rang hollow in Ray's ears.

"Don't take it personally. I worry about all my people."

Ray doubted that very much.

"If you got a problem," the sergeant continued, "you can always talk to me. You know that, right?"

The sergeant's offer sounded emptier than his proclamation of worrying about all his people.

"I'm fine," Ray repeated.

"Okay. Just checking." Newman motioned toward the door. "That's all."

Ray hesitated long enough to watch the sergeant reach for the second piece of cake. He turned and left.

***

"How was your day?" Ray asked Audrey.

"I don't know." She scooped her mashed potatoes with a fork then studied them.

"You don't know?"

Audrey shook her head, then scooped some more potatoes onto the utensil and again studied them. Her hazel eyes were dark, and bags hung under them. Audrey's once brown hair was gray and haphazardly combed.

She had probably taken several naps today, which wrinkled her clothes. They weren't creased when she'd gotten them because he did her laundry. Ray carefully ironed everything of hers as he did his own clothes—a habit born of his days in the military.

Overhead, Bobby Darin's "Beyond the Sea" played.

"What did you do today?" Ray asked.

Audrey tried for a third scoop, but that resulted in most of the potatoes pushing themselves off. She gave up and moved on to the entree. Ray watched as his wife sawed a piece of Salisbury steak. The knife barely cut through the meat, not because of its toughness but rather the lack of strength in her hands.

"Would you like me to cut that?" he asked.

She shook her head once then continued to drag the knife back and forth across the top of the meat.

Ray looked away and watched some of the others in the dining facility. Most were able to feed themselves as Audrey did, but a few needed help. He observed a nurse assist a man bound to a wheelchair. The man was roughly Ray's age, and the nurse resembled his youngest daughter. While she cut and scooped his dinner, the nurse seemed apathetic to the whole thing. Ray didn't blame her, though. Seeing this scene day after day as he did was disheartening. Actively participating in it had to deaden something inside.

The Colonial Springs Assisted Living Community was divided into two wings. Audrey started in the east wing, where less support was needed. Back then, she could still do many things by herself. Now that her disease had progressed further, she'd been moved to the west wing, where total care was provided.

The song on the radio changed to Nat King Cole's "Unforgettable."

Ray frowned. "Do you remember this song?"

Audrey stopped sawing her Salisbury steak and tilted her head to listen. "Yeah." She didn't sound as if she recalled it.

They danced to the song at their wedding.

Ray met Audrey while stationed at Ft. Hood, Texas— his first duty station when he returned home from the war. She had just graduated high school. They married shortly after her freshman year of college. A day hadn't gone by that he didn't feel like the luckiest man in the world.

Now, he hated the damn song because of its expired promises.

"So, Audrey, what *did* you do today?"

"I don't remember."

"Did you go to physical therapy?"

"I don't know."

"It was on your schedule."

Audrey finally freed a piece of meat and sunk her teeth into it. She chewed it with her mouth open. That was a habit she developed recently.

Ray stopped his questions and waited for her to swallow. As soon as she did, she scooped a forkful of potatoes.

"Would you like some?" she asked. She extended the fork toward him.

"I'm not hungry."

That wasn't true. He was hungry. However, Ray didn't eat with Audrey now. He had when she first came to the facility, but that was several years prior. Back then, he and Audrey could still hold some conversation. Like now, it was primarily one-sided, with Ray prompting and Audrey responding. As the months passed, though, Audrey's replies became less engaged until they were like today—mostly filled with "I don't remembers" and "I don't knows."

Eating with her now was a constant reminder of what he'd lost. Therefore, he preferred to sit by while she ate and not pretend it was like their life before.

"Logan is playing tonight," Ray said. When Audrey didn't respond, he added, "Your grandson."

She extended her knife and fork toward him. "Can you help?"

"Sure," he said. He took the utensils from her and pulled the plate closer. He easily cut the Salisbury steak into smaller bites. "Logan is playing tonight," he repeated.

"Who?"

"Your grandson."

Her eyes remained dark.

"Heidi's boy."

"The Realtor?"

"That's right." Ray smiled. "Your oldest daughter. She's a real estate agent."

"I like her." Her eyes did not light up at the statement.

Ray pushed the plate over to his wife. "You do like her." He handed the knife and fork back to Audrey. "We can watch the game on the TV in your room."

Audrey stabbed a piece of meat with her fork then studied it. "What game?"

"The football game. Logan is playing tonight."

She put the food in her mouth. "Who is that?"

***

Upon returning to his north side home, the first thing Ray did was refill a bowl of kibbles. He had no affinity for cats, but William was Audrey's, and she had loved the stupid thing like a child. He would take care of it for her.

When Audrey first went into Colonial Springs, a few of her friends offered to take William in, but Ray politely declined. He should have expected their concern. Throughout their marriage, Ray fussed to Audrey about how much he disliked cats. He didn't really care, though. It was just something he said to get Audrey's attention. She always wanted something to titter over and, as the kids grew older, the cats soon arrived. William was simply the latest to make her happy. Why wouldn't Ray want that?

But Ray liked to poke fun at his wife, especially since it was common knowledge in the family that she did not take it well. When they were young, all the children delighted in teasing their mother.

So, Ray made a stink about whichever cat they had, and Audrey would defend them all. It was a silly game they played until there was no longer anyone at home to tease about the worthless nature of a cat.

An old black tom sauntered into the kitchen to check out the food bowl.

"Well, hello, Billy. What's the verdict today?"

It sniffed the kibbles a couple of times before walking away.

"Good to see you, Bill. There's a new Doberman in the neighborhood. Maybe you should make its acquaintance." When William was out of the room, Ray smirked. "Stupid cat."

He started a small pot of decaffeinated coffee, then

made a peanut butter and jelly sandwich. Ray tossed a handful of salt & vinegar chips onto a plate, then went into the living room, where he turned on the television.

Ray Christy sat on the sofa and silently ate his dinner while watching his grandson play football. The game was already deep into the second quarter.

Chapter 3

"Refill, Ray?"

He peered into his nearly empty cup. "Sure. Thank you."

As she poured coffee, the server craned her head to look at the book that Ray had opened in front of him. "What are you reading this week?"

He closed the novel to show her the title along the spine. The dust jacket had gone missing long ago, and the book's plain brown edges were worn. No words graced its front.

She stopped the pour. "*Don't Stop the Carnival*. Never heard of it."

"It's old."

"Any good?"

Ray said, "It's probably the fifth time I've read it, so yeah."

"I don't think I've ever read anything twice. Seen plenty of movies more than once."

"Same thing."

Her name was Dana, but that's about all Ray knew of her. She had filled his coffee at this particular Shari's Restaurant most mornings for more than a year. She was never sick, never complained, and occasionally sang to herself. It was always the same song, though. Something Ray could never quite make out, but it had the same melody. She was at least twenty years his junior which put her about fifty.

"You must be working today," she said.

"What gave it away? The uniform?"

"But it's Saturday. Is there something special going on?"

"No. Just a regular day."

"Crime never sleeps, I guess."

He saluted her with his cup.

Dana lifted her chin. "What's it about?"

"Excuse me?"

"The story."

Ray put his hand on the book. "It's about Norman Paperman—a guy who leaves his New York job to chase a dream on a Caribbean Island."

"Norman Paperman?"

"Does that sound funny?"

Dana's head bobbled from side to side. "A little, yeah, but you've read it five times?"

"At least."

"Does it have a happy ending?"

"Far from it." Ray's index finger tapped the book. "His dream ends up soured."

"Sort of like life."

"When you think about it, I guess it kind of does."

Dana's laugh was without joy. "That's why I try not to think about it."

She walked away to refill another customer's cup.

***

Ray slowly drove through the Comstock neighborhood. Large trees loomed overhead and cast shadows across the street. The lawns in this neighborhood were lush and trim. The homes were nicely maintained. A couple of them were of mid-century modern construction and seemed out of place with their Craftsman-style neighbors.

No children played outside, which Ray thought

strange. It was nearly ten on a Saturday morning. Ray would have been outside until the sun went down when he was little. His son, Jacob, would have ridden his bike on a day such as this. His daughters, Heidi and Pamela, would have been outside with their respective friends.

Perhaps this latest generation of children was too attached to their electronic devices. Maybe it was the current crop of parents—too afraid to let their kids beyond their sight or too frightened to act like an adult by insisting their children go outside. Whatever the cause, the neighborhood was quiet. All the families were inside.

Ray went by a blue house. It appeared locked up. Cars were not parked out front. Newspapers waited uncollected in the driveway.

He shouldn't stop his car because doing so would further alert onlookers that the home was empty. The vacation check was simply a drive-by—an eyeball test—to see if everything looked okay. However, the stack of newspapers already told a would-be burglar the house was currently unoccupied. It was apparent the homeowner forgot to stop delivery before they left town.

Ray pulled to the side and parked. Then he gathered the newspapers, walked them to the front of the house, and stacked them neatly at the front door. Afterward, he completed a quick perimeter check of the home to make sure the doors and windows were intact and locked.

Once he left the neighborhood, Ray consulted his clipboard. He lined through the address he just passed. Eleven homes requested the vacation checks. This was an activity that Ray usually thought pointless, and he hated doing. Melvin Dolan loved doing them, however. But he canceled this weekend because of a hernia. At least, that's what Sergeant Newman said.

Ray made a mental note to check on Mel later.

The radio in the car squawked. *"Victor one-thirty."*

He again pulled to the side of the road before slipping the microphone from its holder. Ray keyed the Send button. "Victor-130."

"One-thirty, are you available for a call?"

Ray thought anything was better than the vacation checks. "Victor-130. Yes, I'm available. Where do you need me?"

"One-thirty, we've had a Found Property call waiting for some time. Would you divert from what you're doing and handle that? If so, let me know when you're ready for the particulars."

Even recovering lost property sounded more exciting than driving by empty homes.

***

When Ray entered the Denny's on Division Street, a cacophony of loud voices and scraping utensils greeted him. Several families waited in the lobby to be seated. A husband in his mid-fifties frowned. A younger father eyed Ray suspiciously. He ignored them both and approached the cashier's stand.

A server noticed him and hurried over. The nametag on her uniform read *Tyna*. She smiled kindly and said, "I'm sorry, sir. We've got a thirty-minute wait unless you want to sit at the counter."

"I'm here for a pick-up."

"Oh." She looked at the kitchen window. "You called in an order? What's the name?"

"No, ma'am. Someone reported a lost item. I'm here to pick it up."

Tyna faced him again. This time her eyes widened. "Right. I'm sorry. Let me go get it." She hurried away.

The customers in the lobby scrutinized Ray. He was used to that behavior because of his two-tone blue uniform. The patch on his arm read *Volunteer Services—Spokane Police Department*, but it was evident to most people that he was not a police officer. He didn't wear a gun or handcuffs. Senior volunteers carried a radio with them, but Ray left his in the car. It was against policy to do that when out on a call, but what was the administration going to do? Fire him? Hardly. They were already struggling to get participants into the program.

Most citizens regarded the senior volunteers with some sort of friendly attitude, either because of the program's affiliation with the police or due to the age of the participants. Ray didn't care for feigned niceties, though. He just wanted people to be themselves.

These people—the ones waiting for a chance at breakfast—were hungry, and they watched Ray with wariness. He liked that. It was honest and better than a fake smile and a phony handshake. How many of those did his son, Jacob, endure in Albuquerque?

"Here you go."

Ray turned back to the cashier's stand. Tyna held out a woman's wallet. It was long, thick, and yellow. He took it from her then asked, "Do you know how it ended up here?"

She shook her head. "A customer brought it in, I think. Supposedly, they found it in the parking lot. I don't rightly know. I didn't take it."

"Who did?"

Tyna shrugged. "I wasn't here when it was turned in."

"When did this happen?"

"Sometime yesterday afternoon. Maybe early evening. It was my day off."

"Why did you wait to call it in?"

A customer approached with a meal receipt. Trailing behind him was a woman and two young boys. Tyna acknowledged the family then took the ticket. "How was breakfast?" she asked.

Ray stepped back to let the father complete the transaction. While he waited for Tyna, Ray opened the recovered wallet and looked inside. It contained a state identification card for Margaret Kelley. There were also a couple of department store credit cards, some photographs, and other items. There was no cash inside.

He studied the ID card. Margaret appeared to be roughly his age. Ray consulted the listed birth date to confirm. She was a few years older than him. Margaret probably no longer drove, which is why she only had the ID card and not a driver's license.

Ray closed the wallet and tucked it into an arm pit. He realized it was the same thing Audrey used to do with a wallet whenever she carried one. He pulled it out and held it in his left hand—the right always remained free, a habit from his Army days.

When the family walked away, Ray stepped back to the cashier's stand.

Tyna looked around him to the nearest group of customers. "Give us a minute, folks. We're clearing off your table now. Once it's ready to go, we'll get you seated." She returned her attention to Ray. "Sorry about that."

"Nothing to be sorry for. I'm interrupting your business." Ray held up the wallet. "This was turned in yesterday. Why wait to call it in?"

"People forget stuff here all the time. They usually come back for it pretty quick. We figured that would happen again. When the owner of the wallet didn't show up last night, I called it in this morning. We don't want to be holding it due to the credit cards and stuff. You know—liability reasons and all."

"The owner of the wallet is Margaret Kelley."

Tyna nodded. "I saw that."

"Do you know if she came inside to eat?"

"We checked our records. There was no credit card transaction with her name on it. She might have paid with cash, though. We have no way to tell if she did."

"There was no money in the wallet," Ray said.

"That's how it was turned in. I don't know what to tell you."

"Can I speak with the manager who was working yesterday?"

Tyna lifted a single shoulder. "She's off now. You're stuck with me as I'm the only manager on duty."

Ray pulled out his notebook. He recorded Tyna's full name, address, and cell phone number. That was required information for a Found Property report. He closed his notebook and slipped it back into his pocket when he finished. He handed her a generic business card with the Volunteer Services' phone number. "If you think of anything else, please give me a call. My name is Ray."

"Want to stay for breakfast?" Tyna pointed to an open seat at the counter.

"No, ma'am. Thank you, though. I've got work to do."

***

Ray headed toward the property room, which was off Freya Street. The proper procedure was to secure the wallet and let someone else notify Margaret Kelley that her wallet was found.

How long would that be, though? It was Saturday morning. If Ray put the wallet onto property now, it would not be processed until Monday. He believed he knew the priority of things once that day rolled around. A found wallet would fall below handling recovered weapons or sending items to the lab.

Margaret Kelley's wallet could wait a full day or more

before getting logged into the system. And then someone would need to contact her. Since Ray didn't find a phone number for Margaret in the wallet, an evidence technician would need to look it up. What if they couldn't locate it? What would they do then? They'd probably send a letter to Margaret at the address on her ID card. The letter would state the property room had her wallet and that she could pick it up during the appropriate hours.

Considering Margaret didn't have a driver's license, she'd have to get a ride or take the bus.

It meant a whole lot of hassle that Ray could easily avoid by driving to her residence now. Besides, he didn't have anything going on today except a few more vacation home checks. Those could wait.

He detoured at the Greene Street Bridge and headed north. Margaret Kelley lived in the Five Mile neighborhood. It would take a while to get there, but it was still a pleasant autumn morning and a good day for a drive.

Chapter 4

Ray Christy turned off Central Avenue onto North Fleming Street. The neighborhood was like any other in the area—ranch homes constructed in the seventies, older cars in the driveways, and nice yards. Everyone seemed to take pride in maintaining their grass.

According to her ID card, Margaret Kelley lived in the middle of the double block. Even from this distance, Ray could make out the unmarked patrol car. It might have been an ordinary maroon Chevy Impala, but the multiple antennas on the vehicle gave it away. The WSP at the end of the license plate confirmed its owner—Washington State Patrol.

Ray parked and climbed out. He carried Margaret Kelley's wallet with him.

He proceeded up the sidewalk to the front of a house. It was tan with brown accents. The closer he got, the more he became convinced that it was recently painted. The door was open, but the screen remained in place. Ray pressed the doorbell but didn't hear a corresponding ring. The screen bounced when he knocked on it.

A woman came to the door. She appeared to be in her late forties, perhaps early fifties. The gray screen door muted her features. "Yes?"

"Ray Christy, ma'am. Are you Margaret Kelley?"

The woman glanced over her shoulder then back to Ray. "I'm sorry. What?"

"Margaret Kelley?" He held up the yellow wallet. "This was found at Denny's. I'm here to return it."

A man appeared in the hallway now. He strode to the door. "What's going on, Elise?"

"This police officer has Margaret's wallet."

"He's not a cop," the man said. He stepped around Elise and pushed the screen door open.

The man wore blue jeans, a plaid button-up shirt, and black boots. A gun and trooper's badge rode on his hip. His face appeared haggard as if he had not slept well in several nights. "What's this about?"

Ray lifted the wallet. "This belongs to Margaret Kelley. Is she in?"

From behind the trooper, Elise leaned back into view. "She's—"

The trooper cut her off by holding up his hand. "You're a senior volunteer, right?"

"Yes, sir."

The man extended a hand. "Leave it with me."

Ray politely smiled. "I can't do that."

"Why not?"

"Because I'm responsible for it."

"Fine. Then log it into your evidence room." The trooper stepped back inside and pulled the screen door closed. "The fuck do I care?"

"Excuse me?"

"You heard me." The trooper closed the main door.

Ray returned to his car and tossed the wallet into the passenger seat. He should have just logged the darn thing into the property room and saved himself the irritation.

He stared at the car in front of him. What was a state trooper doing here anyway?

It was probably nothing, and he knew he should let it go. But the way the guy talked to him irritated Ray. He'd gone through most of his military career without anyone daring to speak like to him like that.

Was it a fraying of society's moral fabric that allowed men to think they could talk to him in that manner? Or was it the fact that Ray was an old man in their eyes?

It probably didn't hurt that the guy had a badge and gun on his belt.

"Jerk," Ray muttered to himself.

Before leaving, he jotted the Impala's license plate number into his notebook.

***

Ray entered the property room and collected a log sheet and a small brown paper bag.

He could enter all the information on a nearby computer, but forms were provided for those who still liked to do things the old-fashioned way. Ray wondered how soon the old-fashioned way would no longer include blank forms.

It only took him a few minutes to fill in the sheet. It required an incident number, a brief description of the item, and any special handling instructions for a property clerk. Since this was a found property report, Ray entered Margaret's name and address as its owner.

He considered running Margaret's name through the computer-aided dispatch (CAD) system, but it wasn't standard operating procedure with SPD's volunteers. The department didn't want them to run names or otherwise use the system unless it was essential. Supposedly, it was to keep the database secure. However, he was filling out a Found Property report, and he did know who the property belonged to, so this would be deemed essential.

But if the people living with Margaret Kelley didn't care that she recovered her wallet, why should he?

Ray dropped the wallet into the brown paper bag. Then he placed it on a nearby shelf and slipped the evidence form underneath the bag.

He made sure the door was secured when he left the property room.

***

Ray drove by the final few homes on the vacation list, and all of them appeared secure.

Unfortunately, the quiet time in his head only allowed him to replay the confrontation at Margaret Kelley's home. He wasn't angry at himself for how he responded while there. He thought his reaction was fine. And since he had time to calm down, Ray was no longer angry with the way the trooper talked to him.

Men with higher rank due solely to college degrees had often acted superior to Ray throughout most of his military career, but they never talked to him in the manner the trooper did. Now that Ray was seventy-two, though, much younger men, some with no education and no life experience, spoke to him in ways he would never have expected. But that wasn't what bothered him.

What concerned Ray about the interaction with the trooper was how he responded afterward. He let the man get under his skin, and it festered long after. That led to not going the extra mile while logging the wallet into the property room. Ray should have taken a couple of minutes to check Margaret Kelley's name through CAD.

The lack of personal control niggled Ray. Was he getting softer? Thirty years ago, he would have blown off the trooper's slight. Hell, he probably would have done it ten years ago. But today he let it disrupt his actions.

Why was that? He didn't want it to be because of his age. Ray believed that to be a sorry excuse. He would not accept similar justifications while leading men, so he shouldn't let himself off the hook now.

So, what other reason was there? Could it be he was distracted by what was going on with Audrey? That had been occurring for years. Had it reached a boiling point?

Whatever the reason, his lack of personal fortitude disturbed Ray.

When he returned to the Public Safety Building, he parked the Volunteer Services' car in the designated lot. Then he headed over to the Monroe Court Building. He decided he would run Margaret Kelley's name through the system, write a brief report on the found property, and complete a form for the vacation checks. It would only take him ten minutes to do it all, then he would feel right again.

Ray slipped his key into the office door, but it was already unlocked. The lights were on inside.

Typically, the Volunteer Services' office was quiet on a Saturday, but he heard a couple of women talking and laughing. Ray didn't seek them out but instead headed directly toward his desk. A moment later, Irene appeared.

"Look who it is," she said.

"Hello to you."

Standing with Irene was another woman about the same age. Like Irene, she was an attractive woman with bright, attentive eyes.

Irene smiled. "I didn't know you were working today."

"I'm covering for Mel. He's got a hernia or something."

"A hernia? Who said that?"

"Newman."

"Of course, he did." Irene rolled her eyes. "Mel herniated a disk." She grabbed her back as she continued. "He was chopping wood. You know how he is. His doctor told him to stay off his feet for a bit until the pain leveled off, then they'd figure out a plan of action."

Ray smirked. "Mel and his wood."

"I think I would like to meet this Mel," Irene's friend said.

Irene playfully smacked the other woman's arm. "Oh, Ray. I forgot to introduce you. This is my friend, Mary Jo Brakke."

Mary Jo extended a manicured hand, and Ray shook it. Her eyes flared with mischievousness, and her hand held his longer than he would have liked.

"We're going to lunch," Irene said. "Would you like to go?"

"Please join us," Mary Jo said. "I promise not to bite—unless you ask."

Irene nervously laughed. "She's kidding."

Mary Jo wore a low-cut blouse that revealed a tanned and freckled chest.

Ray motioned toward his desk. "I appreciate the offer, but I need to fill out this paperwork."

Irene said, "We can wait if it's only going to be a few minutes. I was showing Mary Jo around. She's always wanted to see this place."

"Thank you for the invitation," Ray said, "but I think I'll pass."

"Are you worried about us?" Mary Jo asked. "I'll be on my best behavior, but I can't speak for Irene. You know how she is."

Ray lifted an eyebrow.

"Don't listen to her," Irene said dismissively, "but you should still come with us. You'd have a great time. We're going to this new place." To Mary Jo, she asked, "What's it called again?"

"Lord Stanley's."

Ray leaned back in his chair. "The hockey bar?"

"You've been?" Irene said.

"I didn't know you liked hockey."

"We don't. Do you?"

He shrugged. "I like it fine."

The two women briefly grinned at each other. Irene

turned back to Ray. "Then you should *definitely* come with us. You can teach us the game."

"I'm sorry. I can't."

Mary Jo's gaze fell to the wedding band on Ray's left hand. "Call your wife and tell her you're going to lunch with some work buddies. We promise to be quiet while you're on the phone."

Irene's hand touched her friend's arm, but her eyes remained locked on Ray. The merriment left her face, and she became gravely serious. "I'm sorry, Ray. You don't have to go. Some other time."

"What?" Mary Jo said. "It's only lunch, and I already promised not to bite—unless you think his wife won't notice." Her smile was devilish.

Irene's eyes widened, and she grabbed Mary Jo's shoulders. She spun her friend around and pushed her away.

"What did I say?" Mary Jo asked over her shoulder.

"Go," Irene whispered. "*Now.*"

The two women moved to another part of the office.

Ray returned his attention to the vacation homes checklist. A few minutes later, the office door opened and closed.

He inhaled deeply and stared at the blank forms. For a brief time, he let his gaze blur. Once he gathered his senses again, Ray removed his notebook to begin the Found Property report. He filled in the necessary information—the complainant, the address where the property was found, and to whom the property belonged.

His mind returned to an earlier question—why was a state patrol trooper at the address on Fleming Street?

If he lived there, wouldn't the guy have said so?

If he was related to Margaret Kelley, why didn't he come out and say it?

Maybe the guy was a detective, and he was there to

follow up on a case. But it was Saturday. And he was dressed casually. Yet if he *was* there in an official capacity, wouldn't a detective have said *that*?

The detective seemed very unfriendly and in a hurry for Ray to leave. Why was that?

And he looked terrible—like he hadn't gotten much sleep lately. Ray had seen that look in the mirror many times throughout his years, and it was never caused by happy events.

Ray stood and headed toward the community computer in the back of the office. This was the only computer attached to the CAD system. It would allow him to run Margaret Kelley's name. He was one of the few volunteers who'd been through the training on the system.

He knew he shouldn't run the woman's name now. Users of the CAD system weren't supposed to check names for personal reasons—they could be disciplined for doing such a thing. A female officer had run afoul of the administration a couple of years ago for running the names of women her ex-husband dated. For Ray, there was no longer an active reason for him to run Margaret Kelley's name. Had he done it while he still had her wallet, he'd surely be in the right. But it was now logged into the property room. It would be up to the warehouse technicians to do that work.

Ray chastised himself for that oversight now. Not only was it sloppy work, it was lazy. He was better than that. And it was caused by letting the trooper annoy him. Again, he admonished himself for it.

But that didn't solve the predicament of checking Margaret's name now.

What was the worst that would happen to him if someone discovered his inappropriate use of the system? He might be terminated from the program. Was he willing to risk it? Looking up Margaret wasn't for any potential romantic or financial gain, but that wasn't a defense for breaking the rules.

From his time in the Army, he knew that following the rules was necessary for success. However, an occasional rule needed to be sidestepped to accomplish a mission. Ray felt this was such a minor issue that no one would ever make a stink about it. And if they did, he felt like he could justify his actions.

Over the past couple of years, Ray developed a friendship with Chief Dillon that might provide him a little air cover if something like this was discovered. But he didn't want to count on it, nor did he ever want to trade on that relationship. The chief was an honorable man who looked at Ray as a friend. Perhaps Dillon did that with others in the department. Ray was too embarrassed to ask and find out. He enjoyed the man's camaraderie and didn't want to jeopardize it by questioning his motives.

Ray opened his notebook and started the computer. He entered the woman's full name—Margaret L. Kelley—and her birth date. Almost immediately, the system returned a short and uneventful history. Margaret was an individual who did not get in trouble with the law.

There were only two entries. The first listed her as a witness to a shoplifting incident over five years ago. Ray skipped that and called up the entry from Thursday. It was a DOA—Dead on Arrival. Detective Parker was listed as the responding investigator.

Margaret Kelley was dead.

Why hadn't the woman or the trooper at Margaret's house told him of her death? They had the chance to do so. Maybe they weren't even supposed to be there. Perhaps they were doing something nefarious.

But the man was a Washington State Patrol detective.

Well, Ray assumed he was a detective. He was in street clothes. Perhaps he was a trooper in a plainclothes assignment. Surely, the man wasn't involved in Margaret's death.

Ray wanted to give the trooper the benefit of the doubt due to his profession, but the guy had been a jerk when they met. Would it be a stretch to imagine the detective doing something wrong? No, Ray decided, it wouldn't.

Cops weren't above temptation. Ray read stories of such things in the newspaper, and Jacob had told him stories that confirmed it.

Ray refocused on the computer. He only had basic access to the CAD system, which allowed him to see incident numbers and the associated history. He could see when a call came in, when officers were dispatched, and who was assigned. However, Ray didn't have access to the software that allowed him to view official reports. If he wanted to know what Detective Parker thought about Margaret Kelley's death, he'd have to talk with the man himself.

And being a detective, Parker wouldn't be in the office until Monday. Before then, maybe Ray could dig a little on his own.

Chapter 5

"How was your day?" Ray asked.

Audrey scooped some peas with her spoon and studied them.

They were seated in the dining facility again. Like most nights, Ray was the only non-resident there. One resident—Mavis Downey—stood at a nearby table and ate her food with her hands. She wore gray sweatpants and an oversized green sweater. Mavis talked while she ate but didn't worry that her tablemates weren't paying attention to her.

Overhead, Mel Torme's "Games People Play" drifted from the speakers.

"Audrey?" Ray said.

She looked up from her spoon.

"How was your day?"

"Good." She looked away and stuck the spoon into her mouth.

"Did you do anything interesting?"

"I don't know." She refused to look at him.

"Did you go to the day room and watch a movie?"

Audrey cut a chicken tender in half with her spoon. "Yeah."

"What was the movie?"

"I don't know." She still didn't look at him.

"Was it *The Maltese Falcon*?"

"I think so."

The nurse Ray spoke with when he arrived told him that's what Audrey had watched earlier in the day.

"Did you like the movie?"

"I don't remember." Audrey used her fingers to pick

up a piece of chicken tender and chewed it with her mouth open.

At the neighboring table, Mavis Downey pulled the green sweater over her head. She wasn't wearing a bra. Ray glanced around for a staff member. None were in the vicinity.

Mavis next pushed down her sweats and stepped out of them. She stood naked before her table. The residents eating with her didn't seem to mind. Mavis picked up a chicken tender and wandered off.

"How was your visit with Pam and Heidi today?"

Audrey chased some peas around her plate with the spoon. Not satisfied that way, she picked them up with her left hand and put them onto the utensil. She stuck the spoon into her mouth.

"The girls, Audrey. They came to visit. Do you remember?"

She stared at him now. "Yes."

He wasn't sure if she really recalled. "Was it a nice visit?"

Audrey's gaze dropped to her plate. She picked up a French fry. "I like these with chili."

Ray smiled. "You used to do that at Wendy's. Do you remember?"

She closely studied the fry as if it held a long-lost secret. Finally, she said, "I went with my husband."

"That's right," Ray said. "You went with your husband."

***

It was shortly after seven, and Ray drove over to North Fleming Street. He wasn't worried about the trooper being there and seeing him. Ray drove his truck now—a late-model Dodge Ram—a ubiquitous vehicle for the region and one that wouldn't call attention to him.

There was no unmarked patrol car in front of the house now.

Ray parked his truck then approached the house. He knocked confidently on the screen door. As before, it bounced with each rap of his knuckles. Soon the door opened, but by a different woman this time. She was a few years older than Ray and badly hunched over. "Yes?"

"Ray Christy, ma'am. I'm hoping to speak with someone about Margaret Kelley."

The woman frowned. "She died."

"Yes, ma'am. Are you her sister?"

"What made you think that?"

He pointed at the house. "This is her home."

"It's my home, too."

Ray smiled apologetically. "Of course. What's your name?"

"Who are you again?"

"Ray Christy. I work with the Spokane Police Department."

"The police were already out here."

"I recovered her wallet earlier today."

The woman's gaze dropped to Ray's empty hands. "Where's it at?"

"I logged it into the property room for safekeeping. It was found yesterday on Division Street, in the parking lot of a Denny's, and turned into the restaurant. Do you have any idea how it got there?"

The woman studied Ray now. "You're too old to be a policeman."

"I'm a volunteer."

"Yeah, that makes sense." She pushed the screen door open. "Want to come in for a moment?"

Ray stepped inside.

"Shut the door behind you, but don't let go of it, or it'll bang."

The woman slowly shuffled away. They went through a living room, then turned down a long corridor where they passed by four rooms. Two had their doors closed, but the other two were open. One was the bathroom. In the other open room sat a man about Ray's age. He strummed an acoustic guitar and softly sang to himself.

At the end of the hallway, they came to a fifth bedroom. The woman pointed to a chair. "Sit there." She sat on the edge of the bed. "Vera Drayton. That's me."

"Nice to meet you, Vera. Who was the guy in the other room?"

She made a disapproving face. "Bob Dylan."

Ray felt slightly disappointed. Did this woman have Alzheimer's like Audrey? He carefully said, "That's not Bob Dylan."

"Oh, I know that." Vera playfully waved her hand at Ray. "But he thinks he is. Don't believe him, though. His real name is John."

"Does he have dementia?"

"Mental issues." She leaned forward and conspiratorially said, "But you don't want to talk to him anyway."

"Why not?"

"He smells."

"Is he related to Margaret?"

"You think they're related because he smells?"

"No." The left corner of Ray's mouth lifted in a smile. "Because you're in the same house."

Margaret's hands gripped the edge of the bed. "Are you sure you're with the police?"

"That's right."

"Then how do you not know about this place?"

Ray looked down the hallway.

"We all live here like a commune. Did you ever do that?"

His attention returned to her. "A commune? No. I missed out on those."

"Too bad. It was a great time. Lots of dope and free love. Although it wasn't really free if you get my drift, but we still had a good time, nonetheless. You were probably in the Army or something. Am I right?"

He nodded.

"Were you in the war?"

Ray served during the Viet Nam War, but he wasn't going to share that information with Vera. He'd learned long ago to keep that mostly to himself. Only his family and the VA needed to know the whole story.

"So, you're roommates?" he asked.

"That's right."

"This is a group home."

Vera's face hardened. "I can take care of myself."

"I'm certain you can," Ray said, "and I didn't mean to imply otherwise. Which room was Margaret's?"

She pointed into the hallway. "The room right there, next to mine. But they've locked it until the family comes to pick up her stuff."

Ray stood and walked to Margaret's room. The door wasn't marked by a number. He put his hand on the knob.

"Hey," Vera said, "you can't go in there."

He tried to twist the knob, but it was locked just like the woman said. "I wanted to make sure it was secure." Ray returned to Vera's room.

As he sat in the chair again, she said, "You don't have a gun."

"I do, but not while I'm working."

"They don't give you a gun? Why not?"

"They say it's for your protection."

Vera smirked. "That's nice of them."

"What happened to Margaret?"

"She drowned in the bathtub." Vera pointed down the hall again. "You can go look where it happened if you want."

"In a minute. Who found her?"

"I did."

Ray put on an empathetic face. "Were you friends?"

"Best friends."

"Did you call the police?"

She pushed herself to a standing position. "Now, I don't believe you. You should already know this. You're not with the police."

Ray held up a three-fingered salute. "Scout's honor."

"You're telling me you were a boy scout, too?"

"It's been a long time, but I was. Should I recite the oath?"

Her scowl softened. "I was a girl scout. Those were the times, weren't they?"

"So, you called the police?"

"I did. They came out and said it was an accident."

"They said that?" It didn't seem like the police he witnessed over the years. They were always slow and methodical during investigations. Pronouncing it as accidental so fast seemed reckless.

Vera returned to her sitting position on the edge of the bed. "Well… one of them said it looked like an accident."

Ray bent forward and put his elbows on his knees. "Do you drive?"

"Don't I wish! Haven't in years. It got to be where I started having trouble judging distances at night. Then the same thing happened during the day." Vera's face brightened. "You still drive, though?"

Ray nodded. "Part of the job."

"That's great. Really great. Good for you."

"Margaret didn't have a driver's license."

"We rode the bus whenever we went somewhere."

Ray cocked his head. "Did Margaret say anything about eating at Denny's?"

"Yesterday, you mean? She was dead."

"Before she died. Would she have told you if she was going?"

"Sure. That's what best friends do. We told each other everything."

Ray pulled out his notebook and pen. "Did she ever go to Denny's?"

"Not that I know of, but that doesn't mean she wouldn't."

"Does anyone ever pick her up?"

"Only on Sundays. That's the day her family comes by to take her to church."

"Would she have gone by herself?"

"To church?"

Ray shook his head. "To Denny's."

"Margaret would have to catch the bus by herself. She wouldn't do that. If she wanted to go anywhere, I would have gone with her."

"What about John?" Ray asked. "Would he have gone with her?"

"Who's John?"

Ray thumbed down the hall. "Bob Dylan."

"Oh, Bob." She held her nose. "No. No one goes anywhere with him."

"Earlier today, there was a woman here named Elise. Would she have taken Margaret?"

Vera shook her head. "The new caretaker, you mean. They don't go anywhere with us. They're kind of standoffish."

"What happened to the previous caretaker?"

"Who knows? Today, it was Elise. They come and go. Sometimes they cover for each other. We're never told when there's a change or a substitute. It's not the best communication around here if you want my opinion. That's what happens once you pass a certain age, but I'm preaching to the choir, aren't I?"

"Does the caretaker live on-site?"

"That's right." Vera pointed down the hall. "The room at the opposite end."

"What was the other caretaker's name? The one before Elise."

"Kayla Reed." She nodded. "Nice girl, but all sorts of problems."

"How do you mean?"

"You know the stuff. Young people drama. Love and money. Money and love." Her hands bounced left and right as she spoke. "It was always something with Kayla, and she just loved talking about it. Margaret and I hated her. It's too bad they're both gone. Margaret would have loved the peace and quiet."

Ray jotted Kayla's name into his notebook. When he finished, he looked up. "And she just stopped showing up?"

"Margaret? She died."

"No, Kayla."

"Oh, right." Vera absently patted her bed. "Kayla was here for part of Thursday, but then she was gone."

Ray cocked his head. Thursday was the day Margaret Kelley had died. "Did Kayla leave before or after you found Margaret's body?"

"Before. Why?"

"Was that like her?"

"To leave and not come back? To leave, sure. But she always came back. Maybe she found a new boyfriend. She missed a whole day once before because of a new man. That's how young people are nowadays. No responsibilities for their actions. Maybe that's how we were, too. I don't know."

"Elise lives here now, though?"

Vera frowned. "She hasn't moved in yet totally. I don't think all of Kayla's stuff is out yet."

Ray made an entry in his notebook. "What about the guy that was with Elise earlier? The state trooper."

Her lip curled. "Jory Bishop. He owns the place."

Ray looked around. "A cop owns this business?"

"And you'd think he'd be nicer about it. Kind of a jerk if you ask me."

"I agree." He wrote Bishop's name in his notebook.

Vera clasped her hands together. "You sure all of this is about Margaret's wallet?"

"Why wouldn't it be?"

"I don't know. People get awfully strange after someone dies. You're not related to her, are you?"

"No."

"Because I can find out."

Ray lifted three fingers in the air again.

"People don't give me enough credit for how smart I am."

"I understand."

"I bet you do."

Ray couldn't think of any other questions, so he stood.

Vera stood as well. "Are you leaving?"

"Yes."

She reached out to him. "You don't have to. Stay awhile. Maybe we can play some cards or something. Do you watch TV? There are snacks in the kitchen."

Ray checked his watch. He didn't even notice the time, but it was the symbolism of the act he was after. "I need to go."

"Got some bad guys to catch?"

"It's getting late, and I have a cat to feed."

Ray left Vera in her room and headed toward the door.

He knew from the early days of Audrey's stay at Colonial Springs that there was no easy way to leave. It had to be done like ripping off a band-aid.

He stopped at the bathroom and lingered for a moment. The tub was a walk-in style that stood over three and a half feet tall. The door would close and allow the tub to fill with water. A person could easily sit upright. Jets inside the walls recirculated the water. The facility Audrey was in had similar types of tubs.

Ray thought it would take some effort for someone to drown.

Had Margaret fallen asleep before slipping under the water? Wouldn't the sudden lack of oxygen cause her to wake?

Did she have a heart attack then slip under the water? That might stop her from having the power to get out on her own.

Or had someone helped Margaret to her demise?

As Ray passed John's room, he heard the occupant strumming his guitar and mumbling, "Gotta serve somebody."

***

Ray reset the trip odometer on his truck and drove toward Division Street.

How did Margaret Kelley get to Denny's? According to Vera Drayton, she didn't drive, and she didn't go anywhere alone. So, hopping a bus by herself seemed unlikely.

If Margaret did not go there, the wallet got to the restaurant by itself. Well, not by itself, Ray corrected himself. Someone else took it there.

So, who was it?

Maybe Detective Parker picked it up at the crime

scene and went to lunch afterward. That seemed unlikely to Ray. It was known throughout the department that Parker was a health nut. He didn't seem to be the type to go for a Grand Slam breakfast, no matter how good it was. Second, why would the detective take her wallet from the crime scene? If it was to secure valuable property, wouldn't he have tracked it down if he lost it?

And if her family only picked up Margaret on Sundays, then someone else came into possession of the wallet.

Could it have been Kayla Reed? Maybe she knew about Margaret's drowning before Vera found the body. And if she knew about the woman's death, then it wouldn't be a stretch to imagine she took the wallet to go have some fun with it. But why didn't she come back? Perhaps she was afraid someone had discovered her theft. Would her boss have known?

Ray turned south on Division Street.

His thoughts moved to the group home's living conditions. The folks who lived there were luckier than Audrey. They didn't need constant supervision as she did. They needed limited oversight and had far more autonomy. It seemed that they could come and go as they pleased.

Ray had heard of group homes like the one on Fleming Street, but he'd never come across one—repurposed houses that brought several people together. The businesses provided assistance such as meal preparation and prescription drug monitoring, but that was about it. He thought changes in the law had pushed out homes like the one on Fleming Street. Was this home grandfathered into the system somehow?

By the time Audrey required help, she had needed to be in a larger facility like Colonial Springs. There were plenty of larger, professionally run facilities around town.

Ray wondered how many small group homes there were like the one that Margaret Kelley had lived in.

Ray pulled into the parking lot of Denny's and checked the truck's trip odometer. It read almost four miles. He stared up at the pylon sign and wondered just exactly how did Margaret Kelley's wallet travel four miles without her?

Chapter 6

Ray skipped church the next morning. To be honest, he skipped services on most Sundays now. Throughout his adult life, he considered himself a lukewarm Christian at best. He only attended because Audrey insisted that he go. Ray felt slightly guilty for not going that morning but knew the feeling would fade the deeper into the day he went. It was always that way.

Right now, though, Ray was more interested in his hash browns and revisiting Norman Paperman's Caribbean adventure.

"How's the book?" Dana asked.

He looked up. "It's good."

"Sorry. That was a stupid question. You told me yesterday that you've read it five times."

"Interested in reading it?" he asked.

"You told me how it ended."

Ray recalled yesterday's conversation. "I think I said his dream soured. That doesn't tell you how it ended."

"That tells me enough. Why would I want to read a sad book?"

"What do you read?"

She motioned toward his coffee cup. "Want me to grab you a refill?"

"No hurry." There was still a third of a cup left.

"So, what do I read?" Dana said. "When I get a chance, which is less than I like, I read paranormal stuff."

Ray canted his head. "Give me an example."

"Vampires and werewolves."

"Horror books."

Dana smiled. "Not horror. Paranormal romances and mysteries."

"There's such a thing?"

"You bet there is."

"I would never have guessed."

Dana glanced around the restaurant as if to see if anyone needed her help. Things were still quiet then. Ray knew it would get crazy as soon as the churches let out. That's why he came early. Her focus returned to him.

"Are you working today?" she asked.

"For a couple hours. After breakfast, I'll go home and get into my uniform."

"Any plans after that?"

"Dinner with my daughters. What about you?"

"I work until one, then I'm done for the day." She briefly studied him. "Can I ask you a question, Ray?"

"Sure."

"You've been coming in here for almost a year now."

He closed his book. "I'd say that's about right."

"But you're always alone." Her eyes flicked to his wedding band.

"I'm not alone." He lifted *Don't Stop the Carnival*.

"I guess what I'm asking is, where's your wife?"

Ray's face flattened.

"I'm sorry," she quickly said. "That came out terrible. What I meant to say— Never mind. It doesn't matter what I meant. You don't have to tell me. I'm sorry for prying."

"She's in a memory care facility."

Dana closed her eyes. "Crap."

"It's okay."

She opened her eyes. "I didn't know. I would never have said anything if I knew."

He tapped the edge of his coffee cup. "I think I will have that refill now."

Dana nodded. "Sure, Ray, sure. I'll be right back."

***

When Ray entered the Volunteer Services' office, the first thing he did was go straight to the computer that shared the CAD software. When the screen brightened, he activated the program and entered 'Kayla Reed.' He didn't have a date of birth, so the system would pull everyone with the same name.

He knew he shouldn't check the woman's history. Ray was clearly outside the scope of the Found Property call and was now violating Standard Operating Procedures. However, the mention of the woman's name by Vera Drayton had plagued his sleep all night.

Who was Kayla Reed, and why had she not returned after Margaret Kelley died? Were the two events linked?

There were three Kayla Reeds in the system, but Ray immediately ruled one out due to her date of birth. Kayla Jennifer Reed was a teenager and likely to still be in high school.

Ray considered a second unlikely—Amber Kayla Reed. She was twenty-one. That one was old enough to be a caregiver, but Ray thought the woman would likely go with her first name.

Therefore, Ray chose the final name—Kayla Dawn Reed. She was thirty-two and had a mild criminal history—some misdemeanor drug possession many years ago and several traffic infractions—mostly speeding. He wondered if the drug possession convictions mattered on a job application anymore now that marijuana was legalized in the state.

He considered printing the entry but worried that it

might register some flag in the system. Instead, he jotted Kayla's information into his notebook.

Ray powered off the community computer, then swung by his desk to retrieve a set of keys.

After selecting a Volunteer Services' car, he soon set out on his vacation home checks. The old Crown Victoria creaked and groaned whenever it hit a bump or went around a corner. It was a former patrol car, so there were a lot of hard miles on it.

As he drove by each home, he checked the addresses listed on his clipboard. Ray didn't normally dawdle, and he didn't do so today either.

The only thing he had to look forward to tonight was dinner with Heidi and Pamela. He would visit Audrey before seeing them, but he'd be hard-pressed to say he looked forward to that. He loved his wife more than anyone ever in his life but visiting her was more duty to the woman she had been than to the woman she was now.

Ray hurried through the vacation checks. He didn't have a reason for being out in the unit's car for more than a couple of hours. However, he wanted to make a detour before turning it in.

He drove several miles over the speed limit as he headed toward the Fleming Street house. Ray narrowly avoided a car full of teenagers that rocketed out of a Walmart parking lot in northwest Spokane. At first, they seemed worried that he was a cop. Then they laughed, and several flipped him the bird before speeding away.

Ray shook his head. He wished he had some authority to stop drivers like those kids, but he was a glorified pencil pusher who occasionally got to leave the office. Ray liked to think that he could still fight with the best of them—a career spent in the Army left him with that attitude. However, age robbed him of the things that were so carelessly blessed on the youth—speed, stamina, and strength came immediately to mind.

He didn't want to consider the rest of the alphabet.

When he arrived at Fleming Street, he turned north. Ray didn't see an unmarked patrol car up ahead and felt confident continuing. He didn't plan to go into the house again and talk with Vera. If he had to qualify why he drove all that way, it was to see the group home once more just to keep it in the forefront of his thoughts.

He often worried that things might start slipping in his mind as they did for Audrey. Whenever he struggled for a word or forgot why he entered a room, there was an immediate flash of panic that he might be getting some form of dementia. That was always followed by his primary worry—who would visit Audrey when he was gone?

Ray wasn't troubled about her care anymore. The folks at Colonial Springs did more than an adequate job of ensuring Audrey's safety. But the girls rarely visited their mother, and they always did it together. He understood why.

Facing the reality of an impending slide into decrepitude isn't something anyone wants. But that's one thing age had brought Ray—the acceptance of his own demise.

As he neared the group home, Ray noticed a gray Dodge Challenger out front. As he passed, the door to the newer muscle car opened, and Jory Bishop stepped out. Ray made eye contact with him as he drove by.

When he passed the Challenger, Ray's eyes flicked to the rearview mirror. Jory rested one arm on the car door and the other on the car's roof. The off-duty trooper watched the Volunteer Services' car until Ray turned and left the neighborhood.

***

"Audrey?" Ray asked.

She looked up from the puzzle piece she held. They were seated at a folding card table in the Colonial Springs' activity room. They were the only ones there.

Her hair appeared freshly washed, and the clothes she wore weren't wrinkled. Sunday was one of the bath days on her schedule. She must have gotten one just before his arrival.

"Aren't you hungry?" he asked.

"No." Audrey's attention dropped to the puzzle that someone else had started. She attempted to click the piece she held into place. It didn't fit. She pulled it back and studied it.

Years ago, Audrey and Ray frequently puzzled during the fall and winter. They would sit together for hours and complete complicated puzzles, often with little conversation. The joy was in being together. His favorite was a thousand-piece puzzle of a kaleidoscope of colors. It was a difficult project, and it took them a long time, but they managed to finish.

Audrey had been a whiz at puzzling, with the ability to intently focus for hours. It was as if she slipped into a meditative state while performing the activity.

Today, she struggled to complete puzzles with limited pieces and large easy-to-match images. Ray spotted more than a dozen that should click together.

Audrey touched the piece she held to another on the table. It didn't fit, but she tried to mash them together.

"I don't think it goes there," Ray said.

"I know." She angrily shook the piece. "I know."

"I was only helping."

Her brow furrowed as her gaze frantically traveled around the puzzle's edge. Audrey's attention moved back to the piece she held. She lifted it up to study it more intently.

"Maybe you should try a different piece," Ray said gently. "I don't think that one is ready yet."

"Lemme do it," Audrey said. Her words sounded mushy, as if she were drunk. That happened when she was distracted or tired.

He sat quietly after that and watched her struggle with the puzzle. After a time, Audrey set the piece on the table and stood.

"Where are you going?" he asked.

"I don't know."

Ray followed her.

They slowly roamed the hallway. Audrey waved at the other residents and staff members. Ray nodded whenever anyone acknowledged him.

Helen Merrill's "You'd Be So Nice to Come Home To" played through the overhead speakers.

They passed a young staff member, spurring Audrey to ask Ray, "Do you know my son?"

"Jacob?"

She nodded.

"Yeah," he said. "I knew him."

"He's going to be a policeman." Audrey's statement did not contain the pride she felt so many years ago. It was a matter-of-fact revelation without vocal inflection or facial contortions. "He's in the academy now."

"Is that so?"

Audrey nodded once but didn't comment on Jacob any further. That's how it was with her now—glimpses into her past that evaporated quickly.

He wondered if she would remember anything more of their son. There were things he hoped she would remember of Jacob. He had been an independent young man who moved to Albuquerque to attend college. He stayed there after graduation because he loved the area.

Ray hoped she would not remember how he died. No parent should outlive a child, especially when their death was a violent one.

He and Audrey fell silent for a bit as they continued down the hall.

"Are you hungry yet?" Ray asked.

"No."

"Then where are we headed?"

"I don't know." Audrey slowly looked around then headed back the way they'd already come.

"Is it okay if I still walk with you?"

She nodded, and they fell silent again.

Audrey waved and smiled at the residents and staff she had greeted only moments before. Ray politely nodded his acknowledgment to the same. Eventually, they returned to the activity room. It was still quiet.

Audrey shuffled back to the folding card table and stared at it.

"Do you want to work on the puzzle again?"

"No."

"Why not?"

"I don't know."

Audrey sat at the table and picked up the same piece she'd struggled with before. She briefly studied it then touched it to another she'd already checked earlier.

As he watched her, Ray wondered if this was what he was doing with Margaret Kelley's wallet. Was he trying to make it fit into something that didn't belong?

Or was it a more complicated puzzle he didn't understand?

Audrey pulled the piece back and studied it again.

Ray imagined himself doing the same.

***

"How was mom today?" Heidi asked.

Ray considered his oldest daughter. She wore a red sweater and blue jeans. Her hair was held back from her face with a large headband. She was a single mom and had been an overachiever since he could remember. Heidi had a busy life with her real estate career and growing son.

He chose his words carefully. If he told Heidi that Audrey was having a tough day, his daughter would worry and ask a bunch of follow-up questions. She still wouldn't see Audrey any more than she did now, though. Ray knew Heidi hadn't accepted the idea of her parents' mortality, let alone her own.

"She was good," Ray said. He accepted the bowl of mashed potatoes that was passed from his grandson. Logan didn't smile and immediately dug into his meal.

"For real good, Dad?" Pamela asked. "Or are you just saying that?"

"*Pam*," Heidi admonished.

"What? Why was my question bad?"

Ray faced his youngest daughter. Pamela was a direct contradiction to Heidi. She wore a Seattle Seahawks jersey and white jeans. Her attitude had always been that of going with the flow. It led to a constant swapping of jobs and boyfriends. Ray could never seem to keep up with where she was working or who she was seeing.

He often wondered if the frequent moves during his military career and the long absences caused by field duty created his daughters' personalities.

The Army gave Ray everything he hoped for in a job—adventure and purpose—but the need to relocate came with it. For Ray, that was a bonus. He'd grown up in Spokane and longed to see the world. When he retired, Ray convinced Audrey to move to the Pacific Northwest. The friends he had grown up with had long moved on to lives of their own. Therefore, it was just them in Spokane—the Christy family. Ray liked it that way.

"Today was like most for your mom," he said, "but there were no tears and no outbursts."

"So, it *was* good," Pam said.

"That's how I'm looking at it."

"Cool."

Ray shoveled some mashed potatoes onto his plate. As he did so, he thought about Audrey's recent experience with them.

"How was your visit with her?" Ray asked.

Heidi said, "It was…" She paused as she struggled to find a word.

"Uncomfortable," Pam suggested.

"Oh, my God," Heidi said. "No, it wasn't."

"Speak for yourself."

Heidi shifted in her chair to face her father. "Mom brought up Jacob."

"What did she say?" Ray asked.

"She talked about him playing football."

"I remember those times," Pam said.

Ray smiled. "You were pretty small back then."

"Still. It was fun going to the games."

Now, Heidi smiled, too. "Jacob was the big man on campus. The girls went crazy for him during football season."

Pam reached over and tousled Logan's hair. "Just like you, huh?"

Logan pushed his aunt's arm away. "They like the guys on offense. Defense never gets the girls."

"Wait until college," Heidi said.

Ray scooped some mashed potatoes onto his fork. "Your mother brought up Jacob with me, too. She remembered him going to the academy."

Heidi touched her father's hand. "Is she doing that a

lot lately? Bringing up Jacob?"

"No," Ray said. "She hasn't brought him up in months."

"What are you going to do if she remembers his death again?"

He shrugged. "The same thing I did last time. I'll calm her down."

"Then she'll forget about it once more," Pam said.

Heidi glared at her sister.

Pam returned her gaze, then lifted her hands. "What? I'm only being honest."

Ray stared at his fork. He wondered what his wife was doing at that moment.

"And how are you, Dad?" Heidi asked.

He looked up. "I'm fine."

"Fine?" Pam said.

"*Pam.*" Heidi's voice lowered an octave.

"What now?"

Heidi's eyes widened in an unspoken message.

Pam crossed her arms. "Are we going to sit here and pretend that whenever dad says 'fine' that everything really is fine? Because we both know it's not."

Ray smiled sheepishly. "It's that obvious?"

"Since I was five," Pam said.

"What's going on, Dad?" Heidi asked.

"Nothing. It's just work."

Heidi rested an elbow on the table. "You mean the volunteer thing?"

"Yeah."

"You're volunteering," Pam said, "if it's too much, fucking quit."

"Pam!" Heidi said.

"What?"

"Logan is here."

Pam motioned to her nephew. "It's not like he hasn't

heard that on the football field."

Logan smirked. "Yeah, Mom. Chill out."

"He's probably even said it himself." Pam grinned at her nephew.

"Is that true?" Heidi asked.

Logan scowled at his aunt before facing his mother. "No. I wouldn't say that. Never."

Heidi pointed at her son. "Keep it that way, mister." She turned her attention back to her father. "So, this volunteering thing. It's getting to be too much?"

Ray set down his fork. "It's not that. There's something I'm working on, and it's in my head."

"What is it?"

Pam leaned forward. "Yeah, Dad. What's going on?"

He dismissively waved a hand. "It's not important. What about you guys? What's going on in your worlds?"

Heidi studied him. "You're deflecting."

"I know," Ray said, "but I don't want to talk about my work. Tell me what's going on with you guys. It's been a month since we've done this. Bring me up to speed on your lives."

Heidi rolled her eyes. "Ugh. The market is the same, and my love life is non-existent."

"Ditto," Pam said. "Well, not the market, but the job is the same."

"Oh my God, Pam. You date."

"Dating is not love."

"Yeah, Mom," Logan said. "That's what I've been trying to tell you."

Heidi stared at her son. "Thank you for the romance advice, Loveline."

Logan's face scrunched. "What the heck is that?"

Pam faced her father. "Dad?"

"Hmm?"

"Do you ever date?"

Heidi's eyes bulged. *"Pam!"*

"What did I do now?"

"He's married—to our mom!"

"I know that, but it's not like mom is coming back."

Heidi's fork clattered on her plate. "Are you fucking serious?"

"Mom!" Logan said with a laugh. "Language."

"Not now," Heidi said. To her sister, she asked, "Are you serious?"

"I'm trying to be."

"It's okay," Ray muttered.

"No, Dad," Heidi said. "It's not. I don't want you out running around while mom is in a home."

Pam shrugged. "She's not going to know the difference."

Heidi covered her mouth.

"When's the last time mom remembered you?" Pam asked. "She hasn't called me by my name in years. She hasn't asked me a question about my life in forever. I would bet everything I own that she doesn't even remember me."

Heidi dropped her hand from her mouth. She appeared hurt. "You bitch."

"Girls," Ray said.

Pam continued. "Why should Dad spend the last years of his life alone?"

Ray pulled back. "The last years of my life?"

"He's not alone," Heidi said. "He's got us. He's got mom."

Pamela rolled her eyes. "When are you going to grow up?"

"I'm your big sister."

"Not in this, you aren't." Pam angrily tapped the table with a finger. "You don't want to deal with it any more than I do, but at least I'm honest about it."

Ray abruptly stood.

Both girls looked at him. Logan kept his head down and continued to eat.

"Where are you going?" Heidi asked.

"Home," Ray said.

"But you haven't finished your dinner."

"If you two are going to argue all night, I'd rather eat with the cat."

Heidi and Pam stared at him.

"If we can all eat in a calm and rational manner, I'll stay."

Pam shrugged. "Works for me."

"I'm sorry," Heidi said. She looked at her sister. "Truce."

"Truce," Pam agreed.

Ray slowly sat. "Let's try this again."

Logan held out his hand. "Pass the potatoes."

"And just for the record," Ray said, "I'm not interested in dating anyone."

Pam held up an apologetic hand. "I was only suggesting."

Ray gently grabbed his daughter's fingers. "Well, stop. I love your mom. That's all you need to know."

Chapter 7

Ray Christy exited the Monroe Court Building. He carried a manila folder with some documents that needed to be delivered to the Public Safety Building. Usually, this was a task for another volunteer, but Ray wanted an excuse to be in the PSB.

As he crossed the parking lot, a woman called out, "Ray!"

He turned in the direction of the voice.

Irene Herbison waved at him then closed her car door. She hurried over.

"I'm sorry about Saturday," she said.

"What about?"

"My friend." She apologetically shook her head. "Mary Jo can be a little much at times."

Ray shrugged. "Don't worry about it."

"But I did. I do."

"There's no reason to." He pointed toward the Public Safety Building. "I need to go."

Irene touched his arm. "Listen, Ray. You're a good guy, and I like having fun with you. But I hope you know there's a line I can't cross. Won't cross. You understand?"

He nodded.

"If you want me to stop with the teasing, then I will."

Ray didn't take long to consider it. "You should probably stop."

She rubbed his arm. "Okay, Ray. I get it."

He jerked his head toward the main building. "I really do need to go. I'll see you when I get back."

Irene smiled. "That sounds good."

Ray walked away.

***

Ray entered the hallway of the Spokane Police Department. He'd been a volunteer long enough that the novelty of being in the main building had worn off.

He walked by the chaplain's office and peeked in. Chaplain Gabriel Green was seated at his desk. The man of God was only a couple of years younger than Ray.

"Hey, Padre."

Gabe turned and smiled. "Ray, what's got you out and about this morning?"

He held up the manila folder. "Making the rounds."

"You're looking good."

"You, too."

"How's life treating you?"

"About the same, Padre. And you?"

"My days are numbered. Only a few weeks left, and then I'm out of here."

"Got any plans for retirement?"

Gabe pointed to a picture of an RV on his corkboard. "The wife and are going to do some traveling. Make up for lost time if you will."

"Sounds like a wonderful way to do it."

The chaplain shifted in his chair. "How's Audrey?"

Ray tapped the edge of the file into his palm. "She's doing well. Thanks for asking."

"If you ever need any help or want someone to talk with…"

"Thanks, Padre. I appreciate it, but I'm okay."

"If you ever change your mind, you know where to find me."

"For a few more weeks, at least."

Gabe grabbed a business card and wrote something on it. When he handed it to Ray, he said, "That's my personal cell phone. In a few weeks, if you want to talk, you call me on that. I'll still be there for you."

Ray slid the card into his shirt pocket. "I might just take you up on that offer."

"Do that."

Ray touched his fingers to his temples and tipped them toward Gabe. Then he continued down the hall. He felt bad for lying to the chaplain, but Ray would never call anyone to talk about his feelings.

***

Ray entered the Major Crimes section. He'd been there once before but didn't know his way around. He wandered slowly by several unoccupied cubicles before he came to one labeled Parker.

A shorter man sat in a swivel chair and was leaning over a desk. He appeared to be deep in concentration as he studied an open file. He wore a white long-sleeve shirt and black slacks.

"Excuse me," Ray said, "Detective Parker?"

The man looked up. "Yeah?"

"Ray Christy." He extended his hand.

Parker eyed it for a moment, then shook it.

"Can I ask you a question?"

"That depends." Parker leaned back in his chair. "What's it about?"

Ray opened his folder and pulled a copy of his Found Property report. He handed it to the detective. "Over the weekend, I recovered Margaret Kelley's wallet from the Denny's on Division."

Parker scanned the report.

"You investigated her death," Ray said.

The detective lifted his head. "And?"

"I wanted to let you know what I found."

Parker considered the report again. "Okay."

"You didn't happen to take the wallet, did you?"

The detective's brow furrowed. "Are you implying I lost it in a Denny's parking lot?"

"No, sir. I was just wondering if you might have taken it, but clearly, you didn't."

"That's right. I didn't."

"Could it have been a homicide?"

The detective raised an eyebrow. "Say again?"

"Could Margaret Kelley have been murdered?"

Parker stood. He continued to look up at Ray, though. "What are you getting after, Christy?"

"Nothing." Ray pointed at the report the detective still held. "It's just that I found her wallet."

"We've established that."

"And she's dead."

"No shit."

"Well, that's suspicious."

Parker cocked his head. "Because you found her wallet?"

"Not just that, no. The group home she lives in is owned by a state patrol detective."

"Yeah, I know. Jory Bishop. What of it?"

"Do you know him?"

The detective slowly inhaled. As he did, Parker studied Ray. "I've never met the man, but why does that matter?"

Ray put his hands on his hips but thought that might be seen as disrespectful. Instead, he clasped his hands in front of him. "Doesn't that seem strange?"

"That I don't know him?"

"That he owns the group home."

Parker half-smiled now. "Cops can't own businesses?"

"Well, no," Ray said. "I mean, yes, they can, but that's not the strange part."

The detective sighed. "Man, I don't have time to waste on your fantasies here. Either blurt it out or let me get on with my day."

"Margaret Kelley died, and then the detective showed up there. He shouldn't be involved in the investigation of her death."

"He's not investigating her death. I am." Parker's face hardened. "Wait. You went to the house? Why?"

"To return the wallet. I didn't know Margaret was dead before then."

Parker rolled the Found Property report and pointed it at Ray. "That house belongs to Bishop. He can be there if he wants. Got that?"

Ray nodded.

"And not that it's any of your business," Parker frustratingly shook his head, "I can't believe I'm explaining any of this to you, but I checked out the man, and he came back clean."

"Why would you do that?"

"What's with all the questions? You're not working this case either." Parker tapped his chest with the report. "I am. Understand?"

Ray lifted a hand. "I apologize."

"I checked him out because it fascinated me that a cop owned a business like that. Is that okay with you? I did it because it seemed cool. And for your information, Bishop wasn't even in town when Margaret Kelley drowned. Her death was an accident. The medical examiner confirmed it this morning. End of story."

"But—"

"But nothing, Miss Marple. You weren't there, so you don't know what you're talking about. Detective Bishop had nothing to do with Margaret Kelley's death. Period.

Now, why don't you dawdle your way back to the volunteer office—" Parker wiggled two fingers to mimic a person walking "—and let us actual cops do our jobs."

"I didn't mean to offend."

Parker smirked. "It'll take a lot more than you to offend me, pops." He dropped back into his chair. "Thanks for the report." He exaggeratedly spun the paper to his desk. "Now, if you'll excuse me, I've got real police work to do."

Ray left the Major Crimes office then.

***

"You want me to look up what?" Dixie Richter said. She held the folder that Ray delivered from the Volunteer Services office.

Dixie was a tall woman and about the same age as Ray. She wore a white sweater, blue jeans, and running shoes. She was also a volunteer and had been assigned to help in the records department. Dixie had gotten the gig due to her previous work history and security clearance.

"It's a homicide report," Ray whispered. He slid a slip of paper across the counter. "That's the report number. I don't know if anything has been filed yet."

Dixie glanced over her shoulder at the paid staff members. They were all in their thirties and forties, and none of them paid any attention to either Dixie or Ray.

When her attention returned to Ray, Dixie whispered, "I could get in trouble for this."

"Don't do it then. We'll still be friends."

Dixie ran her fingers through her short gray hair as she considered the incident number. "What do you want with it?"

Ray looked around before speaking. "I'm trying to figure out something, and the homicide detective working the case won't talk with me."

A sly smile appeared on Dixie's face. "You're like Father Brown."

"Is that one of the new chaplains?"

She shook her head. "It's a TV show. Never mind. Who's got the case?"

"Parker."

Dixie frowned. "He's a piece of work."

"Tell me about it. I get the feeling he thinks I've aged out of my usefulness."

"There's a lot of that going around." She glanced back again at the full-time staff members. None looked Dixie's way. "They only let me sort and file here. Can you believe that? I was a CFO, for Christ's sake. These stupid cows couldn't amortize their way out of a paper bag." She palmed the small piece of paper. "Take a walk. Come back in five."

***

Ray left the building. It wouldn't look good for him to be seen standing around. Not that he was doing anything wrong, but it would lead to questions. Ray learned long ago in his military career that standing around doing nothing led to bad things. It was always better to look busy—be in actual motion or appear to be working.

He could have returned to the Monroe Court Building, but by the time he got there, Dixie might have something for him.

Ray headed for the west doors. On that side of the public safety campus was the juvenile court building, which held both the detention center and its administrative wing. Ray had no business with them.

To the northeast was the concrete monolith that housed the county jail.

Ray headed north toward the public parking lot. Beyond that was the SPD lot.

It was a nice morning, and a short jaunt in the sun would do him well. He and Audrey used to walk together a lot. In their younger years, they even jogged. That was after he left the military and when he still had a lot of pent-up energy that needed expending.

Now, his exercise regimen was mainly a thing of the past. Its falling to the wayside hadn't happened consciously but rather by erosion. One day was missed because he took Audrey to an appointment. Or he skipped going to the gym because he was worried about leaving her alone for too long. His health maintenance seemed secondary to ensuring she was safe.

After she moved into Colonial Springs, Ray had all the time in the world to return to exercising. He tried walking through the neighborhood once. He stopped after about a mile. He blamed the pain in his knee, but the reality was something else entirely. The walks were a stark reminder of how alone he now was in this world. He hadn't been on a walk since.

The morning sun warmed his face, and Ray felt surprisingly good even though Detective Parker's dressing down of him still lingered in the back of his thoughts. When Ray was a first sergeant, no one dared talk to him that way—not even lieutenants or captains. They respected his time in service and the effort it took to get that rank. And the new lieutenants who didn't were quickly advised by their superiors of how experience mattered in a combat unit.

Once Parker started in on him, Ray forgot to mention his thoughts on Kayla Dawn Reed—that maybe she took Margaret's wallet. And if she was willing to do that, perhaps the woman had a hand in the woman's death. But there was no way Ray would go back to Parker and try to explain those thoughts now. He'd keep them to himself for the time being.

Ray wandered into the far north lot where the patrol cars sat in a separate fenced-off area. He checked his watch.

"Good enough," he muttered to himself.

Ray walked with purpose now. He pulled his shoulders back, puffed his chest out, and held his head up. It had been some time since he moved like this, and his upper back quickly told him so by delivering a twinge of pain between his shoulder blades. Ray did his best to ignore it.

As he neared the county jail, Ray noticed a maroon Chevy Impala was parked outside the Law Enforcement Only entrance.

It can't be, Ray thought.

He drifted toward the car to get a better view of the license plate.

The door to the jail opened, and WSP Detective Jory Bishop stepped out. He didn't bother shutting the door—it automatically swung closed on its own. Bishop strode purposefully toward his patrol car. When the detective saw Ray, he stopped.

"What the hell are you doing?"

Ray pointed toward the PSB. "I'm heading there."

"Are you following me?"

"No, sir."

Bishop angrily moved toward Ray.

Ray had been in several fights in his life, but they were many years ago. Today, he was admittedly intimidated by Bishop. Not only was the man more than thirty years his junior, but he also wore a cop's badge and carried a gun. The thumb of justice pressed heavily on the scale for the detective.

Bishop stood nose to nose with Ray. His eyes were

bloodshot, and his breath smelled as if he hadn't brushed his teeth in days. "I don't get you."

"There's nothing to get." Ray did his best to keep his voice from wavering.

"You show up at my business, not once, but twice. That's right. I know you went back and talked to Vera. Now, you're here next to my car. Are you trying to get under my skin?"

"No, sir."

"Well, it's working." Bishop's gaze fell to Ray's nametag, and then it traveled across his chest to the ID badge that dangled from his pocket lapel. "Raymond Christy. I'm going to remember that."

Ray didn't say anything.

Bishop glanced around before saying, "I'm not a guy you want to fuck with."

"I understand." Ray stepped to the side to leave, but Bishop put his hand on Ray's chest to stop him.

"Did you hear what I said?"

"Yes, sir."

"Don't even think about showing up at that house again. Understand?"

Ray nodded.

Bishop dropped his hand away from Ray's chest. "Then be on your way, old man."

Reluctantly, Ray headed toward the Public Safety Building.

***

Dixie Richter approached the counter. "There's not much in the system yet. Looks like just the responding officer's reports."

Ray looked over Dixie's shoulder to the others in the Records section. None of the other employees looked in their direction.

Dixie surreptitiously placed a couple of pages onto the counter.

"Can I take these?" Ray asked.

"I'd prefer if you didn't," she whispered.

Ray lowered his head over the reports.

The new program allowed most officers and detectives to enter the reports directly into the system. Ray knew this was a far more efficient process than the way he wrote his reports. That was an advantage the young had over his generation. They'd grown up with computers. He also thought it was a disadvantage because they wouldn't know how to survive without them. Yet a time hadn't come where they had to do anything close to that. Until that day, the young could gleefully hold onto their technology and lord it over those of Ray's age group.

Dixie provided him with two short reports—both from responding patrol officers. They each wrote that Vera Drayton found Margaret Kelley drowned in the home's bathtub. The officers responded and confirmed this. They then called for a supervisor who alerted Detective Parker. After that, the two officers kept the scene secure until released by the detective.

Each report was less than a full page. One was two paragraphs long.

Ray looked up. "Thank you, Dixie."

"Sure." She quickly put the papers together, tore them in half, then ripped them in half once more. "Did you find what you wanted in there?"

"Not really, but I think I'm still on the right track."

"Let me know how it all turns out." She looked over her shoulder at her co-workers.

Ray also checked to see if anyone was watching them. No one seemed to care that they were talking.

Dixie faced him again. "This was kind of fun, Ray.

Got my blood pumping."

"Yeah."

"Let me know if you need anything else."

He thought about asking her to look up the reports on Kayla Dawn Reed, but he worried that it would be asking for too much right now. Maybe he'd come back tomorrow or the next day.

Ray smiled and tapped the counter twice. "I'll be in touch. Take care."

Chapter 8

Ray started toward the Monroe Court Building but stopped. He'd been replaying the conversation with Jory Bishop in his head when he remembered something that Detective Parker had said.

Parker checked out Bishop because he found it interesting that the detective owned a business. According to the detective, Bishop came back with a clean record. That meant Parker had run him criminally. Had Parker checked the trooper in other ways?

Probably not, Ray decided. Once Parker decided that Margaret Kelley's death was an accident, what other reason would there be to continue digging into Bishop?

Parker didn't have two confrontational run-ins with Bishop as Ray did, so his opinion was colored by the badges they both wore. Ray believed he had a more honest view of the trooper.

He diverted his path and headed toward the Spokane County Courthouse. It took only a couple of minutes to pass through the metal detectors before he climbed the stairs to the Assessor's office. Ray entered the lobby and eyed the clerks.

Ray found who he was looking for at the far end of a line of workers. Donald Faust was engaged in a conversation with a customer. Ray entered the line for service. As he waited, a couple of others joined the queue behind him.

After ten minutes, Ray was at the front of the line, but Donald was still engaged with the same customer.

"Next," a young woman called.

Ray turned to the man behind him. The guy had olive-colored skin and wore a turban. "You can go ahead of me."

"You sure?"

"I'm waiting for that guy over there. He was already helping me."

The man in the turban stepped around Ray and headed to the counter.

In a moment, Donald Faust looked toward the front of the line. He smiled when he announced, "Next."

Ray moved to the far end of the marble counter. A thick piece of Plexiglas separated the two men.

Donald Faust was two decades younger than Ray and probably thirty pounds heavier. He wore a button-up sweater over a blue button-up shirt.

Ray rested an elbow on the counter and watched the other clerks and their customers. He spoke into the opening near the counter. "Hey, Donny. Long time no see. How's Fran?"

"She's good, Ray. And Audrey?"

"She's doing fine. Thank you for asking."

"We've missed you at church."

"Yeah, I know. I'm sorry about that."

Donald shook his head. "There's nothing to be sorry for. It'll be there when you're ready to come back. The men's group, too. You'll always be welcome."

"I appreciate that."

"What can I help you with today?"

Ray changed his position, so his back was to the other clerks. He still leaned on the counter. "I'm hoping you can help me with a thing I'm working on for the department."

"What's that?"

"Can you tell me about a property a guy owns?"

"You can look that up on the internet, Ray. You don't need me." Donald grabbed a notepad and jotted something down. He ripped off the top paper and slid it under the Plexiglas partition. "Go to that website and enter the property address. It'll give you everything you want to know."

"Will it tell me when he bought the property and for how much?"

Donald nodded.

Ray lifted an eyebrow. "Will it tell me if he owns any other property?"

"No. It won't tell you that."

"Can *you* look up that kind of thing?"

"I can. It's public information."

Ray nodded but didn't say anything. He simply stared expectantly at Donald.

"Okay, what's the name?"

"Jory Bishop."

"Jory? Huh." Donald turned to his keyboard and entered the name. "The only thing that comes up is a home in the Nine Mile Falls area. Is that what you're looking for?"

"Maybe. I don't know. The property I'm thinking about is on Fleming Street."

"What's that address?"

Ray told him, and Donald entered it into his computer.

"Looks like it's owned by a limited liability company—Bishop Takes Queen." Donald's fingers danced over the keyboard some more. "And it seems that LLC only owns the one property."

Ray repeated the name of the limited liability company to himself. Then he said, "Okay, thanks for checking, Donny. I appreciate it."

"You bet. I hope to see you at church soon."

Ray nodded and stepped away from the counter. He stopped and quickly moved back to where he previously stood. He whispered, "Try Bishop Takes King."

Donald's brow briefly furrowed. "Are you sure this is for the police department?"

Ray nodded. "Scout's honor."

"All right," Donald said and turned toward his computer. His fingers jumped around the keyboard. "Will you look at that? Bishop Takes King owns a property on Nevada Street."

Ray's heart raced. "No kidding?" He pulled his notebook from his pocket. "Any other properties?"

"No, just the one."

"What's the address?"

"Don't worry about it, Ray. I'll print it for you. Let's run that Bishop fellow's name again and do the same with the Fleming house so we can print those, too."

In just a minute, Ray had three property printouts. "Is that normal?" Ray asked. "For LLCs to own a single property? Wouldn't it make more sense to have those houses under a single LLC?"

Donald shook his head. "A lot of property owners do this. Every property they buy goes into a separate entity. Supposedly, it reduces the risk of litigation or something."

"Really?" Ray studied the pieces of paper. "What about Bishop Takes Pawn?"

Donald shrugged. "I don't know. Let's look." In less than a minute, he smiled. "Ray, if I were a gambling man, I'd bet on whatever you're picking. Let me print this one off, and we'll try the next. What would that be? Rook?"

For the next couple of minutes, Donald checked the remaining chess pieces—rooks, knights, and bishops. There were six LLCs for all. Ray assumed they were all owned by Jory Bishop. The six properties were scattered around Spokane County.

When Donald returned with the printouts, Ray nodded his thanks. "How do I find out if there are any other

LLCs registered to Jory Bishop?"

"We don't have that capability here," Donald said. "That's probably something they can do at the state level."

Ray held up the papers. "Thank you, Donny. This has been a big help."

***

"Hey, Christy," Sergeant Newman said

Ray looked up from his desk. He'd been reading the assessor's reports that Donald Faust gave him. There was a lot of data concerning the size of each house and its accompanying lot, but Ray was most interested in when the properties were purchased. It seemed the first home, Bishop Takes Pawn, was purchased six years ago. How could a guy buy six properties in six years?

"Come here," the sergeant ordered.

Ray left the papers spread out on his desk and entered the sergeant's office.

"Sir?"

Brandon Newman leaned back, and a large set of blueprints rolled up automatically. A few minutes ago, Ray had overheard the sergeant on the phone excitedly talking with someone about a construction start date. He wasn't keeping his new home a secret.

"What are you doing?" Newman asked.

"Uh." Ray glanced back to his desk. "I'm getting ready to handle the vacation checks. Mel isn't back yet. Why? Do you have something else for me?"

Newman crossed his arms. "Were you over in the Major Crimes section earlier? I was talking with the chief's new receptionist and thought I saw you exit their office."

Ray nodded once. "I visited Detective Parker."

"What for?"

"To talk about a case he's working."

The sergeant's eyebrows lifted. "A homicide?"

Ray didn't trust the enthusiasm Newman displayed. Even though Ray had suspicions about Jory Bishop and Margaret Kelley's death, he didn't want the sergeant involved. If Newman understood what Ray found, he might find it worthy of further investigation. In that case, it would be taken from Ray and likely given to Parker. Ray disliked that idea on many levels.

"No, sir," Ray said. "It appears to have been an accident."

"An accident?" Newman frowned. "How so?"

"A woman drowned."

"Oh." The sergeant cocked his head. "And why are you involved?"

"Someone found the woman's wallet in a Denny's parking lot. On Saturday, radio dispatched me to pick it up. I told Detective Parker about it."

"And what did he say?"

"He said thank you."

"That's all?"

"That's it."

Sergeant Newman leaned slightly to the left and looked beyond Ray. "Are you and Irene working on something?"

"Not that I know of. Why?"

"Looks like she's waiting for you."

Ray glanced over his shoulder to see Irene lingering near his cubicle. Her head was bowed as if she were reading something on his desk.

Sergeant Newman cleared his throat to attract Ray's attention. "If you ever have reason to contact Major Crimes again, let me know before you do so. Okay?"

Ray nodded. "Yes, sir."

"I don't want to be caught off guard. You understand."

"I do. It won't happen again."

"Chain of command and that whole thing."

"Sure." Ray wondered if he saluted Newman right now if the man would understand the sarcasm in the act and be offended, or if the sergeant would simply appreciate it and want more of it in the future.

Newman unrolled his blueprints and dropped his attention to them. "Thanks, Ray," he muttered. "That's all."

Ray returned to his desk. Irene Herbison looked up when he neared. "What's this?" she whispered and pointed to the printouts. "What are you working on?"

"Nothing." He collected the papers and put them in the top drawer.

"Who's Joey Bishop?"

Ray didn't bother correcting her. "He's nobody."

Irene canted her head. "Come on, Ray. Tell me what you're working on. I want to help."

Ray harshly whispered, "No." He looked toward Newman, who watched Irene and him with interest. Ray turned his back toward the sergeant.

"What's going on?"

"Nothing." He glared at Irene. "Now, stop asking questions."

She appeared hurt. "Well, excuse me for caring. I can take a hint." Irene stormed away.

"Aw, hell," he muttered.

Ray stood there for a moment and considered going after her to apologize. Irene's feelings weren't his problem, though. She was a grown woman who snooped into his business. She wasn't Audrey nor his daughters. He didn't need to worry about how she felt. He grabbed his keys, the clipboard of vacation home checks, and the printouts of Jory Bishop's properties. Ray headed toward the exit.

Vern Kuehn sat at the reception desk. "Where you headed, Ray?"

"None of your business," he snapped.

Ray yanked open the door and exited the office.

***

Ray performed the vacation checks first. He wanted to shirk his responsibility and get immediately to his own mission, but the duty of the program came first. That was inherent in all of Ray's military training.

He zipped across the city and drove by the various empty homes. Once again in the Comstock neighborhood, Ray stopped his car. He collected two newspapers that lay at the edge of the driveway. He walked up to the front of the blue house and put them on the small porch.

While Ray drove toward the next house, his mind remained preoccupied with various people: Jory Bishop, Irene Herbison, and Audrey. His thoughts jumbled in on themselves, and his attempts to separate them came in starts and stops.

He tried to focus solely on the problem of Jory Bishop. Then he began worrying if he really hurt Irene's feelings. That led to him thinking about Audrey. The cycle started again even when he tried hard to control the direction of his contemplations.

After Ray drove by the final home on the vacation check roster, he moved the printouts for the various Bishop properties to the top of his clipboard. He had ordered them by the rank of chess pieces. Bishop Takes Pawn, LLC went first. That house was located on East Fifth Avenue. It was across town, however.

He wondered if there was a more efficient way to

check the properties.

Ray flipped through the pages until he found a closer house. Bishop Takes Bishop, LLC owned a property on Belt Street. That was less than a mile from where he was now.

He turned and headed in that direction.

It seemed to be a large rancher just north of Wellesley Avenue. Ray checked the assessor's report and confirmed the house to be almost 1,800 square feet. Like the home on Fleming Street, it appeared recently painted tan with dark brown accents. The house also seemed well-maintained, and the yard was recently cut.

Ray didn't know what he should be searching for at this moment. He assumed the house was a group home, but what if it wasn't?

The adage about assuming was a constant refrain during his time in the military. Yet what was his option now? Should he walk up to the door, ring the bell, and ask if it was a group facility? And what if that got back to Jory Bishop?

If the man was angry before then, he would be seriously peeved to know Ray was traipsing around town checking on him.

Which led Ray to realize he hadn't confirmed if Bishop was even involved in the various LLCs that owned these properties. For a moment, Ray berated himself for skipping a step in his investigation. He should have taken a moment before leaving the Volunteer Services' office to confirm Bishop's involvement. However, he really didn't know how to do that, so either he'd have to muddle about on the internet to find out, or he'd have to ask someone for help.

So, that was yet another case of assuming Ray had done. How many times had he told privates and sergeants not to "make an ass out of u and me?" Nevertheless, here he was doing it in an investigation.

But was it an assumption? Could it be correctly labeled as conjecture? After all, the LLCs were all named some variation of Bishop taking a chess piece, and Vera Drayton had told him that Bishop owned the home on Fleming Street.

Maybe Ray was playing word games with himself—conjecture versus assumption—to make himself feel better, feel smarter. He'd never investigated anything before, and the whole thing felt clumsy.

But he was out here now with a Volunteer Services' car and a list of properties owned by LLCs with 'Bishops Takes' in their names. The best thing he could do was drive on, as he would say to his troops. In other words, Ray should simply continue and get a real-world view of the houses he suspected the trooper owned. It was essentially the same thing Ray did for the vacation checks. If it was good enough for that, he should settle for it with Jory Bishop.

Ray selected the next closest property—one on Lindeke Street—and drove away.

***

Bishop Takes Pawn, LLC owned a property on East Fifth Avenue. Ray turned at Sherman Street and headed east. Interstate 90 ran parallel to the road.

He had only one more property to check after this, and then he'd head back to the office. The first thing he'd do when he returned would be to confirm that Jory Bishop was indeed either the owner or a partner in the various LLCs.

But what would that prove?

If Jory Bishop did indeed own these six properties, the only thing he might be guilty of was being a shrewd businessman.

When Ray found the Fifth Avenue property, he couldn't find a spot to pull over. No parking was allowed on the north side of the street, and spaces were limited on the south. Mostly older, dented cars lined the curb. However, there were a couple of cars that were obviously new and expensive.

Ray double-parked and leaned into the passenger seat to view the property owned by Bishop Takes Pawn, LLC. It was larger than the other properties he'd found. They'd all been ranchers. This one was a two-level house with a basement. If this was an adult care facility, he wondered what kind of folks could live in one with stairs. Maybe they were relegated to the first floor.

Like the other Bishop Takes properties, though, this house appeared to have been recently painted the same tan with brown accents. The lawn was well kept.

The front door opened, and four men walked out. Three were in suits. One was in blue jeans and a plaid shirt. Jory Bishop laughed and said something to the well-dressed men. They all smiled in response.

Ray straightened in his seat, put his car into gear, and quickly drove away. Up ahead, he noticed Bishop's maroon Chevy Impala parked on a side street. Ray thought it too much to hope for that his Volunteer Services' car hadn't been seen by the detective.

Chapter 9

"Where's Irene?" Ray asked.

Vern Kuehn looked up from his computer. "She left."

Ray exhaled forcefully and shook his head.

"Did you need something, Ray?"

"Just to apologize."

"You can apologize to me."

Ray smirked. "For what?"

Vern crossed his arms. "For being a horse's ass when you left."

"You're a man."

"What's that got to do with anything?"

Ray shook his head. "I'm not apologizing to you."

"Men have feelings, too."

"They sure do," Ray said, "but they keep them where they belong."

Vern started to say something, but Ray ignored him and headed toward his desk.

Not apologizing to Irene would needle Ray until the next time he saw her. But he needed to compartmentalize it because there was nothing that he could do about it now. Even though her number was listed on the emergency callout sheet, Ray wasn't going to phone her. An apology was something best done in person. Irene's address was also in her Volunteer Services file, and Ray had access to that, but he would never go to her home—it would send the wrong message. So, he'd have to wait for her to return to the office.

He sat at his desk and completed the vacation house check form. When he was done with that, he set it to the side to turn in. Then he pulled out the printouts of the various Bishop Takes properties.

Jory Bishop had walked out of the house on Fifth Avenue. That should be enough confirmation that he owned all the Bishop Takes properties. Shouldn't it?

Even after all these years, he wished he could call his son and get his opinion.

What would he tell me to do?

Jacob would probably tell him to stop screwing around in an investigation and let the cops handle it. Once he became a police officer, Jacob developed an almost zero tolerance for movies and books with sleuths who weren't trained investigators.

"They don't know what they're doing," Jacob had said. "They're amateurs, and they're going to get someone hurt or themselves killed."

But even with all his training and resources, his son ended up murdered while in uniform.

Ray wasn't some pushover, though. He'd spent his entire career leading men who were trained to kill. He, himself, had killed on the battlefield. Admittedly, that was some years ago. But he wasn't going to fear what might be. He wanted to know that he could still stand up in the face of adversity and do what was needed, what was right.

Maybe he could bring it up to Chief Dillon during their lunch tomorrow. He considered it, but the idea bothered him. Discussing the matter with the chief was tantamount to jumping several layers over the chain of command. Talking about life and family with the leader of the police department was one thing; asking Dillon about an investigation Ray had no business sticking his nose into was another matter.

Still, Ray had two questions that needed answers. Did he have enough information to prove that Jory Bishop owned all the Bishop Takes properties? And more importantly, did it even matter?

Ray briefly pondered the second question but kept coming back to the first. He wanted proof positive that Bishop owned the various LLCs. Maybe the detective's appearance at the house on Fifth Avenue was simply an odd coincidence.

Who did Ray know who could help him look up something like that?

He grabbed his cell phone and placed a call. She answered on the second ring.

"Hey, Dad."

"Heidi, are you busy?"

"I'm working, but I've got a few minutes."

Ray glanced around to make sure no one was listening. "If I want to find out if someone is in an LLC, how do I do that?"

"Why do you want to do that?"

"It's a work thing."

"Why do the volunteers want you to look up LLC members?"

Ray massaged his temples. "Look, honey. Is that something I can do or not?"

"Sure," Heidi said. "There's a state website that you do that with, but if a person doesn't want you to know who's inside the LLC, they can have it hidden by using a registered agent."

Ray tapped the space bar on his keyboard to bring his computer to life. "What's the name of the website?"

"Hold on. Let me put you on speakerphone so I can use both hands." He heard a keyboard clicking on the other end of the line. "Here it is. Are you ready?

Ray awkwardly held his cell phone between his ear and shoulder. He set his fingers on the keyboard. "Go ahead."

As Heidi recited the website address, Ray typed it in.

He hit the Enter button, and the screen changed to the Washington Secretary of State—Corporations page.

"Now," Heidi said, "click on the button that says Business Search. Do you see it?"

"Should I click on the one that says Advanced Business Search?"

"Less is more, Dad."

Ray hovered the mouse pointer over the Advanced button but went with Heidi's advice. He clicked the button that said Business Search.

She said, "Now scroll down until you see Corporation Search, then enter the LLC name you want to know about. You can input only part of the name if you want. That'll give you more results to pick from. That's what I normally do."

He rolled down to the appropriate place and entered Bishop Takes Pawn. Ray was about to hit enter when he backspaced and deleted Pawn. Then he hit return. The following entries were returned.

Bishop Takes Bishop, LLC.
Bishop Takes King, LLC.
Bishop Takes Knight, LLC.
Bishop Takes Pawn, LLC.
Bishop Takes Queen, LLC.
Bishop Takes Rook, LLC.

Next to each was a principal office address and the name of its registered agent—Jory Bishop.

"Did you find what you needed, Dad?"

"Yes," Ray said. "I did. Thank you, honey. I'll call you later."

After they ended the call, Ray printed the screen. Now, he had his proof that Jory Bishop was involved with the various properties, but it still didn't answer his second question.

Did it even matter?

He was about to close the window when Ray hit the back arrow and returned to the initial page. He entered Colonial Springs.

Quickly, the results came back.

Colonial Springs III, LLC with a principal address in Nevada. Its registered agent was another LLC—Temple Advantage Unlimited.

Ray back arrowed once more and entered Temple Advantage Unlimited but was greeted with the message—*No Results Found.* What did that mean?

He pondered it for a bit and finally decided that Temple Advantage had to be an out-of-state company. Ray closed the internet browser. He couldn't be sure, but Ray felt fairly confident that Jory Bishop wasn't an owner of his wife's care facility.

That brought him considerable relief.

***

Ray Christy stepped out of the Monroe Court building just as Irene Herbison entered.

"Hey, Irene."

"Ray," she said frostily.

Irene continued to the elevator.

He turned around and followed her. "Listen, I'm sorry."

"Don't be." She didn't look at him.

"Well, I am. I didn't mean to come off so abrupt. It's just that I'm working on this thing and—"

The elevator dinged.

Irene said, "It doesn't matter, Ray. I'll get over it."

As the doors opened, she stepped in. She pressed a button for an upper floor. He didn't follow her in.

Instead, Ray quietly watched her until the doors closed.

"Hell," he muttered.

Ray continued into the parking lot. He didn't mean to upset Irene, but he had. She was really mad now.

He climbed into his truck and started the engine. He dropped the pickup into gear and was about to pull out of his parking spot. That's when he saw the maroon Chevy Impala.

Jory Bishop sat behind the wheel. The two men made eye contact.

Ray wasn't sure what to do.

Should he continue to drive out of the parking lot?

Should he exit his truck and go back inside the Monroe Court building?

Or should he go up to the man and talk to him?

No, he most definitely should not do the last. If the detective had ill intent for him, what could Ray do about it? Nothing.

But Ray's question about what to do proved moot. The Impala slowly drove through the parking lot. As it did, Bishop's gaze stayed fixed on Ray. When the car passed Ray, Bishop broke eye contact. The car entered Monroe Street and headed north.

Ray sat there for several moments until his heartbeat returned to normal. When it did, he left the parking lot and turned south.

It wasn't the direction he wanted to go.

***

"Have you ever been on a roller coaster?" Audrey asked.

It was a strange question, and it caught Ray off-guard. "A roller coaster? Sure. Why do you ask?"

They were in Audrey's room at Colonial Springs. She

rested in the recliner while Ray sat in a wooden chair at the small table.

She pointed at the TV that silently ran a news report about a roller coaster in Florida. Audrey seemed transfixed by the motion on the screen. Her mouth slowly drooped open, and her eyes grew wide.

"Audrey," Ray said.

She turned slowly to him. Her mouth stayed agape, and her eyes remained big.

"Is there anything you want me to bring you?"

Audrey blinked, and her brow furrowed. She closed her mouth and swallowed.

"Do you want some more cookies?"

"No."

"What about some crackers? Would you like some Ritz?"

"No."

"I'll bring you anything you want."

"Okay."

"What do you want?"

"I don't know."

Her attention returned to the TV.

"I had dinner with the girls last night."

Audrey's mouth slowly opened. Ray eyed the TV. A commercial for a pest control company was on. It featured a cartoon spider. He continued to watch it until it ended. When it did, Audrey stood.

She said, "I have to go to the bathroom."

"Okay."

Audrey stared at him.

"I'll wait for you."

She didn't move.

"Are you wanting me to leave?"

"Yes."

Ray poured some kibbles into a bowl then set it on the floor. "Hey, Billy Boy," he called. "Come and get your dinner."

William appeared from around the corner. The cat took his time getting to the bowl. It stuck its nose into the dish but didn't eat. William looked around then left the room.

"I'm glad I could be of service," Ray said.

He thought about making something to eat for himself, but he really wasn't hungry. If he ate now, it would solely be out of habit, and that didn't appeal to him.

Besides, seeing Jory Bishop in the Monroe Court Building's parking lot bothered him. What business did the man have coming to his workplace? None. Ray had done nothing wrong, so Bishop had no business being there.

Ray took a step out of the kitchen when the realization hit him.

This is what he'd done to Bishop. Not only had he shown up at the house on Fleming Street a second time, but he'd talked with one of his residents. Then Ray drove by the house on Fifth Avenue where he was now certain Bishop had seen him.

Why else was Bishop in the Monroe Court Building's parking lot?

Of course, this also meant Bishop had inferred that Ray checked on him. The man must know that Ray knew of his other properties.

If Bishop was indeed innocent in Margaret Kelley's death as Detective Parker insisted, then the man had a right to be sore. No wonder he showed up at the Monroe Court Building.

Ray slowly sat at the kitchen table.

Now that Ray was thinking objectively about things, the state patrol detective could have done a lot worse than just sitting in his car. He could have waited for Ray to leave the parking lot then pulled him over. Or Bishop could have gotten one of his trooper buddies to do it. Then they could have given Ray a citation for something. Jacob once told him that finding a traffic violation was the easiest thing to do. No one could operate a vehicle perfectly.

Or if Bishop didn't want to contact him directly, the detective could have spoken with Sergeant Newman. Ray might have gotten in trouble for badgering the man. He wasn't sure if what he did rose to the level of harassment, but nowadays, just hurting someone's feelings was cause for termination of employment. Ray wasn't worried about getting kicked out of the volunteer program, but had he done something that rose to the level of a criminal charge? He didn't think so.

Ray stared into the kitchen. Questions and worries raced in and out of his mind until he latched on to one—why did Bishop make a show of being in the parking lot?

After some thought, Ray decided that the detective wanted him to know that he knew what Ray was up to. But why?

Again, Ray pondered it, and the best he could come up with was that Bishop didn't want any trouble. He just wanted Ray to ease up.

Ray struggled to understand his feelings in the situation. Would he be happy backing off? Probably not, because it sure felt like something was off with the trooper. But what choice did Ray have? He hadn't proved anything so far except the detective was good at business.

Although maybe that wasn't true. The man had been good at acquiring properties. Perhaps he wasn't good at running a business. A woman had died while in his care, after all.

The doorbell rang, and Ray looked at the clock on the wall. It was nearly nine.

Who shows up at this time of night? Ray wondered. Even Pamela had the good sense to not come over that late without at least a phone call first.

Ray stood and approached the door. He peered through the peephole. The porch light must have burned out, but there was enough ambient light for Ray to see. Standing on the other side of the door was Jory Bishop. The detective's face remained passive.

Fear cut through Ray.

"Mr. Christy," Bishop said to the closed door. "I know you're on the other side. Please open up. I only want to talk."

Ray continued to watch through the peephole.

Should I get my gun? he wondered. Ray owned a Smith & Wesson revolver that he kept in his nightstand. His attention remained glued to the man on the other side of the door.

Bishop inhaled deeply then blew it out through barely parted lips. He glanced around before turning back to the door. "Mr. Christy, if you don't want to talk tonight, that's cool. I'll leave my card." The detective reached into his shirt pocket and pulled out a business card. "Please come by my office tomorrow. I'd like for you to stop bothering me and my employees."

The peephole limited what Ray could see, but he imagined Bishop wedging his business card into the space between the door and the jamb.

"Good night," Bishop said. He turned and stepped off the small porch.

Ray opened the door, and a business card fluttered to the ground. "Detective."

Bishop turned slowly around. "Mr. Christy."

Ray kept his hand on the door in case he needed to close it quickly.

The detective stepped back onto the porch. He appeared haggard. Bishop wore a lightweight jacket. His right hand was bare, but a glove covered his left hand. The right glove poked out of a pocket. "I'm sorry for coming by so late."

Ray didn't bother to hide the suspicion from his face. "Why are you here?"

"Please stop following me."

"What about you showing up at my work?"

Bishop nodded. "I did that to let you know what it was like. A trooper showing up at your work," he glanced around, "at your home, well, it must be very unsettling."

"It was. It is."

"I'm sorry. That's how it feels with you showing up at my businesses. So, can we stop all this silliness?"

Ray frowned. "I don't think what I did was silly."

"Of course not." Bishop clicked his teeth as he thought. He leaned slightly to the left and looked over Ray's shoulder. "Nice home."

"May I ask you something, Detective?"

Bishop's attention returned to him. "What's that?"

"How did Margaret Kelley's wallet get four miles away from where she died?"

"I honestly have no idea."

"Maybe Kayla Reed stole it."

Bishop's features hardened. "That's a big allegation."

"But it seems like one you've considered."

"Are you a mind reader?"

"How could you have not considered it?"

A car drove by, but Bishop did not turn around. "Margaret Kelley drowned," he said. "A detective in your department even said so. That's good enough for me."

"You don't think someone might have had a hand in

her death?"

Bishop pointed at himself. "Are you saying it was me? I was in Seattle when it happened."

"Maybe it was Kayla."

The trooper's eyes darkened. "A bigger allegation than the last. It was an accident, Mr. Christy. Don't go saying otherwise."

"Because it would be bad for business?"

"That's right."

Ray cocked his head. "Who were the men with you at the Fifth Street house?"

Bishop pulled the glove from his jacket pocket. "Leave it alone."

"My daughter is a real estate agent, and I've seen her work before. Those men looked like buyers. Are you selling that home?"

The detective tugged the glove into place. "You've got it all wrong."

"I don't think so."

Bishop looked down at his shoes. "Listen, I came here to make nice, Mr. Christy. Can we do that? Will you stop bothering me and my business?"

Now that the detective was there on his porch, Ray had no intention of stopping. Something was off with Bishop, and Ray felt it. If he couldn't convince Detective Parker of it, perhaps there was another detective in the Spokane Police Department who would listen to him. And if not a detective, maybe there was an officer. All he needed was one person who saw the situation as he did. And if none of them would listen, he'd jump the chain of command and go to the chief.

But the best thing Ray could do for himself right now was to lull Bishop into a false sense of security. He didn't need the man to be any more suspicious than he already was. Therefore, Ray said, "Yeah, sure, Detective. I'll leave it alone. I'm sorry I bothered you."

"Why do I get the feeling you're shining me on?"

Ray shrugged. "I don't know what to tell you."

"Okay, fine. We'll let it be." Bishop bent and picked up the business card from the ground. He handed it to Ray. "In case you have questions."

"Thank you." Ray accepted the card with his free hand. "I might take you up on that offer."

The detective opened his right hand as an invitation to shake.

Ray's left hand released the door as he transferred the business card into it.

When Ray's right hand slipped into Bishop's, the detective's grip tightened.

Ray's eyes widened in surprise. "Hey."

Bishop's face darkened. "You should have stayed in your lane, old man."

The trooper punched Ray in the throat.

PART II

Chapter 10

Quinn Delaney tossed his keys and cell phone onto the kitchen counter. Next, he removed his badge and gun and carefully set them down. When he opened the refrigerator, he considered the items inside. There was leftover turkey meatloaf from the previous night's dinner. Or he could make a grilled cheese sandwich and maybe heat up some tomato soup to go with it.

None of that sounded good right now. Quinn decided he wasn't hungry. What he wanted was a distraction from what felt like a long day of work. He shut the door and headed to his bedroom.

He changed into a long-sleeved t-shirt, shorts, and running shoes. Quinn grabbed his Bluetooth headset and returned to the kitchen for his cell phone. The small headphones were many years old, which was evident by the wire connecting the two earpieces. Most people now wanted the cooler and far more expensive white earbuds, but Quinn's old headset still did the job even though the left earpiece was cracked. He would replace them when they eventually stopped working.

Quinn stepped out of his apartment, pulled the front door shut, and trotted down the stairs. He didn't even bother stretching. He simply started jogging. He'd pick up his pace the longer he ran and the looser he felt.

Recently, Quinn discovered a series of podcasts dedicated to the overturning of wrongful criminal convictions. There were many of them, but the one he enjoyed the most was *America the Convicted*. Each season, the show's hosts investigated a case they believed ended in a wrongful sentence. They then dismantled the case that the police and the prosecuting attorney built. Afterward, the hosts showed who they believed committed the crime and why the evidence pointed in that direction. It was a professionally done show and made for convincing entertainment.

Quinn hoped none of his cases ever appeared on the podcast or any of the others like it.

At the second mile, his legs and hips finally felt loose. He increased his pace. A mile later, he settled into the run and thought he might run for ten miles tonight—five out and five back. It wasn't a distance he ran daily, but he tried to run it once a week. When he got home tonight, he'd be hungry. Thoughts of the leftover meatloaf competed against the podcast. Quinn forced himself to focus.

His phone rang and interrupted the podcast. He didn't break stride as he slipped the phone from the carrying case around his bicep. The call screen showed a familiar number. He answered it. "Quinn."

"Detective, this is Annie in Dispatch. Where are you?"

"Running."

He didn't bother to slow, nor did he turn around. He wouldn't do such a thing until he knew the reason for the call. There had been plenty of calls in his past that were for information only. Quinn checked for traffic and crossed the street. His stride was long, and his breathing was smooth. He felt strong tonight.

"Detective?"

"Yeah?"

"I need you to focus." Annie's voice was gravely serious.

"I am."

"No, you're not. Please stop running."

"Okay." He slowed to a walk. "What's going on?"

"Do you know Ray Christy?"

"Never heard of him. Who is he?"

"One of our senior volunteers."

Quinn stopped completely now. "What happened?"

"Someone broke into his home."

A car with a rattling muffler drove by. Quinn waited until it faded in the distance. "Is he okay?"

"He's dead. According to the officers on scene, it looks like he was beaten to death. His daughter found him. She hadn't heard from him in a few days and got worried."

"What's the address?"

After she told him, Quinn said, "Hold on." He called up a notepad application on his phone. Quinn entered the address. "Got it."

"The chief is aware of this one."

A truck with a loud exhaust passed by. Quinn's hands covered his headphones. "He's made aware of every homicide," he said.

"You're not understanding what I'm saying, Quinn. He's on his way to the scene."

"Why?"

"Because Ray volunteered for the department, and the chief is acting like this is an officer-involved."

Quinn started walking toward home. "Listen, I'm a few miles from my house. Let the scene commander know that it's going to take a bit for me to get there."

"I will."

"Let Marci know, too."

"She'll be late, also. I caught her in the middle of class."

"We're both going to be late. Great."

"Better hurry, Quinn. I'm serious about the chief. He sounded weird when I talked with him."

"Weird, how?"

"Like he just lost a friend."

Quinn ended the call, and the podcast automatically started. Now wasn't the time for leisurely storytelling. He took a moment to find a playlist of classic rock and roll.

Then Detective Quinn Delaney ran as fast as he could toward his apartment.

***

Quinn finished a second peanut butter and jelly sandwich as he arrived at the crime scene. It wasn't the dinner he'd hoped for, but he needed fuel. On the driver's seat were two protein bars. He had a bad feeling that this crime scene might run into the next morning.

The sun was setting as he pulled onto East Ermina Street. Porch lights were on for most of the homes in the neighborhood. However, the exterior of the house with police officers in the front yard remained dark.

Multiple patrol cars lined the street. Their emergency lights were off. Quinn imagined the flashers might have remained activated after the officers first arrived, but there was no need to leave them on for this long. All that would do was attract more attention, and there was already enough.

Near the closest patrol car was an evidence van. The crime scene technicians beat him to the scene. They usually took the longest arriving. It wasn't the first time the forensic investigators beat him to a scene, but Quinn didn't like it when it happened. There wasn't much he could do about it since he essentially gave them a forty-five-minute head start. Even though he showered quickly and hastily prepped a couple of sandwiches, there was no way he could make up for the lost time it took him to run back to his apartment.

A black SUV was parked at the edge of the crime scene. Quinn didn't even need to check the L-100 license plate to know that it belonged to Chief Liam Dillon.

Parked behind the large SUV were two Chevy Impalas belonging to Captain Gary Ackerman and Lieutenant George Brand.

With his chain of command already on scene, Quinn knew questions about his response time would be lobbed his way. Of the three leaders, only Captain Ackerman had been a Major Crimes detective. He would remember that detectives had lives away from the job and that a homicide investigation didn't start until the assigned investigator arrived. The scene should simply be secured until that happened.

They would all question Quinn's sense of urgency, of course. He most certainly had one, but he couldn't live the job every minute of the day. That was a myth created by Hollywood. However, in moments like this, even the department's brass would likely cling to it and hold it above his head.

Quinn exited his car and looked around. His partner hadn't arrived yet. He didn't want to start without her, but he didn't have a choice. From the trunk of his car, he removed several pairs of latex gloves, a pair of shoe covers, and a sketchpad.

He walked toward the edge of Raymond Christy's property.

Chief Dillon approached with Captain Ackerman and Lieutenant Brand in his wake. Dillon wore the department's dark blue uniform while Ackerman sported a tailored suit—the uniform he donned daily.

Brand was the only one who seemed to have been off duty. He wore jeans, a plaid shirt, and a winter vest—a nattily dressed lumberjack. It was a strange juxtaposition for a crime scene, and the lieutenant appeared uncomfortable that he was not attired as either of his supervisors. He shoved his hands into the pockets of his puffy vest.

"What took you so long, Delaney?" the chief asked. His irritation was easily discerned. "And don't say traffic because the three of us all arrived before you."

"I was running."

Dillon studied him, which made Quinn slightly uncomfortable.

The chief was a stocky man in his mid-fifties. His bald head and scowl provided him an intimidating presence. He had the body of a former weightlifter who had grown soft around the middle. "Running," he said distastefully.

"I had to get back to my apartment before I could get ready to come out here." Quinn wasn't the antagonist type, especially not with the chief. "I apologize for the delay, sir."

The chief glanced about. "Where's your partner?"

"She had class."

"Of course." Dillon's lip curled. "One of ours gets murdered, and we get the detectives who want to be Carl Lewis and Chuck fucking Norris. Where's Nash and Higgins when I need them?"

Both Ackerman and Brand stared at the chief, but neither said anything.

Chief Dillon looked at the ground and shook his head. He lowered his voice. "Goddamn it. That was uncalled for. I'm sorry, Detective."

Quinn remained silent.

When the chief regained his composure, he looked up. "How well did you know Ray Christy?"

"I didn't, sir."

"He's been a volunteer for years. How could you two never have met?"

"If we did, I don't remember him."

Dillon rubbed his hand over his mouth. "Ray was a good man. Retired Army. He reminded me of my father."

His eyes misted, and his jaw tightened. "I think that's what drew me to him."

Ackerman shuffled his feet while Brand turned completely away. Quinn didn't break eye contact with the chief.

Dillon continued. "Ray and I had some nice talks over the years—at the volunteer banquet, impromptu chats in the hall. I took him to coffee and lunch a few times. It's probably stupid for a man my age to want a surrogate father..." He reached for his mouth again but dropped his hand just before it touched his face. "He had a son who was a cop in Albuquerque." The chief eyed Ackerman. "Did you know that, Gary?"

The captain shook his head. Lieutenant Brand mimicked the same motion.

"He was ambushed during a traffic stop several years ago. That's why Ray joined the volunteer program here. He wanted to understand why his son did what he did. Why he died the way he did." Dillon's voice wavered, and he covered his mouth.

Now, both Ackerman and Brand looked away.

"We were supposed to have lunch on Tuesday. When he didn't show, I called him and left a message." Tears welled in Dillon's eyes. "I didn't follow up after that. I got involved in my own bullshit. Ray might have been in there—" the chief pointed at the house "—since Tuesday. We could have found him faster had I followed up. Maybe he would even still be alive."

Dillon's hands shook, and he rolled his lips into his mouth. He struggled to maintain composure. Ackerman put his hand on the chief's shoulder. Dillon closed his eyes. In a moment, the chief nodded, and the captain removed his hand.

"Detective," Dillon said but stopped.

Quinn waited for him to continue.

The chief swallowed with some difficulty then inhaled deeply. "Detective Delaney, you find whoever did this."

"I will."

"You goddamn better." Dillon pressed a finger against Quinn's chest. "Make it your best work. Do you understand?"

Quinn nodded once.

"If you need anything, and I mean *anything*, you let me know." Dillon's face hardened. "If either of these guys," he thumbed toward the captain and lieutenant, "give you a hard time with what you need to solve this case, then you come directly to me. I'll get it for you, and then I'll deal with them. Do you understand?"

"Yes, sir."

"If anyone gives you grief, you come to me. I'm not going tolerate any bullshit on this." The chief eyed Lieutenant Brand. "Do you understand?"

Brand nodded.

Dillon looked to Ackerman and patted the captain's arm.

"I understand, Chief," Ackerman said.

"Ray Christy was my friend," Dillon said to Quinn, "but above that, he was a member of this department." The chief's voice broke. "Let's treat him like it."

Dillon walked off toward his vehicle with his head bowed.

Captain Ackerman studied Quinn. "Is there anything you need, Detective?"

"Where's the daughter who called it in?"

"Sitting in her car." The captain pointed to a Honda. "A chaplain is sitting with her now."

"Are officers canvassing the neighborhood for witnesses?"

Ackerman nodded. "There are a couple right now. No feedback so far. Anything else?"

"No."

"Then I suggest you get to work." The captain looked back toward the chief. "We're all under the microscope on this one."

Chapter 11

Quinn slipped under the yellow line of *Caution—Do Not Cross* tape at the edge of the property. That was the outer perimeter of the crime scene. The second line of tape at the house marked the inner perimeter. An officer stood near the front door and logged anyone who entered.

A woman called, "Delaney!" which forced him to stop and turn.

Marci Burkett trotted toward him. She wore a light jacket, blue jeans, and black boots. Like him, it appeared she'd taken some time to shower and change before heading to the crime scene. She normally wore only light make-up and tonight was no different. Even in this low light, however, Quinn could see the swelling around her left eye. It was almost closed shut.

He leaned and studied her face. "What happened?"

She tried to pull her bangs over the eye, but the layered bob style she wore her hair in didn't want to cooperate. "Inadvertent strike."

Quinn cocked his head.

"It's stupid. I kicked the inside of a guy's leg. He twisted and flailed his arm as he went to the ground." She pantomimed a guy whipping his hand into the air.

"And he smacked you in the face?"

Marci shrugged. "It happens, but I should have expected it. I'll remember it next time."

"Did the chief talk with you?"

"No, but Ackerman did. This one is really on the radar, huh?"

"Aren't they all?"

"For someone, sure." Marci looked toward the house.

"But they're saying this guy was a senior volunteer. You ever meet him?"

"No, but I don't think I could name a single one of them."

Marci shrugged. "Me neither."

They walked together toward the front of the house. A young officer with a clipboard stood at the bottom of a small set of stairs. Both detectives announced themselves, and the officer jotted their names onto the entry log. Quinn and Marci then ascended the steps, where they each slipped a set of covers over their shoes. Both then tugged on a pair of latex gloves.

"Ready?" Marci asked.

Quinn studied the neighborhood once more. The street was filled with law enforcement vehicles. The houses across the street and those down the way were lit up with porch lights. Most had their window curtains opened, and shadowy faces peered through them at the police activity.

He turned and studied the porch light of Ray Christy's home. Quinn reached up and turned the bulb until it sat firmly in the socket. It did not illuminate.

Marci stepped into the house, and the light suddenly shone brightly. Quinn turned his face away. The light quickly went out. He knew Marci hadn't turned it off for his comfort. Oily fingerprints were an excellent heat conductor and burned off a bulb. If the killer had carelessly left his prints behind, the detectives would want to make sure they did everything possible to preserve the evidence. Quinn might have already smeared any fingerprints by simply turning the bulb into place.

Marci reappeared. "There's blood on the switch plate."

"The killer loosened the bulb before he came inside but then flicked the light switch off before leaving?"

"Or maybe it was off when he arrived, and he unscrewed it so Ray couldn't turn it on." She stepped back so Quinn could enter the house. She pointed at the three light switches on the nearest wall. Blood smeared across the white plate.

"Maybe," Marci said, "the killer flicked them all off when he left but wasn't thinking about the porch light. Instead, he was worried about the house lights. You know, so he didn't backlight himself."

Quinn studied the light switches. "The killer also wouldn't want the house lit up all night since it would call additional attention to it."

Marci shrugged. "I'll buy that."

"When was the last time anyone saw Ray?"

"No idea."

"The chief was supposed to have lunch with him on Tuesday. Ray never showed."

Marci raised an eyebrow. "The chief was breaking bread with a volunteer? What's that about?"

"They were friends."

"That explains the microscope we're under." Marci leaned down to study the door jamb. "There was no forced entry." She stepped back outside. "Our suspect arrives and unscrews the light bulb." She demonstrated the action. "Probably rang the doorbell, too." She pretended to press the button. "Then Ray opened the door."

Quinn stood where he assumed Ray Christy might have been. The two detectives faced each other.

"So either Ray invited his visitor in," Quinn said.

"Or the killer forced his way in." Marci pushed him back.

Now the two of them stood shoulder to shoulder and studied the interior of the house. There was a small foyer that opened to a living room. Beyond it appeared to be a kitchen and dining area. A hallway led somewhere off to the right.

In the middle of the living room lay a body.

Next to the body stood Geri Utley, a crime scene technician. She wore a hazmat suit, and a camera dangled around her neck. "Are you two ready?"

"Have you photographed the house?" Marci asked.

"Already done. And I've photographed the body in place. You guys took your sweet time in getting here." She leaned forward as if to study Marci. "What happened to your face?"

"Nothing. What happened to yours?"

Geri lifted the camera. "Say cheese." She didn't take a photograph, however. Geri was a professional, and this was simply a moment of humor to let off some steam.

Quinn thumbed behind him. "Geri, get your guys to fingerprint the porch light."

"Will do. The switch plate is already on our list."

The detectives moved toward the body.

Ray Christy lay on his back with his arms splayed out to the side. Blood covered his entire head. Quinn bent over to study Ray's face.

A portion of the dead man's left cheek appeared to have collapsed. His eyes stared up at the ceiling. His mouth was partially open, and a couple of teeth appeared to have been knocked out.

Quinn looked up at Marci. "This guy look familiar to you?"

"Nope, but he's kind of messed up. Maybe he looked different without the broken face."

Quinn continued to study the fallen man. "Someone was seriously pissed at him."

"Revenge, maybe?"

"It's as good a motive as any."

He patted Ray's front pockets. Nothing was in them. Then Quinn reached under the body and removed a wallet. Inside were Ray's driver's license, a credit card, and seventy-four dollars. He eyed Geri. "How is the rest of the house? Is it undisturbed like this room?"

"Nothing looks ransacked. If the house was burgled, it was the cleanest act I've ever seen."

Quinn handed the wallet to Geri. "Please log this into property."

"Anything else?"

He eyed Marci.

She shook her head. "Let's walk the house."

The detectives took their time surveying each room. The sensation of being in a stranger's home no longer bothered Quinn. In the earlier portion of his career, it felt odd to trudge through a person's life. Now, he had no problem digging through a closet, picking through a drawer, or searching a computer of someone he'd never met. It was simply a game of hide and seek. Someone had hidden something he must find. Most of the time, he didn't know what was hidden and wouldn't realize right away he'd discovered it.

In the first bedroom, they found a black cat. It sat in a corner and watched them. When Quinn moved toward it, he said, "Hey, kitty." The cat hissed. "Must not like me."

Marci stepped forward, and the cat hissed again. "It's not only you."

The furthest bedroom appeared to be the master. A Volunteer Services' shirt hung over a bedpost. Marci lifted the shirt and felt the pockets. From inside the right pocket, she pulled a business card. "It's from Chaplain Greene." She turned it over. "And it's got a cell number on it." She returned the shirt to the bedpost but kept the card.

On the nightstand, Quinn found ninety-six cents in coins alongside a coverless book. He lifted the novel and inspected the spine. He showed it to Marci. "Ever hear of it?"

"*Don't Stop the Carnival*? Sounds dumb."

"I agree." Quinn flopped the book onto the top of the nightstand. Then he opened the drawer. Inside was a Smith & Wesson .38. "Hello, there."

Marci peered into the drawer. "Didn't help him much, did it?"

"Maybe he didn't think it was necessary."

Quinn left the drawer open. He would have the forensic team secure the weapon.

"You ever think about it?" Marci asked.

He glanced at Marci. She stared at the nicely made bed.

"Dying?" he asked.

"Getting old."

His brow furrowed.

"I think about it," Marci said.

"You do?"

"Sometimes, and it scares the hell out of me."

"Why?"

"It's probably stupid." She shrugged. "But a day will come when I can't do what I can do now."

Quinn knew what she meant. Marci had a reputation in the department as a fighter. She'd trained in a couple of martial arts systems since she was young and looked to challenge herself against bigger men and more accomplished fighters. Even when she lost on the mat, which was exceedingly rare, she won because her legend grew. They'd worked together for a few years, but Quinn still didn't know what drove her.

"When that time comes," Marci said, "I don't know what that will do to me." She tapped her chest. "In here."

"You'll deal with it. Like everyone else has."

Marci looked at him. "Getting old sucks."

"Said every person ever." He led them out of the room.

In the kitchen, Quinn found a cell phone. Several unanswered phone calls from 'Pam' were on it. He showed it to Marci. "Is she the daughter that found him?"

"That's what dispatch told me."

Quinn slipped the phone into an evidence bag. A thought occurred to him then. His eyes scanned the kitchen.

"What are you looking for?"

"Keys. Mine are usually with my phone."

Marci set off toward the bedrooms. Quinn searched the kitchen again then returned to the living room. Geri Utley was still there. "Did you see a set of keys?" he asked.

"Did you lose them?"

He shook his head. "Not mine. The victim's." Quinn motioned toward the body.

"I don't think I saw any."

Quinn headed into the garage. Inside was a late model Dodge Ram. He opened it and peered inside. No keys dangled from the ignition nor were there any in the center console. He returned to the house.

Marci waited for him in the living room. "Well?"

"I'm not finding them."

"Me neither, but we shouldn't jump to conclusions."

Quinn shook his head. "Of course not."

"Maybe Ray had a special place he put his keys."

"Let's ask the daughter."

***

As Quinn and Marci approached the silver Honda, a woman in her mid-thirties climbed out of the driver's seat. She wore a Seattle Seahawks sweatshirt, jeans, and running shoes. Another woman in her sixties climbed out of the other side. The passenger wore a chaplain's uniform and walked around the car to stand with the driver.

When the detectives neared, the older woman extended her hand. "I'm Chaplain Roland."

Quinn and Marci both shook hands with her.

The chaplain turned to the woman she'd been sitting with. "This is Pam Christy."

"Ms. Christy," Quinn said, "I'm Detective Delaney, and this is my partner, Marci Burkett."

Pam nodded.

"I'm sorry to do this here," Quinn said, "but we've got a couple questions. It's important that we get these answered now. We'll follow up later, too. Do you understand?"

Another nod.

Quinn asked, "Did your father live alone?"

"He did. My mother is in a home."

"She's where?"

Chaplain Roland softly said, "Colonial Springs. Her mother, Audrey, has Alzheimer's."

Quinn jotted the information into his notebook. He didn't know if it would prove valuable, but it was better to have the info and not need it than the other way around. He asked, "Do you know anyone who would want to harm your father?"

She shook her head. "My dad wouldn't hurt anybody. I don't understand why this happened." Tears welled in her eyes.

"Did your father share any problems he's had recently?"

"Problems? No." She looked toward the chaplain. "We've been trying to figure that out, too. We can't think of anything."

Quinn eyed Chaplain Roland. "You knew Mr. Christy?"

She nodded once, a barely perceptible motion. "He was a very nice man. Everyone around the station liked him."

Quinn glanced at Marci. Her shrug was barely perceptible.

Pam burst into tears, and she covered her face. Chaplain Roland put her arm around her.

"It's okay," she whispered. "It's okay."

"Pam," Marci said, "did your father keep his keys anywhere specific in the house?"

She looked up from her hands. "What?"

"His keys." Marci rotated her wrist as if opening the lock to a house. "Where did he keep them?"

"I don't know. They were always just out." Her brow knitted. "The kitchen maybe. I'm sorry. I don't think there was just one spot."

"Since we can't find his keys, do you have a key to the house?"

She nodded. "I used mine to get in."

Marci glanced toward the house. "It was locked when you arrived?"

"Yes. Why? Do you think that means something?"

"I don't know," she said. "It might mean nothing."

Quinn cleared his throat. "Can we get your house key? We'll need to secure it when we're done, and we may need to return later."

Pam went to her car and reached inside. This might be deemed an officer safety concern in other circumstances, but the woman had just found her father murdered. Quinn didn't rate her particularly high as a threat. She returned with a ring of keys. With shaking hands, Pam found the correct key and pulled it off.

Quinn slipped it into his front pocket then handed her a business card. "Ms. Christy, if you think of anything that might help, please give me a call. We'll be in touch for a follow-up interview."

When Pam took the card, the tears returned once more. Chaplain Roland wrapped her arms around the grief-stricken woman and enveloped her.

The detectives walked away without looking back.

***

"What did you learn?" Chief Dillon asked. Captain Ackerman and Lieutenant Brand stood on either side of him.

Quinn eyed Marci before speaking, "We don't have a lot to go on."

Dillon's face soured.

"But we know a few things. First, there was no forced entry, so we believe Ray knew his killer. Second, the light bulb was unscrewed on the porch which leads us to think that the killer preplanned the attack. And finally, we believe that Ray's keys are missing."

The chief folded his arms over his chest. "His keys?"

"Yes, sir."

"Do you think the killer plans on returning to the house at another time?"

Quinn shrugged. "It's possible, but if the killer wanted something from Ray's house why not take it right then and there?"

"Maybe it was too big to take," Lieutenant Brand offered. "Maybe the killer needed additional help."

"Perhaps."

Captain Ackerman eyed Quinn. "But you don't think so?"

"I don't know. Maybe the keys are only lost, and we haven't found them. I don't want to jump to a conclusion."

Chief Dillon pointed at the Christy house. "One of

ours is dead in there, Detective. Feel free to jump to a conclusion."

"His keys are missing."

Marci smacked Quinn's arm with the back of her hand. "Hey. Don't the volunteers wear security badges?"

***

Quinn and Marci returned to the house along with Chief Dillon, Captain Ackerman, and Lieutenant Brand. They began a systematic search for Ray Christy's keys and his department-issued security badge. Each of them wore footies and latex gloves.

Geri Utley remained in the living room with the body. The medical examiner's transport team was on the way.

The five of them broke the house into sections—the garage which included Ray's truck, the furthest bedroom, the nearest bedroom, the kitchen, and the living room.

It took about twenty minutes for everyone to reconvene in the foyer. The consensus was that the keys and security badge were not in the house.

Lieutenant Brand asked, "Could Ray have left the security badge in the Volunteers' office?"

"It's possible," Ackerman said, "but not his keys. He'd need those to drive home at the very least. Maybe he could get into the house via the garage, but the truck goes nowhere without them."

Chief Dillon faced the lieutenant. "I know this isn't your bailiwick, George, but I need you to take the lead on this. Post an officer on the Monroe Court Building tonight and notify the Volunteer Services' sergeant immediately. Change the locks on that office tomorrow." He lifted a finger for each task. "Cancel Ray Christy's security badge ASAP and contact IT to find out if it's been used in our buildings recently."

Brand nodded. "Yes, sir."

The lieutenant was known widely through the department as a mildly functional leader but a damn effective administrator. He was going to get a chance to prove the latter yet again.

Dillon turned back to the detectives. "Okay, you two. It's your show now. Figure this out in a hurry."

Chapter 12

When Quinn awoke Friday morning, he didn't bother following his normal routine. There wasn't time for sipping coffee and browsing through his favorite blogs. Today, he simply rolled out of bed and got ready for the office.

Every homicide investigation required an investigator's best work and taking time to recharge was important. Whether that meant relaxation or exercise was up to the detective involved. The act of getting away from the case files was important. But today was not about taking care of oneself, Quinn knew.

Hot water splashed into his face. He opened his mouth and let water accumulate. It quickly filled, and he spat it out.

Unfortunately, he felt apprehensive. Making Ray Christy's case into something he dreaded working on wasn't fair to the dead man. He put both hands on the wall and leaned forward so the water could work on his tight shoulders. Quinn knew why he felt anxious—Chief Dillon.

It was natural for Lieutenant Brand to keep a watchful eye on Quinn's workload. That was his job. And Captain Ackerman occasionally stopped by to explain how important a case was. It wasn't long ago that a group of young men terrorized the city by playing the knockout game. Ackerman inserted himself into that case because it was so sensational that it became a media circus.

But this was different. Chief Dillon was personally involved. The man had never interfered in any of Quinn's cases. It was only natural that the chief wanted Ray

Christy's killer found. He had a friendship with Ray and looked at him as a surrogate father. However, Quinn shouldn't allow that relationship to dictate any of his actions.

If he and Marci bent to the chief's pressure, they might make a mistake or cut a corner.

Quinn turned his back and let the water pulsate on his neck. He closed his eyes and thought about his partner.

Marci wouldn't cave under pressure from the chief. She'd likely do the opposite and push back, which created its own problems. That was her style. His was to go with the flow while Marci tried to divert the whole damn river.

So, Quinn needed to be on guard for pressure from two sources—Chief Dillon *and* his partner.

He shut off the water and climbed out of the shower.

***

Marci leaned back from her cubicle when Quinn walked in. She motioned toward the cup in his hand. "You splurged today."

He had stopped at a drive-through coffee stand on the way into the office. "Time was of the essence. Are we the only ones here?"

"Too bad they don't give out brownie points to the ones who turn on the lights."

Quinn dropped into his chair. "Your eye is looking better."

She touched her cheek. "Still noticeable."

The area around her left eye was swollen but it was no longer closed. She'd applied make-up to hide the bruising, but it only succeeded in muting the discoloration.

Quinn said, "It looks like a bee stung your face."

"Maybe I should wear sunglasses."

"So you can look like you're recovering from a hangover?"

"Yeah." Marci smirked. "Probably not."

"Wear them and tell people you're a vampire."

Marci's smirk morphed into a frown. "I'll live with it."

"Maybe they'll think you're a movie star."

"Enough."

Quinn turned to his desk. "That won't work. Movie stars are normally gregarious." He looked at her again. "Go with vampire."

"It's a black eye, dumb ass, not a broken arm. I can still choke you out."

He laughed as he started his computer. "What's the plan of action this morning?"

"Besides choking you out?"

"I'm being serious."

"Me, too." Marci faced her computer now. "I guess we do what we always do first. Write up our notes, then review the reports submitted by the responding officers."

"I mean after that. I think we get over to Volunteer Services."

She briefly considered his words then shrugged. "Whatever."

"You don't seem overly motivated."

Marci looked at him. "I hate we're doing this because of the chief."

"We're not doing it for him. We're doing it for Ray Christy."

"We didn't know the guy."

"We don't know any of our victims." Quinn leaned back in his chair. "Besides, how many of the cops do you even know in the department now?"

"Yeah, okay."

"If something happened to one of them, we'd go after it like a dog with a bone."

Marci rolled her eyes.

"What?"

"I hate when you're right."

***

Shortly before eight, Lieutenant Brand walked into the Major Crimes office. He stopped by Quinn's desk. "Anything new?"

"No, sir. We've gone over our notes from last night and reviewed the reports from the officers who were on-scene."

"Learn anything?"

Marci turned to face the lieutenant. "It was the same stuff they told us last night."

"Which was?"

She flashed a look of disbelief to Quinn before continuing. "The officers canvassed the area. None of the neighbors remembered seeing anything remotely suspicious. No strange cars. No hinky outsiders."

"Hinky?" the lieutenant said.

Marci stared at him.

"Basically," Quinn said to call the lieutenant's attention to him, "we've got a body, and that's it."

Brand's lips moved back and forth as he thought. He grunted a couple of times to himself, then looked around. When his gaze returned to the detectives, he said, "There are a lot of eyes on this one."

"We know," Marci said. "We were there last night." She didn't bother to hide her irritation. She and the lieutenant never got along. Quinn believed it because Marci was a woman of action, and Brand was a man of documentation.

"See that you do your best to wrap it up quickly."

Before Quinn could respond, Marci said, "Just what do you think we do, Lieutenant?"

"I think you solve cases, Detective." His gaze slid to Quinn. "Sometimes faster than others."

"We're focused on this one," Quinn said.

Marci abruptly stood. "We're focused on them all."

"That's good," Brand said. "Maybe you can focus a little tighter this time around."

Without waiting for another response, Brand continued to his office.

"Can you believe that guy? Focus a little tighter." She mimed choking a person with both hands. "I'll show you a little tighter focus, you fat bastard."

"Why do you let him get to you?"

Marci pulled back. "He doesn't get to me."

"If you say so." Quinn stood. "And you know it's going to be this way until we find Ray Christy's killer."

"What if we don't?"

"Maybe property crimes won't be as bad the second time around."

"Screw that," Marci said. "We're solving this one." She grabbed her suit jacket. "Let's go."

***

As Quinn and Marci exited the west doors, Chaplain Gabriel Greene ascended the stairs. He appeared distraught and stopped when he saw them.

"Detectives."

"Chaplain," Marci said.

Quinn nodded. "Gabe.

"Is it true you're investigating Ray Christy's murder?"

"It is," Marci said. "Did you know him?"

"I did. He was a nice guy. Although that probably

doesn't help you much, does it? What kind of info can I give that could help in your investigation?"

Marci stepped aside and motioned for the chaplain to ascend the final step to the landing.

"We found your business card," she said, "in Ray's shirt pocket. What was that about?"

"He stopped by on, oh, what day was that?" Gabe looked upward. "Monday, probably. He poked his head into my office to say hello. We chatted for a couple of minutes, and I gave him my card. I told him to call me if he ever needed to chat."

"Was he upset about something?" Marci asked.

"Not that I could tell. Ray would occasionally talk with me about his wife."

"Audrey," Quinn said.

"That's right."

"Was he a religious man?" Marci asked.

"No," Gabe said. "We never spoke about God. I think he enjoyed talking with me because we both served in the military."

"So," Marci said, "he stopped by on Monday just to say hello. Nothing more?"

Gabe nodded. "As far as I can tell, yes."

"And how often did he do that?" Quinn asked.

"Whenever he was in the PSB."

"How often do you think that was?"

"Once a week, maybe."

After they said their goodbyes, Quinn and Marci watched Gabe enter the Public Safety Building.

"Did you hear Gabe?" Quinn asked. "Ray was in the building once a week, and we didn't know him."

Marci shrugged. "So? How many of the records employees do you know? Same with dispatch."

"I used to know them all, I think. But I only know them by their faces now." Quinn's brow furrowed.

"Besides Annie, I'm not even sure who is still in dispatch."

"That's how it goes with what we do. We're hermits, not social butterflies."

"I guess." Quinn looked into the parking lot. "Where are we headed?"

"Why are you asking me? I thought you wanted to go to Volunteer Services."

"I do, but you led us through the west doors."

Marci cocked her head. "I did?"

"I followed you."

She shrugged. "Must have been on autopilot. Let's walk around the building. It's a nice day."

Quinn trotted down the steps. Marci followed him.

"You ever do that?" she asked. "Just do something by habit and realize it's not what you wanted to do?"

"I'm sure everyone has done it at one time or another."

"I hope that doesn't mean I'm losing my mind."

He smiled. "Trust me. If you start, I'll let you know."

Chapter 13

"I guess Ray Christy was an all-right guy," Sergeant Brandon Newman said. His gaze shifted from Quinn to Marci. "The other seniors seemed to like him."

They were seated in the sergeant's office with the door closed. When Quinn and Marci first arrived, Volunteer Services buzzed with hushed conversations. They stopped immediately when the staff realized why the detectives were there. After taking a few minutes to quietly look through Ray Christy's desk for his security badge, the three of them moved into the sergeant's office.

Quinn shifted slightly in his chair to turn his body toward his partner. Almost immediately in their conversation, he noticed Newman's propensity to eye Marci while speaking. Quinn knew she saw it, too. They'd been partners long enough to know when to silently step back and let the other assume the lead in asking questions, even with a member of their own department.

"You don't sound overly fond of the man," Marci said.

Newman's smile seemed disingenuous. "What did I say? I said he was all right. That's supposed to be a compliment."

"Did he do something you didn't like?"

"No." The sergeant bent forward and rested his arms against his desk. "It's just that I have nothing in common with these people." Newman lifted his chin toward the outer office.

"These people?" Marci asked.

"You know what I mean."

"Sure."

Newman raised an eyebrow. "The explorers and co-ops are hopped on hormones and Netflix. The seniors are like my befuddled grandparents. And the reserve officers mean well but come on. Really? They're like the national guard, except the guard puts in more time than the reservists do."

Quinn wasn't a fan of the volunteer program, but even he saw its merits. The fact that Newman was put in charge and carried this attitude amazed him.

Marci consulted her notepad. "What was the last day that Ray Christy reported in?"

"Monday."

Pamela Christy found her father's body on Thursday evening. The chief was scheduled to have lunch with the man on Tuesday. Ray might have been dead for three days before he was discovered.

Marci asked, "Did Ray come in every day?"

Newman smiled. "Can I ask what happened to your eye?"

"No," she said flatly. "Did Ray usually come in every day or what?"

Newman's smile faltered, and he glanced nervously at Quinn. His attention quickly returned to Marci. "I didn't mean to offend you. It just looks painful, is all."

"It's not. Will you answer the question?"

The sergeant sat upright, and his arms slid down the edge of his desk until only his hands remained touching. "Ray came in most days. There were occasional times he missed for family things."

"So, Monday through Friday?"

"Yeah."

"Would you call him dependable?"

"I would." Newman nodded. "He was probably our most dependable volunteer."

"And you didn't think it weird that he didn't show up for several days?"

"Not especially, no. He's a grown man. People call out all the time."

"Call out?"

Newman rolled his eyes. "I'm sorry. It's what the college kids say when they call in sick."

Quinn had been on the SWAT team. 'Call out' had an entirely different meaning to him. Marci glanced at him, so he asked, "Ray called in sick then?"

"No," the sergeant said. "He just didn't show."

"And you still didn't worry?"

Newman flopped back into his chair and crossed his arms. "We've had people no-show before. The explorers do it all the time."

"We're not talking the high schoolers," Quinn said, "but volunteers of Ray's generation."

"Well, not really, no. They're pretty good about giving notice." Newman's gaze slid back to Marci. "Am I in trouble?"

"Not with us."

"Should I get a union rep?"

"What for?" She jotted something into her notepad. "We're trying to establish a timeline for Ray's murder."

The sergeant touched his chest in an act of sincerity. "I certainly wouldn't want anything bad to happen to Ray or to anyone else in the program, for that matter. I care about all of them. They're like my family."

Quinn easily detected the insincerity in the statement, especially after the sergeant's comment about not having anything in common with the volunteers.

Marci asked, "What kind of things did Ray do for the program?"

"A little of everything. He seemed to like helping out with special events the most."

"Could Ray have been killed because of something he worked on?"

The sergeant frowned. "What kind of trouble can the seniors get into? If he was a reserve officer, maybe. You think somebody wanted revenge because Ray gave them bad directions or something?"

Marci rested an elbow on her chair. "We believe his keys were stolen along with his security badge."

"I heard. The lieutenant called me last night. City Services is hoping to get the locks changed today. But you don't really think someone wants to break in here, do you? What's there to take?"

"Was anything missing from the office in the last few days?"

"Not that I noticed. That's why I don't think it involves our office."

Marci's pen hovered above her pad as she thought of her next question.

Quinn looked up. "Did Ray use a notepad?" He motioned toward Marci's. "When we looked through his desk, we didn't come across one."

Newman shrugged. "Maybe he did. I don't know for sure."

Marci turned to Quinn with an unspoken question. He shook his head then they both stood.

She said, "Thank you for your time, Sergeant."

"You bet." Newman stood now and leaned with his hands on his desk. His eyes settled completely on Marci. "If you ever need anything, just let me know."

Quinn thumbed toward the outer office. "We're going to talk with some of your people."

"Understood." Newman didn't bother looking at Quinn. "Help yourself."

Marci started for the door but stopped. She faced the sergeant. "By the way, congrats on that Life Saving

Award."

Newman straightened and puffed his chest. A smile spread across his face. "Thank you. It was a total shock."

"Too bad the guy died." She exited the office.

Quinn watched the smile dissolve from Newman's face before he followed his partner out the door.

***

Due to the time of day, there weren't any explorers or co-ops in the office. They were still attending high school or college classes. And reserve officers normally didn't show up until the later shifts when there was a higher probability for more exciting calls.

There were twenty-three senior volunteers in the office that morning. According to the first woman that Quinn talked with, that number was substantially higher than the normal daily turnout, which was only a handful. It appeared that Ray's death motivated many to come in as a show of moral support.

Marci and Quinn split up to interview the various volunteers. The first three seniors that Quinn talked with couldn't offer anything more than Ray was a nice guy who helped others whenever they needed a hand.

Quinn looked around for his next person to interview when he saw a petite woman waiting patiently. Her eyes were red from crying, something that many of the others hadn't done.

He extended his hand, and she timidly accepted it.

"Detective Delaney," he said.

"Irene Herbison."

"Ms. Herbison, did you know Ray Christy?"

Tears welled in her eyes. "Ray was my friend. We worked together on some projects."

"Like what?"

"Oh, we did all sorts of things. Picking up mail. Working the info booths at the courthouse and the Public Safety Building."

"Sergeant Newman said Ray liked working the special events."

Irene crinkled her nose. "Ray hated those events, especially Hoopfest. Too many people. But he did it because he was a team player." She wiped her eyes.

"What can you tell me about him personally?"

"He was a nice man who loved his wife."

"So, you knew him well?"

A sad smile hinted at the corner of her lips. "I would have liked to have known him better, but that's not how life worked out."

Quinn motioned toward a chair. "Would you like to sit?"

She shook her head. "I'm fine. How are his daughters?"

"We've only talked with one—Pamela. She discovered Ray."

Irene covered her mouth. "The poor girl."

"Do you know of anyone who wanted to hurt Ray?"

"No."

"How did he seem lately?"

"Normal, I guess." Her brow furrowed. "Except Monday. He was secretive for some reason."

Quinn raised an eyebrow. "How so?"

"He was working on something that he wouldn't tell me."

"Do you have any idea what it was?"

"Not really, but I saw some printouts of properties. He got upset when I looked through them."

"Why do you think he got upset?"

"I don't know. That was very unlike him."

"Where did you see those printouts?"

"His desk."

Quinn walked over to Ray Christy's desk. Irene followed him.

"Show me where you saw them," he said.

"They were spread out." Irene waved her hand over the desk.

Marci walked over to them. "What's going on?"

Quinn quickly relayed what Irene had told him. He then looked through the desk drawers again. "There aren't any printouts of properties in here." To Marci, he asked, "Do you remember seeing something like that at Ray's house?"

She shook her head. "But I wasn't looking for them either. They might have been in plain sight, and we glanced right over them. Or maybe they were in his truck."

"I don't remember seeing them either. That's not saying they couldn't be there." To Irene, Quinn asked, "Do you remember any names on these printouts?"

"Just one because it struck me as odd— Joey Bishop."

"Why was that odd?"

"There was a famous comedian by that same name. You probably don't remember him. He ran with the Rat Pack. You know—Dean Martin, Frank Sinatra, Sammy Davis. I think he passed away fifteen years ago, but I might be wrong on that. The timing, not his passing."

Quinn wrote the comedian's name in his notepad.

***

As the two detectives were about to walk out of Volunteer Services, the man sitting behind the reception desk stood. His hands were clasped and dangled in front of him. "My turn?"

Quinn looked at Marci.

She said, "I thought you did."

"Not me." Quinn turned to the older man and studied him now.

He had a flaccid face with bushy, unkempt eyebrows. Short, wiry hairs protruded from his ears. But his eyes were bright and earnest.

"I'm Detective Delaney, and this is my partner, Detective Burkett."

"Vernon Kuehn, but you can call me Vern. Everyone else does."

Quinn smiled politely. "All right, Vern. Did you know Ray Christy?"

"Oh, sure. I know everyone in the program since I captain this here chariot." Vern jostled the receptionist chair. "It's not exactly a glamorous assignment, but someone's got to do it."

"How did Ray seem lately?"

"Like normal, I guess."

"And how's that?"

The older man suddenly seemed uncomfortable. "I don't want to speak ill of the dead. You understand."

"Vern," Quinn said. "We need to know anything you can tell us. We're trying to solve his murder."

Vern mashed his lips together then nodded several times. "Uh-huh, sure. Well, I guess it will be all right in that case. If you really want to know, Ray was sort of an abrupt person."

"Abrupt?" Marci asked.

"As in rude."

No one had described Ray that way to Quinn. He glanced at his partner. She shook her head.

Quinn asked, "Why do you think he was rude, Vern?"

"Because whenever I asked him a question, he'd shut me down with some snide comment. Like he didn't want me in his business which I wasn't trying to get into if you want to know the truth."

"Everyone else described him as nice and helpful."

"Well, I think different. If you want to know the real of someone, watch how they treat the person on the front desk. You'll get a good understanding of what's inside them." Vern wiggled the chair again. "And Ray Christy was kind of a jerk."

***

Quinn opened his desk and retrieved a small envelope. Inside was Pamela Christy's key to her father's house. "Do you want to ride with me up to Ray's place? I want to see if I can find that missing paperwork and his notebook."

"I'll stay here and run that Joey Bishop name through the system. Then maybe I'll put some work in on our other cases so that they maintain some forward momentum."

"I'd appreciate that. See you in a bit."

Quinn turned and bumped into Captain Ackerman.

The captain took a half-step back and appraised the detective. "How's it going, Delaney?"

"Fine."

"That's it? No new developments?"

"None yet."

Ackerman eyed Marci. She stared back at him. Eventually, she shrugged, and the captain's shoulders slumped.

He said, "Neither of you've got anything for me to give the chief?"

"Tell him we're working on it," Quinn said.

"That's to be expected."

Marci cocked her head. "Come on, Captain. You know how this works."

"That's right, Burkett. I do. And to help clue you in, here's how it's going to go until you get a suspect. The chief has already been on my back twice this morning which is why I'm here."

"The lieutenant was here earlier, too," Marci said.

"Because I was on his back. Don't you get it? If we don't give the chief what he wants, he's going to be in your space, asking you directly. You don't want that."

The detectives glanced at each other.

Ackerman lifted his hands in an apologetic manner. "I'll tell the man you've got nothing but get me something and get it fast." He turned and left them.

Marci stood. "On second thought, I think I will go with you to Ray's house."

***

They were southbound on Washington Street when Marci asked, "Why didn't you tell Ackerman what we learned at Volunteer Services?"

From behind the steering wheel, Quinn said, "I don't know."

"I know why I wouldn't have. My general distrust of anything covered in brass has already been established. Hell, I don't even like brass doorknobs. But you, Quinn Delaney, are a friend of the administration."

His brow furrowed. "Since when?"

"Since we've been partners, the brass has liked you. Don't pout. You're a likable guy. It's not a bad quality. You were probably the kid in elementary school that got 'plays well with others' on every report card."

"Why are you making this about me?"

"It's what I do."

Quinn changed lanes. "What should I have told the captain? That Ray Christy *might* have had some property printouts. That he *might* have had a notebook that we can't find. That he *might* have been looking into some guy named Joey Bishop. For all we know, Ray was looking at buying a house."

"Have you ever heard of him?"

"Joey Bishop? Why would I?"

"If he was hanging out with Frank Sinatra and Dean Martin, he had to have been a big deal, but I can't picture him. That woman—what's her name again?"

"Irene."

Marci snapped her fingers. "That's right. Irene said Joey Bishop was a famous comedian, but damn if I can't place him."

"When's the last time you watched a Frank Sinatra or Dean Martin movie?"

"I don't know if I ever have."

"There you go."

"But I know what they look like. Sammy Davis, too. Wasn't he a junior?"

"I think so," Quinn said. "But that's the kind of crap we shouldn't give the captain to take to the chief. Give them something of value or give them nothing."

"Like I said, friend of the administration."

"No," he said. "It's better to say we're working on it and let them think we're slow than to give them complete garbage and make them think we're incompetent."

Marci grunted something incomprehensible and faced forward.

Quinn drove in silence.

***

It took the two of them thirty minutes to methodically walk-through Ray Christy's house and search for the paperwork and notebook. Each of them took different rooms.

In the master bedroom, Quinn searched the uniform shirt that hung over the bedpost. Both pockets were unbuttoned and empty. He considered that for a moment. Had nothing been in the pockets to begin with, the pocket flaps would have remained buttoned. Yet both were unsecured. To Quinn, that meant something was removed from each. Marci removed the chaplain's business card from one. Had something been removed from the other? Was that where Ray kept his notebook?

Quinn didn't find the property papers or the notebook in the nightstand or the nearby dresser.

He also searched the truck parked in the garage. Before climbing in, he made a cursory walk around and checked the tool bench and toolboxes. He didn't really expect to find the property paperwork or notepad there, though.

Inside the truck, he popped open the center console. He found detritus normally left in a vehicle—gum, mints, coins, and receipts. He moved to the glovebox. It was surprisingly tidy. Inside were an owner's manual, a flashlight, and a screwdriver.

When Quinn returned to the living room, Marci stood there studying the floor where Ray Christy had likely died several days earlier.

She glanced at him. "Nada. You?"

"The same. What were you thinking?"

Marci's eyes narrowed as she continued to stare at the space on the floor. "Have you ever been beaten up?"

"I've been in a fight."

"That's not the same thing. I'm talking about being unable to defend yourself while someone—" She clenched a fist and held it up. "—hits you. Repeatedly."

Quinn stared at his partner. They'd investigated beatings before—some resulted in homicide while others resulted in serious bodily injury. Marci hadn't responded this way at any of those scenes.

She continued. Her voice seemed distant. "The only thing you can do is hope they stop and pray they don't kill you."

"No," Quinn said. "That never happened to me."

Marci's face slackened, and her eyes took on a faraway look. "You're lucky."

A couple of seconds passed before Quinn asked, "Did that happen to you?"

She blinked and slowly faced him. Her face hardened. "No. I asked if it happened to you. Don't make this about me."

"That's your thing."

Marci pushed him as she walked by. "Are we done?"

Chapter 14

When they returned to the department, Quinn detoured to the Records section, and Marci continued back to the Major Crimes bullpen.

At the counter, Quinn grabbed a Records Request form and caught the attention of a woman in her late thirties. Stephanie Lesh was the head of the Spokane County Records Division. She had long brown hair that fell almost to her waist. She wore a light blue sweater and black slacks.

Stephanie waved politely from across the room and broke away from the conversation she was having with a woman who appeared to be in her early seventies.

"Detective," she said, "what can I help you with today?"

"I'm investigating the murder of a senior volunteer."

"I heard." Stephanie glanced back. "I was just talking about that with Dixie. Horrible news."

"Can you pull anything Ray Christy has worked on recently? Any calls or events he went out on, or any CAD work he did?"

Stephanie nodded. "Sure, we can do that. It'll take some time." She pointed at the blank form Quinn had. "Fill that out, and we'll get on it."

***

When Quinn dropped into his chair, Marci said, "There's no Joey Bishop in the system, but there are a few Josephs. One of them is a frequent flier."

"No kidding."

She handed Quinn an arrest record for Joseph Kieran Bishop. Thirty-two years old. White male. Five-nine. One hundred sixty-seven pounds.

"This guy," Marci said, flicking the piece of paper, "has an impressive history of assault, robbery, and burglary. And he's out on probation right now. Less than two months free. What do you think?"

"Irene said she saw a property printout that said Bishop was the homeowner. Does this guy look the type to buy a house?"

"How would I know? Maybe it got passed down from a dead relative."

Quinn stared at the face in the corner of the arrest record. "But how would he and Ray have met?"

"I don't know. Maybe they were in a book club together. We'll figure that part out after we talk with him."

"Sure."

Marci crossed her arms. "What's your problem with this guy?"

"He seems like a weird one for our victim to know."

"I'm not disagreeing, but we meet freaks daily in this job. Perhaps the senior volunteers meet a wingnut every now and then."

Quinn turned the sheet around to show Joseph Bishop's photograph. "But Ray willingly opened his door to this guy? We're still thinking that, right?"

"Maybe ol' Joe is a bit of a sweet talker and got Ray to open the door. And maybe ol' Ray wasn't so sharp and trusted a bit too much."

"Eh, I don't know. The chief said he was a retired first sergeant. I think he'd be smarter than that."

"Newman's a sergeant. You think that automatically makes him smarter? Let's grab this Joseph guy and squeeze him."

Quinn's expression soured. It was common for criminals to be expert salesmen. They had to be with the life they led. Whatever story they sold, the goal was always the same—to separate someone from their money.

"Then again, Ray still had cash in his wallet," Marci said. "So, it wasn't a robbery." She sounded as if she was starting to talk herself out of an argument for looking into Joseph Bishop.

Quinn offered, "Maybe the killer didn't search the house after they attacked Ray."

"What are you thinking? That maybe they got scared because they took it too far?"

"It's happened."

"But in this case? With the missing keys and security badge?"

"What do you want to do?" Quinn asked. "Keep Joseph Bishop on the radar or pick him up for a look?"

She grimaced. "I'll admit it's pretty thin. All we've got is an elderly lady saying she saw his name on a piece of paper."

"Maybe if we had that paper."

Marci tapped her desk. "But if Joseph Bishop has injuries to his hands and we wait to pick him up until better proof…"

"He heals up and comes up with an alibi—"

"—if he doesn't already have one—"

"—and starts to build a rock-solid defense."

Marci snapped her fingers, then pointed at Quinn. "That's why we should pull this guy off the street."

He reconsidered Bishop's arrest record. He also thought about the podcasts he'd been listening to recently. "What's it going to hurt? The guy's not a citizen."

"That's right. He understands the game. He's been playing it long enough to know the rules."

"Let's ask patrol to locate him."

Marci spun toward her computer. "I'm on it."

Detectives Dallas Nash and Glenn Higgins walked by their cubicles. Both wore dark suits and appeared to be on their way out. They stopped when they noticed Quinn and Marci.

"You guys catch one last night?" Dallas asked.

"Yeah," Quinn said. "Got the potential to be a red ball, too."

Marci looked at the interloping detectives. "Don't let him fool you. It already is."

Glenn glanced between Quinn and Marci. "That bad, huh?"

She nodded. "It was a senior volunteer."

"No shit? Who?"

"Ray Christy. I guess he was friends with the chief."

Sadness crossed Glenn's face. "Ah, man. Really? He was a good guy." Glenn looked to Dallas. "Remember when he told us that story about those MPs in Viet Nam?"

Dallas nodded, then looked from Marci to Quinn then back to her. "We're still buried with that double from Sunday, but if you need us to kick in, let us know. We'll do whatever we can."

Quinn shook his head. "We got this, but thanks. We appreciate the offer."

"Yeah," Marci said. "Thanks, Dal."

Dallas patted her shoulder. The touch wasn't suggestive. She and Dallas were friends. He'd gone through a rough patch with the passing of his wife and was finally looking like he was starting to put it behind him. "Let me know if you need anything, kid. We know how the administration can get."

"Don't I know it," Marci said.

Glenn and Dallas headed toward the hallway.

***

An hour later, Lieutenant Brand arrived at their cubicles. "Delaney, Burkett, let's go."

Quinn glanced over his shoulder. "Where to?"

"We've been summoned." Brand wandered off toward the hallway.

"This can't be good," Marci said.

They followed the lieutenant to Captain Ackerman's office. Brand poked his head in and said, "Ready."

A moment later, Ackerman appeared in the hallway. He eyed the two detectives. "This is what I warned you about." The captain turned and led the procession down the hall to the chief's office.

Ackerman passed Melanie, the chief's new receptionist. She nodded curtly at him, then ignored the rest of them by returning her attention to her computer. At the chief's door, Ackerman knocked twice.

"Enter," Chief Dillon angrily called.

Marci muttered, "Christ."

Lieutenant Brand looked back. "Too late for prayers, Burkett."

Inside the chief's office, the four of them stood in front of a large mahogany desk. Liam Dillon reclined in his chair. "These two," he motioned at Ackerman and Brand, "have blown smoke up my ass all morning, but the basic message I keep hearing is that you two have got nothing. I find that hard to believe."

Quinn's face remained passive, and he refrained from looking at Marci. He believed she did the same.

Dillon shifted his sitting position, and his chair groaned. "Maybe I should I have put Parker and Johnson on this case. They're a couple of hungry dogs. They'd have gotten after this like it was a piece of raw meat.

146

What, Burkett? I see you want to say something. Spit it out."

Quinn's jaw tightened.

"No, sir," she said. "I don't have anything to say."

"That's a first."

Quinn tightened in expectation of a Marci retort, but he still refused to look at her. Thankfully, she didn't respond.

Eventually, Dillon focused on Quinn. "And what about you, Delaney? Nothing to say for yourself?"

"We're investigating Ray Christy's murder like we would any other case, sir."

Dillon slapped his desk, and Brand jumped. Marci snickered.

"I don't want you treating it like any other case. What don't you understand? Ray was my friend. He was a retired first sergeant in the United States Army. That means something."

"Yes, sir."

"And above all, he was one of ours. You treat this case like someone just killed the president in our backyard. You treat this like it's the only death that matters!" Chief Dillon's face was beet red, and he looked away. He stood and turned his back to them.

The two detectives stole a glance at each other. Ackerman angrily shook his head and mouthed, "Knock it off."

"I'm sorry," the chief muttered. His back was still to them. Dillon brought a quivering hand to his temple. When he faced them, the color in his face had dropped to bright pink. "This case means a considerable deal to me and this department. Give me something, *anything*, to hold on to. Even if you think it's inconsequential. Just let me know you're making progress."

Marci said, "We're looking into recent events and

activities that Ray was assigned to."

The chief dismissively waved a hand. "That's what you're doing, Burkett. Tell me you've found something."

"A woman in the Volunteer Services' office said she thought Ray was working on something outside the scope of his assignment."

Dillon stepped around his desk. A look of hope appeared on his face. "What woman?"

Marci said, "Irene."

"Herbison?" Dillon asked. "Nice lady. She thinks Ray was working on something special? Do you have any idea what it was?"

"Irene thought she saw a number of property printouts on Ray's desk."

"Maybe he was looking to buy a home," Lieutenant Brand offered.

Quinn said, "We thought about that. Irene said he seemed protective about the papers. Like he didn't want her to see them."

"But she saw them?" the chief asked.

Quinn nodded. "She noticed a name on one of them—Joey Bishop."

"Like the old-time actor?"

"That's what she said." Quinn shrugged. "But we've never heard of him."

"What are you doing about it?"

"It's a long shot, sir, but Marci found a possible. She requested an attempt to locate through patrol."

The chief's face relaxed. "So, there has been some progress."

"We don't know if it's real progress, though."

"But it's something, Delaney. And that's what I want to see. Thank you for the update." The chief looked to Ackerman. "They're authorized for as much overtime as needed."

The captain nodded.

Dillon studied both detectives. "I assume you two are going to work the case this weekend." It wasn't a question.

"Yes, sir," Quinn said. He didn't have anything happening on Saturday or Sunday, and the overtime pay would come in handy.

Several seconds passed before Marci said, "Yes, sir." Her voice was low, and it sounded as if she spoke through clenched teeth.

"Good," the chief said. He moved back behind his desk. "Are there any other resources you need?"

Quinn stole a glance at Marci before speaking. "Yes, sir. Have we gotten any hits on Ray's security badge being used?"

"Information Services is working on that," Lieutenant Brand said. "They're making it a priority."

"Why the delay?" Dillon asked.

"They're short-staffed. I've been assured we'll have something by Monday."

Quinn asked, "Will that include any security footage?"

The lieutenant responded, "If the badge has been used, we'll get the footage, Detective."

"Thank you, sir." Quinn eyed the chief. "We don't need any additional resources at the time, sir."

"Then you've got everything you need to bag a killer. Thank you for your commitment to this weekend." The chief fell into his chair. "Gary, stay behind."

The lieutenant and Marci led the way out of the chief's office.

***

"Excuse me."

Quinn glanced back to see a tall, older woman standing behind him. Her short gray hair was combed to the right. She wore a pullover sweater, jeans, and soft shoes.

Marci wasn't at her desk. She'd gone down the hall to blow off some steam. The chief's insistence that they work this weekend irritated her. She had planned to attend a martial arts seminar on both days.

"Yes?" Quinn said.

"Hello." The woman extended her hand and smiled nervously. "I'm Dixie Richter."

Quinn remained seated but shook her hand. "Detective Delaney."

"I volunteer in Records." She twisted slightly and looked in the direction of where the division was.

Now, he made the connection. Quinn had seen Stephanie Lesh talking with her earlier. His gaze dropped to her empty hands. "Is there a problem with my request?"

"No. At least, I don't think so." She looked anxiously around. "Stephanie and one of the other girls are working on it right now."

Quinn stood. "What can I do for you, Ms. Richter?"

Dixie lowered her voice. "There's something missing from Ray's history."

"And what would that be?"

"A report I pulled for him."

Quinn cocked his head. "He didn't put in a records request?"

"No. He just gave me a number."

The detective crossed his arms. He fought the frown that wanted to form on his lips. "Why would you pull a report like that?"

"Ray wanted to know about a case that Detective

Parker was working on."

"Pulling a case without the proper documentation is a violation of policy."

Dixie's brow knitted. "Yes, sir. I know, and I knew if I helped Ray that I could get in trouble for it."

"Then why do it?"

"Ray said Detective Parker was dismissive of him."

"Dismissive, how?"

"You're still young, Detective. You'll learn soon enough."

He studied her. Dixie's statement wasn't combative—quite the opposite. She sounded sad, almost remorseful.

Quinn asked, "Do you remember the case number?"

"I'm sorry. I don't. Once I pulled the report, I destroyed his note."

"Did Ray take the report with him?

"No. I made sure he only looked at it with me, then I ripped it up, too. I put everything in the shredder bin. I don't know if that made what I did any better, but that's how I justified it."

"The pieces of the report should still be in the bin."

Dixie smiled apologetically. "The shredding company picked it up a couple of days ago. If I knew something like this would have happened, I would have written down the number."

"But there was no way to know. Did you read it?"

"No, but I saw that it was about an accidental death. I read the page header. That's all. I promise."

"So, Ray wanted to talk with Parker about an accidental death?"

Dixie shrugged. "I guess. He didn't tell me. He just asked to see whatever reports were filed under that incident number."

"Why did you help him?"

"Because we're friends. And truthfully, I know what it

feels like to be diminished because of my age. It doesn't feel nice."

"I would imagine not." Quinn briefly thought about additional questions but decided there weren't any. If he decided on some later, he knew where to find Dixie. "Thank you for coming forward with this information."

Dixie looked over her shoulder before asking, "If you could…"

"Yes?"

"I know what I did was wrong, Detective. I should never have shown that report to Ray, but I did it full well knowing what the ramifications were." She sighed. "However, I like volunteering around here even if it is helping in Records."

Quinn considered the woman. Dixie Richter seemed like a sweet grandmotherly type. Telling Stephanie Lesh what the woman did felt like overkill. She was already remorseful for what had occurred. Dixie appeared to be the type to not do a bad thing twice. Even threatening to tell Stephanie seemed like it wouldn't accomplish much.

Hell, Quinn thought, Dixie might even pray for forgiveness about what she'd done.

"We'll keep it between us," he said.

"Thank you, Detective." Dixie nodded several times then left.

Quinn went deeper into the Major Crimes office. Parker's desk was empty. So was his partner's.

When he returned to his cubicle, Marci was slipping her suit jacket on.

"We've gotta go," she said. "Patrol's detained Joseph Bishop."

"That was fast."

"They're in the parking of the Yoke's on Foothills. They don't have a reason to detain him for long, so we're going out there. I can do this solo if you don't want to come."

Quinn pulled his jacket from the back of his chair. "We're in this together, right?"

***

Yoke's Fresh Market was on North Foothills Drive, just east of Division Street. The regional grocery store sat next to a large Mazda dealership. Quinn pulled into the parking lot and immediately spotted a single patrol car. He stopped beside it.

Standing in front of the patrol vehicle was a young male officer he'd never seen and a female officer he'd known over the years. The two kept a watchful eye on a sketchy-looking male in his early thirties. The guy had long hair, wore a backpack, and held onto a newer BMX bicycle by its left handlebar.

Officer Pauleen Sherman approached the detectives as they exited their car. "We got your boy."

"In record time," Marci said. "How'd you find him so fast?"

"Little Joey Shitbag? Everyone knows this turd. He's not hard to find if you know where to look." Pauleen leaned toward Marci. "Hey, what's wrong with you? You got pink eye or something?"

"I got punched."

"By your desk?"

"Bite me, Sherman. Anytime you wanna hit the mat, let me know."

She waved Marci off. "Sucker someone else with your sadomasochistic invitations."

Quinn motioned toward Joseph Bishop. "Did you check the backpack?"

"We asked, but he wouldn't let us. As long as he keeps it on, it's hard to claim officer safety issues. So, we've called his P.O. She should be here any minute."

"Beautiful." Marci looked at the young officer intently watching the detained man. "Who's the new guy?"

"My recruit. It's his second week in my car. Don't bother to learn his name, though. He won't make it through my rotation."

Marci raised an eyebrow. "I thought you hated being an FTO."

"I do, especially with guys like him. He's a soup sandwich."

"The hatchet woman strikes."

Pauleen smirked. "Someone's gotta do it. Besides, standards must be maintained. This guy barely qualifies to be a Level 1 Reserve Officer. And I, for one, wouldn't want to ride around with him all day if I wasn't getting paid extra for it."

"Chop chop, baby." Marci faced Quinn. "You wanna do the honors?"

"You can have this one."

"Because you think he'll fight?"

"No. Because he smells." He glanced at Pauleen. "Right?"

"They all smell."

"I got the last stinker, Marci. This one is yours."

Marci rolled her eyes. "Fine. Whatever." She approached the detained man. Quinn and Pauleen followed her.

"Joseph Bishop?" Marci asked.

"What did I do? I didn't do nothing."

"Relax," Pauleen said. "Answer the detective's questions, and you'll be on your way."

"I know my rights," Joseph said.

"So do we. Now, answer her questions."

"I'm Detective Burkett," Marci said. "We're investigating a homicide."

"Homicide?"

"As in murder. Yeah."

Joseph looked about. "But I didn't kill nobody."

Marci said, "That's what we need to find out."

Using a single hand, Joseph pulled the BMX tighter to his side. He appeared confused. "In fact, I ain't never killed a single thing 'cept maybe some bugs."

The young officer said, "Drop the bike."

Joseph ignored the rookie, but his arm relaxed and extended outward. The bike now stood at a forty-five-degree angle to him. Confidence passed over Joseph's face. "You got the wrong guy."

Marci said, "We just want to know where—"

"Drop the bike," the rookie ordered.

The detectives glared at the young officer.

"It's new," Joseph said. "I ain't dropping shit."

The young officer puffed his chest and jutted his chin at Joseph. "I told you to drop the bike."

Joseph's face pinched. "Man, shut the fuck up."

Pauleen quickly stepped around the detectives to stand next to the rookie. She lowered her voice. "Get in the car."

"What?"

She snapped her fingers and pointed. "Start your report from the last call." She sounded like a scolding mother.

Everyone waited until the young officer climbed into the passenger seat of the patrol car and closed the door.

Marci asked Joseph, "Now, where were you Monday night?"

"With your mom."

Quinn shook his head. Pauleen muttered, "Not smart."

"You're starting out on the wrong foot," Marci said.

Joseph chuckled. "Lady, I didn't kill anyone, so this whole stop is bullshit. I know the law, and you can't touch me. Besides, it looks like your old man already put you in your place once this week."

Pauleen snorted. "Oh, you're doing great, Joey."

He eyed her. "It's Joe. Nobody calls me Joey."

"What were you doing on Monday night?" Marci asked.

Joseph sucked something imaginary through his teeth. "I already told you—your mom."

An unmarked Chevy Impala pulled up with a woman behind the wheel.

Joseph glanced toward the new arrival then hung his head. "Shit."

"Time to pay the piper," Marci said.

When the woman exited the car, Quinn approached her. He extended his hand. "Good to see you, Yvette."

Yvette Oliver was a corrections officer based out of the West Central C.O.P.S. office. Her blue jacket had gold lettering on the left breast that read *Washington State Department of Corrections*. She also wore blue jeans and black Nikes. Her blond hair fell to her shoulders.

She accepted Quinn's hand. "How've you been?"

"Good. Thanks for coming out."

Yvette lifted her chin in acknowledgment to both Marci and Pauleen. "Ladies. What's my boy up to?"

"We're investigating a homicide," Marci said, "and the name Joey Bishop came up."

"Is that a fact?"

"Hey, yo, Miz Oliver," Joseph said, "it wasn't me. You know I don't go by that."

Yvette moved closer. "How do I know that, Joe? Maybe that's what your girlfriend calls you."

Marci tilted her head. "Is that true? Is that what my mom calls you?"

Yvette scrunched her nose. "Excuse me?"

"Joe here has been going on about how he's hooking up with my mother."

Joseph Bishop lifted his hands in mock surrender, and his bike clattered to the ground. "It was a joke, Miz Oliver. I swear."

"You're not doing Detective Burkett's mom?"

"That's right," Joseph said. He tried to wear a look of contrition, but it looked more as if he were constipated. "I was only teasing."

Yvette crossed her arms. "That's not a very nice thing to tease a woman about, is it?"

Joseph's constipation switched to mild embarrassment. "No, ma'am."

"Then you should apologize to Detective Burkett."

"I'm sorry."

"Not to me," Yvette said. "Her. And say it like you mean it."

Joseph faced Marci. "Yo, I'm really sorry, Detective. And I apologize for the comment about your face, too."

The corrections officer clucked her tongue. "You commented about her looks?"

"I didn't mean nothing by it."

Yvette looked to Quinn. "What do you want to know about this guy?"

"Where was he on Monday night?"

The corrections officer looked at Joseph. "Well?"

"I was at a friend's house sleeping off a drunk."

"What friend?" Yvette asked.

"I don't know his name."

"Which means you don't have an alibi."

Joseph slapped his chest. "I swear to God that's what I was doing. We just gotta find my friend."

"But you don't know his name," the corrections officer said. "Therefore, he's not a friend."

"We just met. You know how it is."

"No, I don't. I know all my friends by their names."
Yvette eyed Quinn. "Well?"

"We don't have a reason to hold him, but we don't
want to lose track of him either."

"Want me to violate him?"

Joseph interlaced his fingers and dropped to his knees.
"Please don't, Miz Oliver. I swear what I'm saying is
true."

"What's in the bag?" Pauleen pointed at the backpack
Joseph wore. She eyed Yvette. "We asked, but he
wouldn't let us see."

"It's my dirty underwear," Joseph said.

Yvette snapped her fingers, then motioned toward
herself. "Let's go. Let's see the bag."

Joseph slowly stood. "Then you'll let me go?"

"Maybe."

"Maybe? What did I do? Nothing. Just out here
minding my own business."

Yvette waved impatiently. "The bag, Joe. Now."

Joseph took a deep breath. "Right. All right. Gimme a
minute." He abruptly hopped over his bike and sprinted
toward the sidewalk. Pauleen and Yvette chased him.

Marci crossed her arms. "He probably doesn't know
Yvette was a sprinter in college."

Quinn shrugged. "Let him find out the hard way."

About twenty feet away, the two women dragged
Joseph Bishop to the ground. It was like two lions pulling
down a slow-moving zebra. After a brief struggle where
Joseph threw punches that hit both Pauleen and Yvette,
the two women wrestled him into handcuffs.

Chapter 15

During the drive back to the station, Quinn filled Marci in on his visit with Dixie Richter. When they returned to the Major Crimes office, they didn't bother stopping at their cubicles. Instead, they went directly to Andrew Parker's and Jessie Johnson's desks.

Parker glanced over his shoulder when he heard them approach. "What the hell are you doing? Sneaking up on a guy like that."

"We weren't sneaking," Marci said. "And you heard us, so settle down. Where's your partner?"

"Following up on an interview." Parker powered off his computer screen before standing. He smoothed his tie while he asked, "What do you two want?"

Quinn said, "To talk about a case of yours."

"Which one?"

"The accidental death."

Parker's eyes narrowed. "Which one? I've got two of them."

Quinn glanced at Marci, then shrugged. "We don't know."

"You don't—" Parker stood. "What the hell is this? You two jerking my chain or something?"

"We got word that one of our victims came and talked with you about an accidental death."

Parker's brow furrowed. "Who?" As soon as the word escaped his mouth, his brows shut up. "The senior volunteer? That's the guy who was beaten to death?"

Quinn and Marci both nodded.

"No shit." Parker dropped back into his chair.

"So?" Quinn said.

"What?"

"Tell us about the accidental death."

"You're barking up the wrong tree."

"How do you know?"

"Because she drowned."

"Who drowned?" Quinn and Marci asked in unison.

"Margaret Kelley." Parker turned to his desk and grabbed a file. "It was an accident—plain and simple."

"Are you sure?" Marci asked.

Parker dropped the file, and his head whipped back around. "Of course, I'm sure."

"Easy," she said. "I'm just asking."

"Well, be nice when you ask. This isn't my first rodeo, princess."

"Listen, jackass—" Marci pointed down at Parker.

He jumped out of his chair. "Jackass?"

"You heard me. We're chasing down everything Ray Christy did because the chief is up our butts. Have you ever had the chief take an interest in you?"

Parker's jaw flexed. "I've had high-profile cases."

"Not like this. And let me tell you something, buddy, you don't want it. We're being micromanaged like you can't believe." Marci lifted three fingers. "The chief, the captain, and the lieutenant hover over us like spy satellites. They watch our every move. So quit being a baby and fill us in on your case."

Parker crossed his arms.

Marci stepped forward and stood nose-to-nose with Parker. "Or should we tell the three wise men how you're being a dick? If this case is going to be a race to property crimes, we'll make sure you beat us there."

Quinn opened his hands in a calming manner. "Chill out, both of you. Let's pretend like we're a team."

Parker moved back and sat on the edge of his desk. His eyes narrowed as he focused on Marci's eye. "I like what you did with your face."

"Want me to help with yours?"

He smiled at that. "Good one."

"I thought so."

Parker inhaled and slowly let it out. "So, the brass has taken an interest in your case."

"It's a dead volunteer," Quinn said. "He's one of ours."

"One of ours?" Parker scoffed. "Save that bullshit for the administration."

"That's how the chief is viewing it."

Marci nodded. "It's true."

Parker rolled his eyes. "Whatever. What do you want to know?"

"Everything you can tell us," Marci said. "Start with the drowning."

"It's so simple it didn't even need a binder." Parker grabbed the file from his desk and handed it to Marci. "A woman reported she found her friend unresponsive in a bathtub. Officers responded along with Fire, who pronounced her dead. Then officers contacted their supervisor, who placed the call for an investigator. That's when I showed up."

Marci flipped through the file. "This was a group home?"

"Yeah, but not the type of place that gives a lot of assistance. Just help with medication and food. The residents can dress and bath themselves."

Quinn pointed to the file. "Is there a caregiver on-site?"

"It's a converted house," Parker said. "And yes, a caregiver is supposed to be there, but she wasn't when I arrived. According to the owner, Elise Morrow was there in the morning and helped everyone with their medication. Then she left. It was a scheduled thing."

Quinn looked to Marci. "What day was this?"

She consulted the date on the report. "Last Thursday."

"A week ago."

Parker nodded. "That's right. Nothing pointed to foul play. There was no bruising on the victim. I interviewed the witnesses. One gal said she was the victim's best friend—her name is in the file. Anyway, this gal said Margaret Kelley seemed normal before going in for her bath. A copy of the ME's report is also in there." He wiggled his finger at the file. "She conducted the autopsy on Monday and ruled that Margaret Kelley had a heart attack then drowned. As I said, it was an accident. Nobody's fault."

Marci pointed at the medical examiner's conclusion in the report so Quinn could see it.

He looked up at Parker. "If the caregiver was there—"

"She wasn't."

Quinn paused before restarting. "If the caregiver was there, could the accidental death have been averted?"

Parker shrugged. "That's more of a civil argument than a criminal one. Supposedly, the caregiver doesn't assist in baths, so she wouldn't have been there when the woman had a heart attack."

Quinn scratched his chin. "Why did Ray Christy come to you about this?"

"Because Margaret Kelley's wallet was found at the Denny's over on Division. Dispatch sent him on the call, and he put it on property." Parker tapped the folder. "His report is in there somewhere."

"And that's all he wanted to talk about?" Quinn asked.

Parker shook his head. "No. Christy decided to play Jessica Fletcher with the wallet."

Quinn and Marci stared at him.

"Your mothers didn't watch *Murder, She Wrote*? Whatever. Christy took the wallet over to the group home in hopes of returning it to Margaret."

Marci looked up from the file. "He didn't know she was dead?"

"That's right," Parker said. "And that's when Christy got it into his thick skull that the group home's owner was involved."

"Why did he think that?" Quinn asked.

"Because the owner is a WSP detective—Jory Bishop."

Quinn and Marci looked knowingly at each other.

"What?" Parker said. "Does that mean something?"

"It connects a dot," Quinn said. "Go on."

"Yeah, well, Christy seemed upset that a detective was investigating a case involving someone who lived in a home he owned. I told him that Bishop wasn't investigating and that I was." Parker tapped his chest. "I also told him that I checked out Bishop, and the guy was clean. Not a scratch on his record. That was Monday morning. The same day I got a heads up from the ME about her ruling on the autopsy. I was just waiting for the report."

"Was Ray satisfied with that?" Marci asked.

Parker shrugged. "I think so. He left, and I thought that was that until you two showed up. I mean, I heard about the murder of a senior volunteer, but I didn't put two and two together."

"How could you not?" Quinn asked.

Parker's face flattened. "I didn't hear his name."

"It was a senior volunteer."

"So? There's more than one of them. Besides, do you know the names of my victims?" Parker pointed to the binders on the shelf above his desk. "Or are you just playing high and mighty right now, Glory Hound?"

Quinn fought the anger rising in his chest. "A real detective would have heard the name of a murdered senior volunteer and maybe wondered if it had something to do with the case he was working."

Parker's face soured, and he flicked the folder that Marci still held. "It was a drowning—a *fucking* accident. And it's closed. Don't make this about me."

"This isn't about you, Parker," Quinn said. "It's about Ray Christy."

Marci handed Parker back his folder. "Let me ask you something."

"What?" he snapped.

"How do you think the wallet got to the Denny's on Division?"

"I have no idea."

"Think someone stole it?"

"Maybe."

"Are you working it?" Marci asked.

"The wallet? No. Why would I?"

Quinn and Marci stared at him.

Parker clutched the file. "How many times do I have to tell you? Margaret Kelley died by natural causes. Her death investigation is resolved. My job is done." He pointed at the binders on his shelf. "Look at those."

"We've got the same binders," Marci said.

"Yeah? Well, those are my priority. If some maggot stole Margaret's wallet, may they burn in hell, but it's a theft. Let Property Crimes handle it. I've got bigger fish to fry."

"Maybe they're related," Quinn said.

Parker emphatically waved the folder. "It's a drowning!" He slammed the file onto his desk. "Now, if you'll excuse me, I've got work to do." He dropped into his chair and turned toward his darkened computer.

Parker sat that way for several moments until he glanced back to Quinn and Marci. "That's your cue to leave."

***

It was a few minutes until five when Quinn consulted the department's internal directory. He picked up his phone's receiver, then dialed the number he wanted.

Quinn had spent the last thirty minutes looking into Jory Bishop. Just as Parker had claimed, the man didn't have any criminal history. That wasn't surprising, given his occupation.

Additionally, he Googled Jory Bishop and found a few news entries related to the trooper. According to several articles in the *Spokesman-Review*, Bishop was a detective working with the Special Investigations Division (SID). Based on the content of the articles, it seemed Bishop's specialty was gangs.

The Spokane Police Department also had a team dedicated to gangs—the Special Investigations Unit (SIU). That was the phone number Quinn dialed now.

It had been a few months since he talked with Sergeant Trevor Hackworth. Quinn and Trevor were never friends, but the two men had been friendly when they were on SWAT many years ago. When Quinn left the team, Trevor remained for another year. He eventually left when it impeded his pursuit of gangs.

When Hackworth's voice mail started, Quinn hung up. Frustrated, he powered off his computer. "I'm calling it."

Marci hung up her own phone and leaned back. "You're done?"

"Yep." Quinn stood and grabbed his suit jacket from the back of his chair.

"I just flagged Margaret Kelley's credit file. If there's

any activity, we'll be notified." Marci began shutting down her computer. "What time are we meeting back here in the morning?"

"How about nine?"

She grunted. "You don't have to sound so happy about it."

"I'm not happy about it."

"You're not unhappy about it."

Quinn faced her. "It's in-the-office overtime. It could be worse."

Marci stood. "I don't need it."

"Go to that seminar if you want."

"I can't do that."

"Sure you can. I'll cover for us this weekend. Go live your life."

Marci pulled her jacket from the back of her chair and slipped an arm into it. "I'm not going to do that. Not only would that be unfair to you, but the three wise men would also hang me out to dry. No, we're in this trouble together."

"Then let's make it a point to interview Ray's daughters tomorrow."

"What about this Jory character?" Marci asked.

"From what I can tell, he's clean. He's attached to a WSP specialty unit. I'm checking into that some more. It might be nothing, but we need to bird dog it, nonetheless."

Stephanie Lesh walked up then. "Looks like I caught you just in time." She extended a stack of papers several inches thick. "Here's Ray Christy's history. If you need more than ninety days back, let us know, and we can pull it."

"Thank you," Quinn said and accepted the papers.

Stephanie nodded before leaving.

Marci asked, "Want to go through that now?"

"Let's read through it first thing in the morning." Quinn took a moment to lock the stack of papers in his desk. "I want to go for a run tonight and clear my head. That way, I'll be fresh to come back at it."

The detectives headed toward the west doors.

***

When Quinn entered his apartment, he tossed his keys and cell phone onto the kitchen counter then set his gun and badge next to them. He opened his refrigerator and considered his options. The turkey meatloaf was still there. How many days had it been in there now? Two? Still good, then. He'd usually eat leftovers without much complaint, but the meatloaf wasn't doing it for him.

He scanned the rest of the fridge, then shut the door. There were other options in there, but none of them intrigued him. Quinn opened a cabinet door and appraised the canned items. He quickly decided he didn't want any of those choices either.

Quinn rested against the counter and crossed his arms. He stared at the closed refrigerator and listened to it hum. He was hungry, but nothing in his apartment sounded good.

The old Quinn would have immediately snatched his keys and gone out for an expensive dinner. There would have been no additional thought to it. Afterward, he would have put the entire thing on his credit card. Maybe he'd have a beer or two with it—craft beers for sure. They were better but more expensive.

That was then. Now, Quinn was trying to live frugally. Most days, he accepted his life. It wasn't glamorous or exciting to live within a budget. And tonight, it felt incredibly constrictive—boring, almost.

Yet, Quinn didn't miss the stress that came with the

missed payments and the foreclosure notices.

Maybe boring was better.

But it didn't feel better.

Quinn walked into his bedroom and changed. He slipped on a pair of shorts and a long-sleeved shirt. Then he put on his running shoes. The soles were showing wear. He'd have to replace them soon.

Ray Christy entered his thoughts. Was that why he felt this way tonight? Was it the fact that the administration took an extra level of interest in the case? Or was it something else?

Occasionally, Quinn brought home cases—not the actual files, but the thoughts of them. They remained in his head until he got a chance to work on them again. He'd be back at the office tomorrow—a Saturday.

He wasn't struggling to comprehend Ray's demise; the man was beaten to death.

So, what was it about Ray?

Quinn returned to the kitchen and grabbed his cell phone. He removed the Bluetooth headset from its charger.

It struck him then.

It was Marci's comment about aging. Ray Christy died at seventy-two. If Quinn lived another three decades, what would his life be like? Would it be filled with leftover turkey meatloaf and nightly runs through his neighborhood? Is that what he wanted for himself?

Quinn exited his apartment, but he stood for a moment staring at the white door.

If his life was to be a series of monotonous nights like this one, could he handle thirty more years of them? It seemed too gloomy to ponder.

Was he depressed?

Quinn walked down the stairs to the sidewalk. Running normally helped his mood, but he had the feeling it wouldn't make these sentiments go away.

Had his life become a simple loop? Work—sleep—repeat. And how did that happen?

Quinn started a podcast and slowly jogged through the parking lot toward the road. The host's voice droned on as Quinn tried to remember where he was last in this story. It took about a minute before he caught up with the latest content.

He ran for half a mile before his mind drifted back to his concerns of depression. Quinn didn't feel that way at the department. And he didn't feel that way while running. Even now, he could sense a lightness coming over him as his body relished the opportunity to move.

It seemed Quinn felt this depression while at home. And if he had to dive deeper into it, it was because of the budget he tried to live within. It wasn't so long ago his finances were screwed up so badly he feared that the department might find out and discipline him.

Fights about money were what tore his marriage to Barbara apart.

Thinking about his ex-wife brought on the old feelings of remorse. It led him to recall a short romance he had with a yoga instructor following the divorce. Had he only been in one short-term relationship since Barbara? That was two years ago.

Was this worry about depression an illusion?

Could he simply be lonely?

Quinn might have scoffed at that question on another day. Instead, he increased his speed and felt his legs loosening. The run didn't clear his head, and he wasn't paying attention to the podcast.

He pulled his phone from the armband and switched to rock & roll. It was an awkward process due to his continued running, but he accomplished it, nonetheless. Quinn pushed the phone back into its holder then turned up the volume.

If a podcast wouldn't distract him tonight, he'd let the music try.

Quinn increased his pace, and his stride became longer.

Chapter 16

The hallways of the Public Safety Building were eerily quiet on the weekend. Therefore, Quinn heard Marci approaching her cubicle long before she arrived.

"I thought we agreed to nine," she said.

"We did."

"How long have you been here?"

"Since eight," he said. "I was restless, so I came in early."

"You should have called."

"Don't worry about it." Quinn waved his hand over several stacks of papers. "This is the info Stephanie Lesh dropped off yesterday. I think I've got it all figured out."

"You solved Ray's murder?"

Quinn shook his head. "No. I think I figured how Ray operated." He put his hand on the largest stack. "This pile doesn't matter."

"You're sure?"

"Mostly."

Marci raised an eyebrow.

"Trust me," Quinn said. "One thing I found is Ray Christy doesn't have a history of running anyone's name outside of a call."

"At least over this period of time."

"That's correct."

Marci moved closer to inspect the piles. "And this is important?"

"It is."

She crossed her arms. "Ray Christy followed protocol is what you're saying. Why is that relevant?"

"Hold your horses." Quinn pointed to a single piece of

paper. "Here's Ray's Found Property report."

"I saw the narrative in Parker's file."

"Right. About an hour after Ray logged out of that call, he ran Margaret Kelley's name through the CAD system." Quinn pointed to another sheet of paper. "He didn't do that with any other call."

"So? I'd still say he was within protocol. Ray probably forgot to run the name before he put the wallet on property. We've all done something similar. He corrected his oversight afterward. Big deal."

"I agree," Quinn said. "And he probably discovered that Margaret didn't have much history—just a witness to a shoplifting incident and her death."

"She's got more history than that. She was an old woman. Probably lived a full and remarkable life."

Quinn smirked. "You know what I mean. Now, here's where things start to get interesting. He ran the CAD report of her accidental death."

"I wonder why he did that."

"Remember what Parker said. Ray didn't know she was dead until he arrived there."

"So, he finds out that Margaret expired, then he came back to the office to figure out how it happened?"

Quinn nodded. "That would be my guess."

"When did all this go down?"

"Last Saturday. The found property call. The pull of the accidental death CAD report. All of it."

Marci nodded. "Okay."

"On Sunday, he checked in for the vacation home checks, but before he did that, he ran two names through the system—Kayla Reed and Kayla Dawn Reed."

Marci eyed him. "Who is Kayla Dawn Reed?"

"No idea, but I checked her out. She's thirty-two with some history drug of possession and moving infractions."

"Low-level stuff," Marci said.

"I Googled her, too, but she's got nothing. Not even a Facebook account."

They both heard the footsteps simultaneously and turned to face the approaching figure. Captain Ackerman nodded his approval. He wore a gray sweatshirt, black jeans, and gray tennis shoes. "Good to see you guys this morning. Any progress?"

"Some," Quinn said. He filled the captain in as quickly as possible on the latest developments.

"What's your mission today?" Ackerman asked.

"We hope to interview Ray Christy's daughters. We've concentrated on his recent work past, but there might be something personal we're missing."

"Good," Ackerman said. "Real good. Do you need any additional resources? Should we assign Parker and Johnson to assist?"

"No," Marci blurted.

Ackerman seemed taken aback. "Got a problem with the young guns?"

"No, sir. We can handle this case without additional interference."

Captain Ackerman rubbed the bridge of his nose. "Additional interference, huh? I'm picking up the underlying message. By the way, your eye is looking better, Burkett."

Quinn could see that Marci was about to reply, so he quickly said, "We're fine on resources, Captain."

"Okay." Ackerman slipped his hands into the pockets of his jeans. "Just so we're clear, we still don't have a solid lead on who killed Ray Christy?"

Quinn shook his head, but Marci's face darkened.

"Easy, Burkett," the captain said. "That wasn't a judgment statement. The chief wants updates, and I need to give him one. I like what you two are doing here. Keep digging through Ray's recent history. Go talk with his family. Be methodical."

"And above all," Marci sarcastically said, "keep you informed."

Ackerman sighed. "No, Burkett. Above all, catch Ray Christy's killer."

***

Quinn and Marci headed northbound on Monroe Street. The in-car police radio crackled with activity. A stolen vehicle had been stopped on the South Hill by members of the Criminal Task Force. Two AK-47s were found in the backseat. Captain Ackerman announced his call sign, then stated he was "on the air" and en route to the stop.

"I hate that guy," Marci said.

"You hate all the brass."

"Especially that guy."

"Even more than Lieutenant Brand?"

She turned toward Quinn. "Why do you have to be like this?"

"I'm helping you keep it real."

"Well, thank you."

"Anytime." He smiled.

She stared at him for a moment longer, then faced the front again. "I hate you, too."

"But I'm not one of the brass."

"You should be."

Quinn laughed. "Oh, you'd love that."

"No, I wouldn't."

They were headed to the house on Fleming Street. This was the address where Margaret Kelley had lived, and supposedly Ray Christy tried to deliver her lost wallet. When they arrived at the location, Quinn parked a couple of houses away. It was a habit he'd learned while on patrol and still practiced.

At the front door, Marci stepped to the left side of the door, and Quinn moved to the right. He opened the screen a bit and knocked. When he let go of the screen, it slammed shut.

"Working a Saturday's not so bad," Quinn said.

Marci shook her head. "You *really* want me to hate you."

The door opened, and a hunched-over woman appeared behind the screen. She seemed to be in her mid-seventies. "Yes?"

"Hello, ma'am. I'm Detective Delaney with the Spokane Police Department." Quinn motioned to Marci. "This is my partner, Detective Burkett. Would you mind if we came in and looked around?

"What's this about?"

"We're following up on Margaret Kelley's death," Quinn said.

The woman pushed the screen door open. "There has been a lot of you people coming through."

Quinn grabbed the screen and held it open. Marci stepped under his arm and entered first. "A lot of us?" she asked.

"That's right. First, there were those young policemen who came out, and then they sent that handsome man out. I sure enjoyed talking with him."

"Handsome man?" Marci's face registered incredulity. "Detective Parker?"

"Oh, not him." The older woman shook her head. "Ray something or other."

"Ray Christy."

The woman smiled. "That's the one."

Marci stepped out of the way so Quinn could enter the house. He released his grip on the screen door, and it clattered shut. He grimaced because he'd let it slam a moment ago.

The woman waved away Quinn's embarrassment. "It happens all the time."

Marci asked, "What's your name, ma'am?"

"Vera Drayton. I live here."

"And Ray Christy visited you?"

She nodded. "Such a delightful man. You folks are lucky to have him."

Marci eyed Quinn before asking Vera, "What did you talk about?"

"Driving."

"Did you talk about Margaret Kelley?"

"Oh, sure. Some."

Marci motioned deeper into the house. "Can you show us where Margaret Kelley drowned?"

"Of course. I'm the one who found her." Vera turned and shuffled away. They turned down a long hallway. The first room they came to was closed. "That's Elise's room. She's not here now."

"Gotcha," Marci said.

"She won't be of any help to you." Vera turned around. "She wasn't here when Margaret died."

"That's what we heard," Marci said.

Vera looked up at Quinn. "Does he ever talk?"

"When she lets me," he said.

"Oh," Vera said, then turned to Marci. "I like you."

She grabbed Marci by the hand and walked to the next room. Inside, an elderly man strummed a guitar. He warbled out, "Gotta serve somebody."

"That's Bob," Vera said. "You don't have to talk with him. He smells."

The man stopped playing.

Vera held a finger to her lips. She shushed the detectives. "He might hear us." She pulled Marci further down the hall. "This is the bathroom."

Quinn stepped by Vera and Marci to inspect a standing tub. It featured a door that allowed for easy entry, a seat, and jets to circulate the water. The design seemed to make it difficult to drown, but not impossible. If a frail, older woman had a heart attack then slipped under the water, the ability to stand in the tub wouldn't make much difference. He stepped out of the bathroom.

"Let's go," Vera said and tugged on Marci to follow. She pointed at the next room. "This was Margaret's. It's locked now."

Quinn reached out and tried the knob.

"Ray did that, too." A final tug on Marci's hand and the two women were in the last bedroom. "This is mine."

Marci held Vera's hand with both of hers. "Thank you for the tour."

"My pleasure."

"Was there anything else you talked with Ray about?"

Vera sat on the edge of the bed and wiggled her feet up and down. "He asked about the owner of this place."

"Jory Bishop," Marci said.

"How did you know?"

"I'm a detective."

The two women smiled at each other.

"Vera," Quinn said.

She looked up at him.

"Tell us about Elise."

"What do you want to know?"

"How is she as a caretaker?"

Vera shrugged. "Good, I guess. She just got here."

"Is that so? When did she arrive?"

"When Margaret drowned. Jory had her come over right away."

Quinn glanced at Marci before asking, "Elise wasn't the caretaker before Margaret drowned?"

"Oh no. That was Kayla."

Marci leaned closer to her. "Kayla Dawn Reed?"

"You really are a detective!" Vera laughed. "I didn't even know her middle name."

"How long had she been here?"

Vera leaned back on her bed and scissor-kicked her feet. "Oh, I don't know. Maybe half a year. A little more. A little less. Give or take."

"When did she leave?"

"The day Margaret drowned."

"And you're sure of that?"

Vera struggled to sit upright. "I think so. Is there a problem?"

"Where did Kayla go?" Marci asked.

Vera shrugged. "I don't know."

At the front of the home, the screen door clattered. Heavy footsteps crossed the floor, and a woman entered the hallway. She appeared to be in her early fifties and was slightly overweight. She wore a hooded sweatshirt, blue slacks, and white nursing clogs.

"That's Elise," Vera whispered.

"Hello," the woman said from down the hall.

Quinn moved toward her and introduced himself.

"What's this about?" Elise asked.

"We're following up on Margaret Kelley. Are you Elise?"

She looked beyond Quinn to Vera and Marci. "What are you doing with Vera?"

"She was the one who found Margaret. We're asking what she remembers about that day. Are you Elise Morrow?"

Elise looked to Quinn. "Yes."

Quinn pulled his notebook from his back pocket. "What's your birthday?"

"Is this really necessary?"

"I like to know who I'm talking to."

Elise sneered. "You know my name. I'm not in the habit of giving my birthdate to strangers."

Quinn flipped his notebook closed. He should be able to locate a fifty-something Elise Morrow in the system. "What can you tell me about this place?"

"It's an adult residential care facility. That's all you need to know."

"When did you replace Kayla Reed?"

"Last week."

"Was that before or after Margaret drowned?"

"Yes." She looked down the hall. "I'd really like it if you stopped bothering the residents."

"Which was it? Before or after Margaret drowned."

Elise faced him again. "Before. I started here the day before because Kayla was fired. It doesn't look good on my record that a resident died on my first day here. Now, if you please."

"Why was Kayla fired?"

She smirked. "How would I know? You'll have to get in touch with my boss."

"That's Jory Bishop, right? Do you have his number?"

Her face soured. "He said not to give it out to anyone, and I'm already in enough trouble with Margaret's drowning." Elise looked down the hall again. "If you're done interviewing Vera, I'd like you to leave."

Quinn could try bullying the phone number from the woman, but why bother? It wouldn't be hard to track down the phone number for a WSP Detective in their Special Investigations Division. He pulled a business card from his pocket and handed it to Elise. "If you remember anything—"

"I won't."

"But if you do, that's my number. Please pass it along to your boss."

"Fine."

"And before we leave, I'd still like to talk with Bob."

Elise's brow furrowed. "Who?"

"The man across the hall."

"Oh, by all means, help yourself."

Elise stepped near her door and inserted a key into the lock. She glanced a final time toward Vera before stepping inside the room. She closed the door behind her and set the lock.

Quinn approached the man playing guitar. "Excuse me?"

The older man stopped strumming and looked up from his chair.

"I'm Detective Quinn of the Spokane Police Department. I'd like to ask you some questions."

The man strummed the guitar, and his fingers danced along the fret. He mumbled some words that Quinn couldn't understand.

"Excuse me?"

Bob kicked back his head and said, "You're a big girl now." His head dropped back down as he continued to strum the guitar and mumble.

"Sir."

The older man paid him no attention and simply mumbled to himself.

"Quinn," Marci said.

He looked over his shoulder. She waved for him to leave the room. He stepped into the hallway.

"What?"

Marci whispered, "He thinks he's Bob Dylan." She tapped her temple. "Mental issues. We're not going to get anything from him."

Quinn took a final look at the singing older man, then followed Marci out of the group home.

Chapter 17

While they drove, Quinn placed a phone call. It was answered on the first ring.

"Hello?"

"Ms. Christy? This is Detective Delaney. We met the other night."

"I remember."

"Are you available for a follow-up interview?"

"Do you know where I live?"

"You gave me your address. We can be there in ten minutes if that's all right."

"I'll see you then." She hung up without waiting for his response.

Marci dialed a number next. When it was answered, she said, "Hey, Annie. It's Marci. Yeah, Quinn and I are out in the field right now. I need a favor. Put an Attempt to Locate out on a Kayla Dawn Reed. I don't have her date of birth, but you should be able to find her."

Quinn changed lanes.

"Uh-uh," Marci said into her phone. "I appreciate it. Great. Thank you."

When she hung up, Marci said, "Let's see if Pauleen and her soup sandwich of a rookie can find this one."

"You think that recruit will make it through the weekend?"

"I hope not. It's better to wash them out quickly than coddle them."

"Better for them," Quinn agreed. "And better for the department."

They drove up to a portion of the South Hill known as Lincoln Heights. Pamela Christy lived in an apartment on

Thirty-first Avenue. She opened her front door before either detective had a chance to knock. "Come in. I'm sorry for my appearance."

Pam looked as if she hadn't slept in days. She wore an oversized Seahawks t-shirt that fell to her bare thighs. Quinn assumed she wore a pair of shorts underneath.

He closed the door after they entered.

The three walked into a living room that was decorated with Seahawks memorabilia. Posters and a framed jersey hung on the wall. Team knickknacks were everywhere.

Quinn and Marci sat on a tattered couch. Pam settled into a worn leather recliner. A pair of white shorts were revealed when her shirt pulled up around her waist.

A glass coffee table stood between them. On it was an empty coffee cup, two opened containers of Red Bull, and a cell phone.

Quinn said, "Thank you for making time for us."

"I wondered when you would call."

"We'd like to continue our conversation from the other night."

"The other night," she said, "I haven't stopped thinking about it."

Quinn pulled out his notebook. "Has anything new come back to you? Something that might help us."

Pam looked down at her hands. "I still can't believe he's gone. I haven't left my apartment since." The cell phone on the coffee table buzzed once. Pam motioned toward it. "My sister won't leave me alone. She's blowing up my cell."

"What for?" Quinn asked.

"To make sure I'm okay." Pam looked up. "She didn't see Dad. I don't know if I'll ever be okay with it. I can't get it out of my head."

He softly asked, "What's your sister's name?"

"Heidi. Same last name. It used to be Durbin, but she changed it back to the family name after her divorce."

Quinn jotted the sister's name into his notebook. "Can you give me her number? We'd like to talk with her as well."

Pam recited the phone number from memory.

An older black cat wandered into the room. It took a cursory look at both Quinn and Marci before leaving the room.

"My father's cat," Pam said. "William's not exactly a people person."

The cell phone on the table buzzed again.

"Are you sure you don't need to get that?" Quinn asked.

"If I text her back, she'll just call me because she knows I have my phone. I don't want to talk with anyone." She appeared apologetic. "Except you guys. This is important, I know."

Quinn nodded his thanks. "Was your father having any money problems?"

"I don't think so, but that's a question you should ask Heidi. She's more in tune with that stuff."

"What about Heidi?"

"What about her?"

"How is she with money?"

Pam shrugged a single shoulder. "She's fine." A thought seemed to register with her. "Wait. You don't think Heidi had anything to do with this, do you?" Pam's voice raised with anger. "Because I can tell you she didn't. She loved Dad. I loved Dad."

"We're looking for an explanation as to why your father was murdered, and we have to ask questions like this. I hope you understand."

Pam reluctantly nodded.

Quinn asked. "Who's the executor of your father's will?"

"Heidi," Pam said, "but I'm telling you there's no way she was involved with this. Talk with her. You'll see."

Quinn held up an apologetic hand. "These are normal questions, Pam."

Marci slid forward to the edge of the couch. "Your father was well-liked among his peers and others on the department. From what we've heard, he enjoyed volunteering."

Pam shrugged, then shook her head. "Yeah. Maybe. I don't really know. I think he did it to be close to my brother. Do you know about him?"

Marci said, "We heard he was an officer and killed on duty."

"In Albuquerque." Pam tucked her legs underneath her. They disappeared beneath the large t-shirt. "Jacob was killed during a traffic stop. My dad was proud of him, but I don't think he fully accepted his death. I mean, he knew he was gone. It wasn't like that. It was more that Dad wanted to understand why Jacob wanted to be a cop. I thought the whole thing was pretty simple."

"Yeah?" Marci's face was open and inviting.

"It was the same thing that drove my dad to serve in the Army." She waved at the Seahawks banner. "It's the reason my nephew is so focused on football. It's what men do." She made eye contact with Marci. "Some women, too. I guess. I'm sorry. I'm rambling."

"It's okay."

"I'm probably not much help."

"You've been very helpful," she said. Marci looked to Quinn. "Anything else?"

He stood. "I think we're good. Thank you for your time. If we need anything additional, we'll be in touch."

***

"Yes, I'm the executor of his will," Heidi Christy said.

They were seated in the living room of her South Hill home. She lived across from Manito Park on Tekoa Street. The house was in stark contrast to her sister's apartment. Expensive-looking artwork hung on the wall. The floors were real hardwood, not imitation plank. White leather furniture lay interspersed around the room. It was the house of a successful adult.

Quinn and Marci sat on separate recliners. Heidi had the couch to herself.

"Have you seen the will yet?" Quinn asked.

"Yes." Heidi dabbed her eyes. "I saw it before Dad's passing. The assets are to be split fifty/fifty. It's nothing fancy. Why do you ask?"

"It's a standard question in situations like this. What about your mom? Shouldn't the assets go to her? Washington is a community property state."

Heidi shook her head. "When mom's disease first appeared, my parents understood there was no reversing its course. People with Alzheimer's don't get better. So, they met with an elder law attorney about how to prepare mom's estate. It was a long process to get her ready to go into a home. I can't imagine how anyone does it without the help of counsel."

Quinn looked up from the notes he'd written. "Is there anyone who would want to hurt your father?"

"Not that I know of, and I thought about this. I wish there was someone that I could point you to and say that's the guy so we could be done with this, but there's not. My parents got along with the neighbors their whole lives. They went to church even though I think that secretly Dad only did it for Mom. Basically, my parents lived a drama-free life." Her shoulders slumped. "Except for what happened to Jacob. Did Pam tell you about him?"

Both Quinn and Marci nodded.

"He was so much older than us. You probably noticed the age difference between Pam and me. We're seven years apart. Well, Jacob and I were eight years apart. My parents weren't much for having children in a hurry."

Quinn said, "Pam thought Jacob's death was one of the reasons your father volunteered."

"He never said, but that's my thought, too."

"Was your father having money problems?"

"None. He was very careful with his finances. He didn't owe anyone anything. Their house had been paid off for years. Same thing with his truck. After mom went into Colonial Springs, he sold her car. He was a pragmatic man when it came to money."

Quinn jotted a note into his pad. He noticed Marci doing something similar. He looked up. "How did your father seem lately?"

"Fine." A sad smile crossed her lips.

"Something funny?"

"He always said 'fine' even when things weren't. Pam called him out for it on Sunday."

"What happened Sunday?" Quinn asked.

"Family dinner. Here. The four of us. Logan, my son, was with us." Heidi glanced over her shoulder to another portion of the house. "If you don't have to talk with him, I'd appreciate it."

Quinn shook his head. "We won't need to. Did you do that—the family get-together—every Sunday?"

"No. We should have, but it got a little tense every time we were all together."

"What made the get-togethers tense?"

"Mom." Heidi shifted in her seat. "Sucks to admit that to you guys, but it's the truth."

"Would you mind explaining why?"

Heidi puffed her cheeks before answering. "Dad saw her every day. He loved her. It was a sweet thing to be a part of when growing up. But Dad never stopped loving Mom even when the disease robbed her of who she was. He wanted Pam and me to see her more, but we're not good at it. We've each got our insecurities that I won't bore you with, but Pam is a little more calloused about it than I am. Regardless, seeing our mother that way isn't..." Heidi looked away. When her gaze returned to Quinn, she said, "Well, that's why we argued."

Quinn imagined Ray sitting and talking with his wife. "Would your dad talk with your mom about things?"

"He talked with her all the time."

"I mean, would he share things that bothered him, things that he was working on?"

"He might. It's unlikely she would comprehend much of it, even less if she remembered any of it. One thing is for sure—Dad wouldn't tell us his problems. That's what he did at dinner on Sunday. Or didn't do, I should say."

Quinn perked up. Marci leaned in at Heidi's last statement.

"What happened?" Quinn asked.

"Dad seemed distracted, maybe a little upset. When I asked how he was doing, he said fine, of course, which led to a little tiff. Afterward, he said he was working on something for the volunteer program but then changed the subject."

"Any idea what it was regarding?"

Heidi squinted. "Not really, but on Monday, he called me while I was working. He wanted to know how to look up members of an LLC. Do you know what I'm talking about?"

Quinn nodded.

"I do that frequently for my job, so I walked him

through the process. It took maybe three minutes at the most. Maybe I should have spent some more time with him, maybe asked him what it was concerning, but I was in a hurry." Regret filled Heidi's eyes.

Quinn said, "Did he mention the name of the LLC?"

"He didn't, and I didn't even think to ask." She covered her mouth. "Please tell me this isn't the thing that got him killed?"

"Whatever it was," Quinn said, "it couldn't have been just that."

Heidi looked away. Tears welled in her eyes. "I was busy," she muttered.

Quinn pulled out a business card and laid it on the coffee table. "If you think of anything else, please give us a call."

She nodded as tears streamed down her cheeks.

The detectives left then.

***

When they arrived back at their cubicles, the red light on Quinn's phone blinked.

"We're calling it a day, right?" Marci said.

"In a minute."

Quinn lifted the phone's receiver and pressed the voice mail button. The system notified him he had one new message. It played automatically.

"Detective Delaney, this is Jory Bishop."

Marci grabbed her keys and stepped toward the hallway.

"You were by my business today."

Quinn snapped his fingers then held one up in the air—a non-verbal message for Marci to wait.

"Would you mind giving me a call to let me know what this is about? I'd appreciate it." Bishop provided his

phone number after that.

Quinn pressed the button to replay the message, then set the phone to play over the speaker. He placed the receiver back where it belonged.

"What's going on?" Marci asked. Her eyes brightened when she heard Jory Bishop's name.

Quinn pulled out his notebook and copied down the phone number. He saved the message then hung up. "What do you think?"

Marci pointed at the phone. "Call him—*now*."

He set the phone to play on speaker again and dialed the number. It rang loudly throughout the Major Crimes section. Neither detective would do this during the week, but since they were alone on a Saturday, no one was there to complain.

When the call was finally answered, there was traffic noise in the background. "Bishop."

"Jory Bishop, this is Detective Delaney."

"Hey, Detective. I heard you were at my business today. Something I can do for you?"

"We're following up on Margaret Kelley's death."

"Detective Parker already handled that."

Quinn eyed Marci. "We're assisting him. Can you come down to the station tomorrow and answer a couple of questions?"

"I'm on a tight schedule tomorrow with my business. I hope you understand."

Marci flashed a dubious look, then made an obscene gesture with her hand. Quinn rolled his eyes.

Bishop said, "But maybe we can meet for breakfast. How does eight at the Wall Street Diner sound? That way, we both get what we want."

Quinn raised his eyebrows, and Marci nodded. "Eight sounds fine," he said.

"See you then."

The call ended.

"That was interesting."

"Maybe it's nothing," Marci said. "And all we'll get out of it is breakfast."

"There could be worse ways to earn overtime."

"You and the overtime." She headed for the exit. "Friend of the administration. What did I tell you?"

***

Quinn tossed his keys and cell phone onto the counter then unclipped his badge. He didn't set it down, though. He simply stared at the hunk of silver.

How many days in a row had he performed this same post-work routine? There was no way to know because he'd done it for years. Oh, it varied slightly while he was married to Barbara because she didn't like the gun left in the kitchen, but the effect was the same: enter the house and drop his gear in one spot. It was an old habit, but did that make it bad?

No. It made it safe and boring.

His mind returned to the fact that he had not dated anyone since shortly after his divorce. Is that what happens when you trudge through life? he wondered. Go to the office, keep your head down, return home, go to bed, wake up, go back to the office.

The sad truth was he didn't even care that a woman hadn't been in his life. Why didn't he? He *should* care. It *should* matter.

Quinn disgustedly flipped his badge into the living room. It bounced off the couch and clunked against the wall. He then pushed his keys across the counter. They slid off the opposite side and fell to the floor. Quinn angrily snatched the cell phone and raised it above his shoulder, ready to huck it across the room.

He paused. It was a fragile piece of department-issued equipment. If they thought he'd broken it purposefully, then he'd be responsible for its replacement. He dropped the cell to the counter with a clatter. That bit of self-control pissed him off. He hadn't thrown the phone because of what it might cost him.

He went to his bedroom and removed his gun and its holster. Quinn set them on the dresser and contemplated going for a run.

"No," he muttered to himself.

Quinn returned to the kitchen to retrieve his keys. Irritation flooded through him when he realized the keys were on the other side of the counter where he had pushed them. After collecting the set, he left the apartment. Quinn hadn't bothered to change his clothes.

He headed down to his car. He'd sold his truck a while back and bought a used Toyota Camry. Right now, he didn't care that it was paid off. He only cared that it was safe and boring.

Is this who he'd become? Safe and boring Quinn Delaney—alone and driving a car he didn't like simply because it was affordable.

Why did thinking about this bother him tonight?

He didn't know, but he wanted to get away from these brooding thoughts.

Quinn started the car, and its four-cylinder engine quietly came to life. The truck he used to own had a big, throaty roar. He also used to own a boat and an ATV. They were gone now, too—victims of his credit purge of over a year ago.

Now, he didn't own anything remotely fun. He revved the Toyota's engine, and it softly purred.

Quinn had been a member of SWAT and acted like a fool at many team parties. Barbara, his ex-wife, used to love going to gatherings with him. No one invited him to get-togethers anymore. Or did he just quit attending, and the invitations eventually stopped as a result? Now, he spent his weekends watching broadcast TV alone since he no longer had a cable subscription and no one to sit with anyway.

He gripped the steering wheel. Quinn wanted to do something stupid, something dangerous. His hands tightened before he shook himself back and forth.

Quinn hollered inside his car.

When he ran out of breath, Quinn rested his head against the steering wheel. He listened to the engine hum. He could barely hear it.

That was the sound of safe and boring.

Quinn turned off the engine.

He hated this car.

But he remained sitting behind the wheel for some time after that.

Chapter 18

When Quinn turned off Wall Street onto Princeton Avenue, he drove slowly past the little parking lot. There were no spots available. He continued half a block to the east before squeezing his unmarked car between two oversized pickups. He noticed Marci's patrol car across the street. She'd beaten him to the meeting.

It was a bright, crisp morning. Only a few of these would remain before the region's weather turned sloppy with rain and snow. If he wasn't working, Quinn might have taken advantage of a day like this and gotten outside. Maybe he would have taken a drive and left town. When he was married, he and Barbara would have gone up to Green Bluff to experience the fall festival. In his mind, that was a romantic event, and he couldn't imagine doing something like that alone.

Safe and boring, he thought.

But why couldn't he go to Green Bluff by himself?

Quinn pulled open the door to the Wall Street Diner and entered. A cacophony of voices, scraping utensils, and kitchen noises greeted him. He scanned the small restaurant until he saw Marci sitting at a table. He walked over and sat next to her. There were three place settings already on the table. Marci held a cup of coffee between her hands.

"I knew this place was going to be slammed," she said, "so I got here thirty minutes ago."

A server walked over and smiled at Quinn. "Coffee?"

"Please."

She turned to Marci. "Still waiting for your third?"

"Yes."

The server hurried off.

"What's the bet that Bishop doesn't show?" Marci asked.

"He'll show."

She sipped her coffee. "Yesterday, you said he was in a specialty unit. What's it do?"

"Looks like something with gangs. I'm going to talk with Hackworth tomorrow and see if he's dealt with him."

"Maybe we're barking up the wrong tree."

"That's what Parker said." Quinn shrugged. "And we'll know soon enough."

The server returned with a cup of coffee. She was followed by a man in a green flannel shirt, blue jeans, and black boots. He was unshaven and dark bags were under his eyes. His short dark hair looked recently washed but uncombed.

"Detective Delaney?" the man asked.

Quinn nodded.

Jory Bishop looked at the server. "I'll take a cup, too. Just black. And gimme a cheese omelet with some hash browns." He glanced at Quinn and Marci. "You guys eating?"

Quinn shook his head. "I'm good."

Marci waved her hand.

"That's it," Bishop said to the server then sat across from Quinn. He eyed Marci. "Who are you?"

"This is my partner," Quinn said. "Detective Burkett."

Bishop's brow furrowed. "I've heard of you."

Marci smiled at Quinn. "Our reputation precedes us."

"Not him," Bishop said. "You." He motioned toward her eye. "What happened to your face?"

"Genetics."

Bishop smirked, then turned to Quinn. "They sent two of you to follow-up on the drowning of one old woman.

Parker must've fucked up his report or something."

"We've been asked to make sure everything is above board."

"Above board?" Bishop frowned. "If that isn't the most noncommittal bullshit I've ever heard. What's this really about?"

"Tell us about Kayla Reed," Quinn said.

Bishop seemed mildly perplexed by the question and was just about to respond when the server returned with his cup of coffee. She set it in front of him. He mumbled his thanks then lowered his eyes as he sipped from the mug.

Quinn studied Bishop's hands. There was no damage on the knuckles or fingers.

Bishop set his cup down. "Kayla Reed was a caregiver."

"What happened to her?" Quinn asked.

"Why are you asking about Kayla? I thought you were following up on Margaret's drowning."

"Maybe we're not convinced she drowned."

Bishop rolled his eyes. "What game are you playing, Delaney?"

"I'm not playing any game."

"Yeah, you are." Bishop leaned forward. "The medical examiner stated Margaret had a heart attack and drowned. Case closed."

"How do you know that?"

"You think only the PD has inside sources? Get real. And why is she really here?" Bishop motioned to Marci. "To witness this conversation?"

"She's my partner."

"But it's Sunday." His brow relaxed. "Oh, I get it. You guys shacked up last night. Is that it? Played a little spank and tickle, and now you bring her along as cover with the administration. Your secret is safe with me. I promise not to tell."

Quinn cocked his head. "You still haven't answered my question. What happened to Kayla Reed?"

Bishop's lip curled. "She quit." He snapped his fingers. "Just like that."

"No notice?"

"That's what this means." He snapped his fingers again.

"Kayla was gone when Margaret Kelley drowned?"

"Yeah. She quit the day before."

"Vera told us that Kayla was there that morning."

Bishop shook his head. "Vera gets confused. Don't put too much stock into what she tells you."

"And you were out of town?" Quinn asked.

"That's right. In Seattle."

"Doing what?"

"None of your fucking business is what I was doing." Bishop stabbed the table with a finger. "Margaret drowned. Case closed. What's this about, Delaney? What are you really after?"

"You don't seem upset about Kayla's disappearance."

Bishop smirked. "Disappearance? She didn't disappear. She quit the day before, just like I told you. Want her number?" He pulled out his phone. His index finger jumped around the screen for a moment. He read off a number, and Quinn jotted it in his notebook.

Marci set her cup of coffee on the table. "Tell me about your business."

Bishop faced her. "Excuse me?"

"It's a group home, right?"

"Technically, it's an adult residential care facility. Licensed and regulated by the state." Bishop slipped a finger through his coffee cup's handle. "Why do you want to know about it?"

"You must have to jump through a lot of paperwork."

Bishop toasted her with his cup. "You wouldn't believe."

"What happens when there's a death at your facility?"

The mug hovered at Bishop's lip. "They send out an investigator."

"Has it happened before?"

"Has what happened?"

"A death."

Bishop plunked the coffee cup on the table. "They're old and feeble, Burkett. Their end is inevitable. It's better when they kick off at the hospital or when their family takes them home to be with hospice, but yeah, people die. It happens."

"So, you're experienced with the state's investigative process is what you're saying."

The trooper nodded. "That's what I'm saying."

Marci said, "Were you upset about Margaret's death?"

"Am I supposed to be?" Bishop looked at both detectives. "Don't take this wrong, but she wasn't my family. She was a customer, renting a room, that's it. Am I sad for her? Sure. But am I going to get all weepy-eyed that she's gone? No. I've got shit to do."

Quinn crossed his arms and watched for Marci to give him an opening. She noticed him waiting and nodded slightly. He asked, "Did you meet one of our senior volunteers when he tried to return Margaret Kelley's wallet?"

Bishop grinned. "Oh, so that's what this is about."

"I'll take that as a yes."

"Yeah, I met him. Ray Christy, right?"

"That's right. How did the meeting go?"

Bishop's face flattened. "Which one?"

"How many were there?"

"There were two." Bishop sipped his coffee. "The first was when he came by the house to return Margaret's wallet. I told him she died and—"

Quinn interrupted. "You told him she drowned?"

Bishop seemed to think about that before saying, "Yeah. Why?"

"Because Ray came back to the station and pulled the report on her."

"Maybe he was looking for an incident number." Bishop looked to Marci. "Anyway, I told him he could leave the wallet with me. I said I'd put it in her room— you know, for the family to deal with. But ol' Ray claimed he couldn't do that—that he had to put it into evidence. That seemed like an acceptable choice, and I told him so. We ended the contact then."

Quinn was intrigued by Bishop's response. Up until then, the man had been emotional—at times, cocky and belligerent. But now, he spoke like he'd practiced a monologue.

"And the second meeting?"

"We spoke in the jail lot. I'd just booked a baby banger on a felony warrant, and when I came out, Ray was at my car. We chatted for like maybe a minute, and then he went into the Public Safety Building."

Again, the way Bishop described the second meeting came off as if he had practiced the delivery.

Quinn asked, "What did you speak about?"

"I asked if he was following me." Bishop noticed Quinn's confusion. "It was a joke. You don't get it either. I guess my jokes don't always come off the best." Bishop leaned forward. "Wait. Is all this about Ray?" The trooper waggled a finger back and forth between Quinn and Marci. "About my conversations with him? Did he step out of line in your department or something?"

Quinn shook his head. "We're not investigating Ray."

The trooper shrugged. "Too bad. The guy is an asshole if you want my opinion. He's not a good reflection of your volunteer program."

Quinn thought about addressing Ray's death right then, but he eyed Marci first. By the look on her face, he imagined she was considering the same thing. Instead, she asked, "How many care facilities do you own?"

The server arrived and put Bishop's breakfast in front of him. She asked, "Can I get you anything else?"

He shook his head. "I'm good. Thanks." Bishop grabbed the saltshaker. "Why's it matter how many facilities I own?"

"Just making conversation," Marci said.

"Well, I'm ready to eat my breakfast, and so far, this doesn't look like you two are following up on Margaret's drowning. I'm not sure what you're after, but I'd like to eat in peace."

"So your answer is…"

"I'm eating." Bishop salted his omelet.

Quinn nodded at Marci then stood. She followed his lead.

Through a mouthful of hash browns, Bishop said, "I'll cover your coffees."

"No," Quinn said. "We'll pay for them on the way out."

The trooper chuckled. "Whatever, Delaney. Enjoy your day."

At the cashier's stand, the two detectives watched Jory Bishop eat.

"He doesn't know that Ray is dead," Marci said.

Quinn crossed his arms. "Either that or he had time to practice. A couple of his answers sounded rehearsed."

Marci handed him a five-dollar bill then stepped toward the door. "Pay for the coffees. I'll meet you downtown."

***

After Quinn parked his car, he detoured to the large concrete building known as the Spokane County Jail. He stopped at a secured door and pressed a buzzer. He looked up into a camera and smiled. A moment later, a lock audibly disengaged. He pulled open the door.

Quinn entered the sally port and locked his gun in one of the holding bins. He slipped the oversized key into his pocket and passed through the booking lobby before getting to the jail processing desk. Several Spokane County Sheriff's deputies moved about behind a large circular structure. One of the jailers noticed Quinn and stepped toward him.

"What can I do for you, Detective?"

"I'd like to speak with the sergeant."

Sergeant Craig Truitt sat behind a computer and stared intently into the monitor. He perked up when he heard his rank. "Detective Delaney, welcome to the salt mine."

Quinn motioned him over with a slight jerk of his head.

Truitt's brow furrowed, but he stood and approached. "What's going on?"

The detective turned away from the other jail staff and lowered his voice. "Do you have a camera on the parking lot?"

"A portion of it." Truitt rested his elbows on the counter. He lowered his voice to match Quinn's. "Why do you ask?"

"I'm investigating a homicide, and there's an interaction I'd like to see if you caught. How long do you keep the logs?"

"They're kept for sixty days then dumped. The files are huge. Do you know the date and time?"

"Not exactly."

"You're not suggesting we watch two months' worth

of video, are you?"

Quinn glanced at the other staff. A couple took some interest in the two men. He lowered his voice even further. It was barely a whisper now. "Can you tell me what time a certain WSP detective was here? Particularly when he was booking a suspect on a warrant?"

Truitt straightened and stared at Quinn. Several moments passed with neither man saying anything. Then the sergeant stepped around the counter.

"Follow me," he said.

The two men walked into the sally port and to the furthest wall. Truitt said, "The guys can still watch us on the camera, but they can't hear us now. What's this about?"

"Do you know Jory Bishop?"

"Of course. You're not telling me you suspect him of a homicide?"

"Honestly, I don't know. This might be a whole lot of nothing, and, quite frankly, I hope it is. But his name came up during an investigation, and some of the things he's said seem a little odd."

"A little odd?"

Quinn nodded.

Truitt looked around the sally port even though they were the only two there. He rubbed his face as he thought. "What is it you're looking for?"

"Bishop said he talked with one of our senior volunteers in your parking lot. It occurred after he booked a gang member on a warrant."

"And this is important, why?"

"The guy who was murdered was our senior volunteer."

Truitt rested his shoulders against the concrete wall. "Technically, you should get a warrant for this."

"Why?" Quinn asked. "There's no right to privacy in

the parking lot. None in here either."

Truitt appeared pained. "C'mon, man. You know how the county attorneys are.

"I don't even know if this will lead to anything."

"Still," the sergeant said, "you're asking me to maybe violate some protocol here."

"Then do me this favor. Would you see if the confrontation exists in the system? If it does, save it."

Sergeant Truitt nodded. "All right, Delaney. I'll look for it. If I find it, I'll let you know." He walked toward the jail lobby.

Quinn headed for the exit then walked across the campus to the Public Safety Building. When he walked into the Major Crimes office, Marci was already at her desk and working.

"What took you so long?"

"I stopped by the jail to see if they had some footage of Bishop's conversation with Ray Christy. They're going to look for it."

"Good idea. Not going to sit?"

"I'm going to run up to Colonial Springs and see if Ray's wife might be able to shed light on anything."

Marci frowned. "Serious? That's a long shot."

"It's one we should take."

"Like shooting for the moon."

"I know but—"

"She's not going to remember anything. That kind of thing only happens in the movies."

Quinn shrugged. "You're probably right, but do you want to tell the chief that we didn't even try? Feel free to do so."

Marci pushed her chair back.

"You don't have to go."

"I thought we already discussed this. Besides, it's Sunday."

***

Upon their arrival at Colonial Springs Assisted Living Community, Quinn and Marci met with Deanna Galimore, the on-duty manager. She had a small office just off the now-quiet dining facility. Pictures of nature settings hung on the walls. Quinn had the feeling the company provided the photos, and the office was shared by multiple members of the staff.

"Audrey Christy?" Deanna asked. "May I ask what this is in regards to?"

Quinn said, "Her husband is dead."

"Ray died?"

"He was murdered."

Deanna stood and covered her mouth with both hands. "Oh my God," she said through her fingers. "That's terrible."

Both Quinn and Marci nodded.

"Poor Audrey."

"Yes, ma'am," Quinn muttered.

The manager confusedly glanced around her office. When she collected herself, she said, "Are you here to notify Audrey?"

Quinn eyed Marci before saying, "We hadn't planned to do that, but we can."

"If you want us to do that, we've done it for other families."

"No one from the family has been here in the last few days?"

Deanna shook her head. "No. His girls—how are they doing?"

"They're taking it hard," Quinn said. "We'd like to ask Audrey a few questions to see if Ray might have said anything to her."

"Sure, sure. Of course. I'm allowed to discuss her medical condition with family only, but I'll tell you this much—don't get your hopes up." Deanna sat again and consulted her computer. "She's scheduled for a bath in the next hour. If you're not done by then, I'll have the nurse come back."

"We'd appreciate that," Quinn said.

Deanna stood once more. "Audrey is a very sweet woman, but her ability to recall most things is gone. Please be patient when talking with her."

"We will."

"Why don't we handle the notification? That way, if she does react poorly, you'll have been able to ask your questions."

Quinn nodded his thanks.

They followed Deanna down a long hall to a small room. "This is Audrey's. She lives alone."

Inside, Audrey sat in a recliner with her feet up. She stared at a flat-screen television as a football game played silently. She wore a gray t-shirt and blue slacks. One brown slipper lay on the floor while the other dangled from her left big toe. Her silver hair was uncombed.

Deanna cheerfully said, "Good afternoon, Audrey. How's the football game?"

"Good," Audrey said.

"Who's winning?"

"I don't know."

Deanna moved in front of the television and pointed to Quinn. "Audrey, this is Detective Delaney."

Audrey's head moved slowly to make eye contact. Quinn nodded.

"And this is Detective Burkett."

Marci smiled politely at the older woman.

"They'd like to ask you some questions. Is that okay?"

Audrey nodded.

Deanna leaned into Quinn's ear. "Stand in front of the TV when you talk. It'll help with her focus. Please come by my office when you're finished."

After the manager left, Quinn moved to the spot she previously stood. He said, "We'd like to ask you some questions about your husband, Ray Christy."

Audrey blinked.

"Do you remember Ray, Audrey?"

"Yeah." It didn't sound convincing.

Marci sat on the edge of the bed and studied Audrey.

Quinn asked, "How has Ray seemed lately?"

"I don't know."

"When was the last time he came and saw you?"

"Who?"

"Ray—your husband."

Audrey frowned. "I don't know."

Marci gently said, "Audrey?"

The older woman faced her.

"Do you know where you are?"

"Yeah."

"Where are you?"

Audrey stared at her.

"Where are you, Audrey?"

"I don't know."

Marci reached out and patted her arm. Then she stood and walked over to Quinn. "We're not getting anything here. We'll tell the chief we tried, and that's it."

Quinn nodded.

"Do you know my son?" Audrey asked.

Both detectives looked at the older woman.

"He graduated from the academy yesterday. He's going out on patrol soon." She spoke the words mechanically.

"We don't know him," Quinn said. "But I'm sure he'll do a fine job."

Marci walked out of the room. Quinn stayed a moment further, then moved out of the way of the TV. "Enjoy the game, ma'am."

Audrey didn't speak. Her mouth slowly fell open as she stared at the television.

***

Quinn went out to dinner that evening. At first, he wanted to go to a fancy sit-down restaurant, but doing that by himself held no allure. So, he decided to go to an old haunt—a place he hadn't been since high school.

Dick's Hamburgers sat at the corner of Third Avenue and Division Street. There was no lobby, so everyone was forced to order at the outside counter. Even a chilly fall evening wasn't enough to scare away the customers. He had to wait in line for several minutes before he ordered.

Quinn considered inviting a friend but quickly realized there wasn't anyone he wanted to eat with. He had a lot of associates, but no one close enough to be called a friend. Marci could probably be categorized as such, but it would come with an asterisk since they were 'work friends.'

No, Quinn thought, that wasn't even true. He and Marci were partners. They had a different bond than friends—closer in a way due to the things they saw and experienced. But they would never see a movie together or play a round of golf. It's not what they did.

Quinn stood near a support post and watched the various customers. All walks of life were represented at Dick's—young and old, rich and poor, drug addicts and churchgoers. If there was ever a local eatery that could be considered a neutral zone, Dick's would be it.

A woman in her early thirties watched him. She was

attractive with short brown hair, and she wore a black EWU sweatshirt with faded blue jeans. She sat with a group of women. Quinn thought the woman looked familiar, but he couldn't place her. He smiled, but she didn't return the gesture. The woman continued to stare until Quinn turned away.

He had considered asking Barbara to dinner, but the last time they spoke, she mentioned she'd begun dating someone. Quinn didn't need another weird thing between them. It already felt strange that Barbara wanted the divorce, and he didn't. He still missed her and wished they hadn't separated. She felt differently.

For a moment, Quinn thought about calling the yoga instructor he had the brief fling with. But after their short relationship ended, they hadn't talked. There wasn't a connection deep enough to keep either of them fighting for the other. Quinn only thought of her because he was lonely, and that was no reason to rekindle something that fizzled out so quickly.

"Two Whammy's, fries, and a Diet Coke," the cashier called.

Quinn stepped to the counter, paid for his order, and grabbed his food. Then he sat at the end of one of the long picnic tables. He removed a Whammy and unwrapped it. Before he could bite into it, the woman in the EWU sweatshirt approached him. She was now smiling.

"I think I know you."

Quinn nodded. "You look familiar, too."

She tapped her sternum. "Mona Shaw."

"Quinn Delaney."

"Did we go to high school together?"

"I would have remembered," he said. "Plus, I'm probably ten years older than you."

She smiled. "I don't think so, but I swear I know you

from somewhere. What do you do for a living?"

It was then Quinn remembered her. But she wasn't Mona Shaw back then. She was Mona DeCaro, and her fiancé had tried to kill her. He could envision the bloody pictures of her naked body now. If he thought hard enough, he could pinpoint the five places where her boyfriend had stabbed her. She lost a kidney and had to have a section of her bowel removed. For a time, she lay in critical condition, and the doctors didn't give her much chance at surviving.

He was new to Major Crimes, and his partner interviewed her when her condition stabilized. Quinn stood back and took notes. She was on painkillers at the time. That's why she didn't vividly recall him. And since it was so long ago, that was why it took him time to place her. If he remembered correctly, Mona had long, blond hair back then.

"I work for the city," he said. It was a noncommittal answer.

Mona's lip's twisted, and her brow furrowed. "Maybe you just have one of those faces."

"Maybe."

She pulled a business card from a back pocket and set it next to his burger. "I own a salon in the valley. My cell number is on the card. If you remember how we know each other, maybe give me a call."

"I will."

"Or even if you don't remember. You know." She shrugged before returning to her friends.

Quinn stared at the card for a moment. Then he put the uneaten burger back into the bag. He also tossed the business card inside. He walked to his car and got in.

He was northbound on Division Street when he rolled down his window. Quinn reached into the bag and pulled out the business card. He'd seen this woman lying wounded on a hospital bed. He'd seen the evidence photos of her naked body before and after the surgeries. Quinn would never get those images out of his head.

It was no way to start a relationship.

Maybe they could just be friends.

It was a stupid thought. Quinn threw the business card out the window.

Chapter 19

An email alert popped up on Quinn's computer screen and diverted his attention. It was labeled *Monroe Court Security Camera*. Instinctively, he turned to Marci, but she was out of the office attending Ray's autopsy. The medical examiner called first thing in the morning and said that she had moved up the postmortem.

Marci and Quinn were both going to go, but Lieutenant Brand caught them as they were leaving.

"Where are you headed?" he asked.

"Ray Christy's autopsy," Quinn said.

"And it requires both of you?"

Marci and Quinn glanced at each other to formulate a response, but the lieutenant beat them. "One," he said and held up a single finger. "One goes, and one stays. The captain told me about your additional interference comment, Burkett. This is one time I think it's warranted."

Quinn turned to her. "Rock, paper, scissors?"

"You'll catch the next one," she said over her shoulder as she headed toward the exit.

Now, Quinn opened the email from the IT section. Inside was a short paragraph of text and a hyperlink to a file. The email read:

Found your man, but you're not going to get much out of it. He used Ray Christy's security badge and key to access the building at 3:39 a.m. on Tuesday morning. He walked into the parking lot so there's no video footage of an associated vehicle. Sorry.

Quinn clicked the included link. It took a second for the video to start.

A hooded man wearing sunglasses and gloves entered the parking lot. On the lower right corner of the screen was a time stamp. It showed 3:38 a.m.

Thirty seconds later, the video screen changed as the man walked into the lobby and headed directly to the stairwell. A moment later, he disappeared behind the door.

The video jumped to a new angle, and the man reappeared in the third-floor hallway. Now the time stamp showed 3:40 a.m. Only the back of the man was visible as he walked toward the door of the Volunteer Services' office. He faced the door, inserted a key, and quickly entered.

Once more, the video jumped, and the man exited. The timestamp now read 3:52 a.m. He'd been inside for twelve minutes. Nothing appeared to be in his hands. The man still wore sunglasses, and the hoodie remained cinched tight around his face. He returned to the stairwell.

The next cut on the video showed the man leaving the building. The timestamp read 3:53 a.m. The video's final scenes were of the man leaving the parking lot.

Quinn pulled out his notepad and re-watched the video.

***

Quinn walked through the department's parking lot, crossed Adams Street, then entered the building on West Gardner Avenue. Inside the small waiting lobby, he approached a steel door. He opened his wallet, held his security card to the entry pad, and a lock was released.

The building hummed with activity. Quinn nodded and smiled at various people until he made his way to the office of Sergeant Trevor Hackworth, the head of the Spokane Police Department's Special Investigation Unit.

Hackworth was bent over a file with a brown felt tip pen in his hand. Overhead fluorescent lights shone brightly. He looked up from his paperwork and frowned. "Quinn." The sergeant capped his pen. "To what do I owe this pleasure?"

"I want to pick your brain."

"You and everybody else." Trevor tossed his pen onto the desk, then he crossed his arms. He leaned back in his chair. The overhead lights danced on his bald head. "What is it you think I can do for you?"

"You ever run across WSP's Special Investigations Division?"

"Occasionally. Why?"

"Ever met a guy named Jory Bishop."

Trevor's chair creaked as he leaned forward. "Why are you asking?"

"His name came up in an investigation."

"Came up, how?"

"He's the owner of a group home."

Trevor's nose crinkled. "Like for the elderly?"

"Exactly."

"Okay, weird, but I didn't know that was a crime."

"It's not, but a woman drowned in his building, and we're asking some questions about it."

Trevor nodded knowingly. "Let me guess. Bishop's being a dick."

"That's a succinct way of putting it."

"Don't take it personal. Work around gangs long enough, and it'll change you."

"Has Bishop ever been in the Monroe Court Building?"

"How the fuck would I know?"

Quinn stared at him.

"Don't get your panties in a bunch," Trevor said, "Yeah, maybe Bishop had reason to be over there. I don't know. CTF is in the building. Maybe his group has dealt with them."

The Criminal Task Force was a specialty unit that existed on the second floor of the Monroe Court Building.

Quinn asked, "So, what's your read on Bishop?"

"Based on the limited contact I've had with him, I wasn't impressed. He's more bark than bite. If you want, I can reach out to his supervisor and ask for his input."

"Hold off on that. I might be stirring a pot that doesn't need to be stirred."

"Let me know if you change your mind." Trevor grabbed his pen and tapped its bottom on the desk. "Where's your Mini-Me?"

"She's at an autopsy. Why do you ask?"

"It's weird not to see you two…together."

Quinn frowned. "Don't be a jerk, man."

"You know how the department talks. I'm just looking for the inside scoop."

"She's my partner. Nothing more." He turned to leave.

"A pleasure, Quinn. As always."

He didn't stop to look back.

***

Quinn crossed the Public Safety campus and headed toward the Monroe Court Building. He went up to the second floor and entered the office of the Criminal Task Force. The place was set up in a bullpen fashion with desks scattered about.

Only Detective Nayla Senai was in the office. She

stood at the copy machine and looked over her shoulder when he entered. "Hey, Quinn."

He approached her. "It's quiet in here. Where's the rest of the team?"

"The boys are watching a house."

"Why aren't you out with them?"

"I'm writing the warrant."

Quinn nodded in understanding. "Detective duty, huh?"

"You got it. What can I help you with?"

"Just a quick question. Has CTF ever worked with WSP's Special Investigation Division?"

"We bump into them occasionally. They're not our cup of tea."

"Why's that?"

Nayla motioned toward the copier. "Can we do this later? I need to finish."

"This will only take a minute. Why isn't SID your cup of tea?"

She turned to the copy machine and swapped out another document. She pressed the Copy button. The machine hummed to life. "SID likes to think we work for them."

Quinn knew that feeling when dealing with larger law enforcement agencies, whether it be Washington State Patrol or the Federal Bureau of Investigations. In their eyes, bigger automatically meant better.

"Have you ever dealt with a guy named Jory Bishop?"

Nayla pulled her documents, and its copies from the machine then returned to her desk. "Bishop? Yeah, we've dealt with him. Why?"

"Has he been in this building?"

"Once or twice."

"Would he have reason to go to the third floor?"

Nayla dropped the papers on her desk. "Excuse me?"

"This is important. At any time when he was here, was there a reason for Bishop to go to the third floor?"

She sat on the edge of her desk. "Last year, the restrooms down the hallway were remodeled. We had to go upstairs or downstairs to use the bathroom. Most of us chose to go upstairs because it had less foot traffic. If Bishop visited during that time, and he had to use the restroom, he might have gone upstairs, too."

"Thank you, Nayla. That's what I needed to know." Quinn headed to the door.

"Or," she said, "he might have held it until he got back to his office."

***

Marci looked up from her desk when Quinn returned. "There you are. The captain was asking for an update."

"What did you tell him?"

"Pound sand. What do you think I told him?"

Quinn dropped into his chair. He flipped back a couple of pages and found a phone number he'd written yesterday. When he dialed it, the call immediately went to voice mail. Quinn waited patiently then said, "Hi Kayla, this is Detective Quinn Delaney with the Spokane Police Department. When you have a moment, please give me a call." He recited his phone number.

Marci turned as he hung up. "Kayla Reed?"

He nodded. "Straight to voice mail again. That was my third message for her."

"Maybe she doesn't want to be contacted."

"Maybe." Quinn lifted his chin toward her. "By the way, how was the autopsy?"

"Did you really ask that?"

Quinn raised an apologetic hand. "Let's try again. What did you learn at the autopsy?"

"That's better. Ray Christy was one messed-up guy. Broken zygomatic and maxillary bones on the left side of his face. Left eye ruptured. Three teeth knocked out. Two broken ribs. The guy sustained a lot of damage before he died."

"Sounds like he was tortured."

"I thought so, too, which got me thinking; why do you torture someone? I think there are two reasons—for revenge or to get information."

"Don't forget pleasure," Quinn said.

"The psychos, right. So, three reasons, but normal people would only do it for revenge or information."

"Normal people wouldn't torture anyone."

Marci's head bobbled left and right. "Why do you do this to me?"

"I'm trying to be precise."

"I'll show you precise."

"So, you're saying revenge or information are likely motives for torture."

"Those are my thoughts. The ME said she'd expedite the report for us. I told her about the pressure we're getting from the brass."

Quinn nodded. "Let me show you what I've learned." He turned to his computer and called up the video from the IT department. "Here's the security footage from the Monroe Court Building." He played it and let Marci watch without his commentary.

As soon as it started, she said, "Dude looks like the Unabomber."

When the video ended, Marci asked, "How long did that take? Fifteen minutes?"

"Exactly. Here are my thoughts." He pulled out his notepad and restarted the video. "The guy was familiar with the building."

"How so?"

"First of all, he's wearing a hooded sweatshirt, sunglasses, and gloves. He knew there were cameras inside."

"Eh," Marci said, "that's a leap. He could have assumed that of any building. Let's be honest. Almost every office building has security cameras now."

"I'll give you that, but I should have led with this nugget. You saw him walk through the parking lot. Why? I think it's because he knew there was a camera on the lot."

"Still a leap," Marci said. "Maybe he assumed that most office buildings have cameras covering their lots. Or maybe the guy didn't even have a car."

Quinn appreciated her arguments. It's what a prosecuting attorney would do when they presented their case. "Okay but look at how he moves once he's inside. He avoided the elevator and headed directly to the stairwell. Why do that?"

She crossed her arms and watched the video. "Well, there aren't any cameras in the elevator, or they would have included the footage."

"Right. I think the stairwell gave him an escape route that the elevator wouldn't."

"I don't know. You could say that once he entered the building, he was already trapped."

"For whatever reason, the guy had to risk entering the building."

"You're assuming that because of how he's dressed."

Quinn pointed at the monitor. "And the fact that he went immediately to Volunteer Services."

"So this guy killed Ray Christy for his keys and badge to enter the Volunteer Services office."

"Yeah."

"Why?" Marci asked.

"Ray had something he wanted."

"Another leap."

Quinn smirked. "How so?"

Marci tapped the monitor. "Maybe this guy killed Ray to get access to the office because someone else had something he wanted."

"But Sergeant Newman said nothing was missing. Everyone checked, remember? The only one who couldn't say if something was gone was Ray Christy."

Marci stared at the screen. "What time did the suspect enter the building?"

"Three thirty-eight," Quinn said. "An hour after the second power-shift team secured and a couple of hours before graveyard would come in. An hour earlier, and there would have been cops all around this building."

She faced him. "Okay, that's a good one, but that doesn't mean the suspect is a cop or knows our schedule. It just might mean he got lucky."

"How about this one—do you know who has been in that building before? Jory Bishop."

"How do you know?"

"I talked with Nayla Senai." He filled her in on the conversation with Sergeant Hackworth that led him over to the CTF office.

Marci shook her head. "It's circumstantial. Jory Bishop being in the same office building as the Unabomber—" she tapped the monitor "doesn't mean he killed Ray Christy."

"It might mean just that."

"I don't disagree, but you and I have been in that building along with thousands of other people."

"But we didn't have motive to kill Ray Christy."

Marci cocked her head. "Did Bishop have a motive?"

Quinn raised his hands in frustration. "No idea."

She pointed at the screen once more. "But you're thinking this guy is Bishop?"

"Again, I have no idea. It could be. Maybe."

"But back to an earlier question, where did this guy park his car—assuming he had a car?"

Quinn stared at the looping video. "How far could he have parked then walked in? Maybe a mile?"

"Why not more?" Marci's lip curled. "I think it's time we go ask for additional resources."

***

They stood outside Lieutenant Brand's office. Through opened window blinds, Quinn could see the man working on his computer.

"Aren't you going to knock?" Marci asked.

He eyed her. "You knock."

"He's your friend. You knock."

Quinn pointed at himself. "How's he my friend?"

"You're a climber. Everybody sees it."

"I've been in the unit longer than you."

"I didn't say you were a fast climber."

Quinn smirked. His knuckles rapped against the door.

"Yes," the lieutenant called.

After entering, neither Quinn nor Marci bothered to take a seat.

"Do you have an update?" the lieutenant asked.

"We do," Quinn said, "and we've come for a request of additional manpower."

He described the recent video from the Monroe Court Building. While he spoke, the lieutenant wrote on a notepad. Brand asked a single clarifying question: "When did the suspect enter the building?"

When Quinn finished explaining the video, Brand leaned back in his chair. He pulled his wire-rimmed glasses from his face and rubbed them with a cleaning cloth. "Any idea who the hooded man is?"

"No."

Marci glanced at Quinn.

"What about you, Burkett? Any ideas?"

She faced the lieutenant. "No."

"And this lack of identification is why you'd like additional manpower?" Brand slipped the glasses back onto his face.

"We'd like officers to canvass the surrounding neighborhood to see if any businesses—"

"Maybe apartment complexes, too," Marci said. "Some of them have those doorbell monitors."

Quinn continued. "We'd like officers to ask those entities if they have security footage of a hooded man leaving his car on the night in question."

The lieutenant frowned. "That's a big ask."

"That's why we came to you first," Marci said.

Quinn picked up her insinuation. If Brand couldn't deliver, they would go to Captain Ackerman then Chief Dillon. For a man who thrived on order and the chain of command, the chief's invitation for the detectives to go directly to him must have rankled the lieutenant.

Brand inhaled deeply. "I didn't say it couldn't be done, Burkett. I simply said it was a big ask." He turned to Quinn. "I think a mile radius around the Monroe Court Building should suffice. Don't you?"

Quinn nodded. "I agree."

Brand's gaze settled on Marci. The two had never gotten along. "Any problem with that distance?"

"No, sir," Marci said. "We appreciate your help."

He cocked his head. The lieutenant seemed confused by her sincerity.

Marci exited the office. Quinn figured it best to leave without any further discussion.

Chapter 20

When Quinn returned to his cubicle, an email from IDENT awaited him. It had also been sent to Marci.

"Here we go," he muttered.

"The fingerprints?" she asked without looking at him. "I'm already reading it. Looks like we struck out."

No prints were found on the light bulb on Ray Christy's porch. Either the killer wore gloves to unscrew the bulb, or it had been loosened previously, and the prints wore off in the weather. Quinn chose to believe the former.

The forensics team also hadn't found any unmatched prints in Ray's house. Both daughters were identified. They took Pamela Christy's prints that night since she was already on-scene. And Heidi's fingerprints were on file since real estate agents submitted them as a background check requirement before the state issued their license.

Quinn's phone rang. The caller ID screen showed it was the Information Desk in the lobby of the Public Safety Building. He answered it, "Delaney."

"Detective, this is Stan Gifford at the Info Desk."

"Yeah, Stan."

"There's a gentleman out here by the name of Donald Faust. He's requesting to speak with you."

"What's it about?"

"He says it's about Ray Christy."

***

Donald Faust was fifty-one years old with a doughy

but pleasant face. He wore a blue sweater over a pink collared shirt. In front of him on the small table was an 8" x 11" envelope. His hands rested on it. He and Quinn were in Interview Room #1. A fluorescent light hummed overhead.

Quinn finished asking for Donald's particulars—name, date of birth, and address. He looked up from his notepad. "You went to church with Ray." Donald had mentioned he knew Ray from church while they walked from the lobby to the interview room.

"That's right, but I think it was Audrey who really went. Ray sort of tagged along."

"How long have you gone to that church?"

Donald shrugged. "I grew up in it, so, wow, must be going on forty-five years."

That astounded Quinn. "A long time."

"I was lucky to have been brought up in the Word."

"How long had Audrey and Ray been going?"

Donald's eyes went to the ceiling as he thought. "They showed up about twenty-five years ago, but my math might be wrong. It must be more than twenty years—I'll give you that. They were a nice couple. It's sad what happened to Audrey. Are you aware of what she's experiencing?" A look of guilt flashed over Donald's face. "I should visit her. She's probably lonely without Ray."

Quinn eyed the envelope under Donald's hands. "What can I do for you, Mr. Faust?"

"I saw the news." He absently rubbed the edge of the envelope. "They said that Ray had been murdered—that anyone with information should come forward."

Quinn didn't make a habit of watching or reading the local news. He barely paid attention to national reporting, for that matter. The department's Public Information Officer would have gotten the information out to the media.

He asked, "And you have information that might be helpful?"

Donald lifted the envelope. "I work in the assessor's office. Ray came over last week and asked for some help."

Quinn thought about the timeline leading up to Ray's death. The latest he'd been able to get anyone to confirm they'd seen or spoken to Ray was Monday. "What day was this?"

Donald shrugged. "I'm not a hundred percent sure, but probably Monday. Maybe Tuesday."

"Tuesday?" Quinn jotted a note on his pad.

"I can't be positive."

"What did Ray want?"

"For me to search for the owner of some properties."

Adrenaline burst through Quinn's system. "Properties?"

"I told him he could do that on his own, but he wanted to know if the legal owner had more than one. That's not an easy thing for a citizen to find out on their own, but we can do that quickly, so I helped him."

"Why did you do it? Because of the connection through the church?"

Donald shrugged. "Would that be so wrong? Besides, property ownership in our state is public information, so it's not like I was doing anything improper. Ray told me he was working on a thing for the police department. That's exactly how he described it, by the way—working on a thing."

Quinn wrote that down. "What's in the envelope?"

"I remembered the ownership names. They were kind of hard to forget."

Donald slid the envelope to Quinn. He opened it and scanned the various papers inside. At the top of each page was listed the ownership of that certain property.

Quinn's heart raced when he saw the first one—Bishop Takes Bishop, LLC. He looked up.

Donald continued. "So that's what Ray asked me to search for. He didn't tell me why he wanted them. Looks like a bunch of houses. Think it means anything?"

Quinn flipped through the pages until he stopped on one with an address he knew—a house on Fleming Street. It was owned by Bishop Takes Queen, LLC. Quinn knew that Jory Bishop owned this house. He could reasonably assume that Jory Bishop owned the other Bishop Takes properties. Quinn didn't look up when he asked, "Did Ray ask for anything else?"

"He also asked for any other property owned by some guy named Bishop, but I can't remember his first name. I'm sorry. I tried running a search by just the last name, but you'd be amazed at how many Bishops there are in Spokane County. I even found some more LLCs with the name Bishop in it. I thought about printing everything off and bringing it to you but decided that I should bring just what I gave Ray."

Quinn asked, "Was the guy's name Jory Bishop?"

Donald shrugged. "It might have been. It sounds familiar now that you say it. But I run so many names daily that it's hard to remember one I did four hours ago." Donald pointed at the pages Quinn held. "However, those LLC names were outstanding. I played a lot of chess with my kids when they were little, so those names stuck with me."

Quinn slid the papers into the envelope. "Would you do me a favor?"

"For Ray—anything."

He pulled a business card from his pocket and handed it to Donald. "Find those other Bishop LLCs you mentioned. I'd like to see those, too."

***

Back at his desk, Quinn tossed the envelope to Marci. She awkwardly caught it.

"What's this?" she asked.

"Ray Christy went to a friend in the assessor's office. He asked the guy to look up a property and found that."

Marci opened the envelope and pulled out several pages. She flipped through them.

Quinn sat and rested his elbows on his knees. "Notice anything about Bishop Takes Queen?"

"It's the house where Margaret Kelley died." Marci straightened. "Ray's daughter said he wanted to know how to look up individuals in an LLC." She waved the papers. "What do you want to bet it was for these?"

"If I bet against, I think I'd lose."

Marci spun to her computer.

While she worked, Quinn called his computer to life. A new email was there from Sergeant Craig Truitt. It was titled *Video*. Inside were two lines of text with an attached video file.

> *Is this what you want?*
> *If so, write a warrant to cover my ass.*

Quinn started the video, and it filled his screen. The image was of the parking lot directly to the west of the jail. Ray Christy entered from the top right. On the bottom of the screen, a door swung open, and a man appeared. Due to the camera angle, only the man's head and back could be seen.

The man took several steps and stopped. Ray pointed toward the left side of the screen. The other man stalked toward Ray.

When they stood nose-to-nose, the two men turned slightly. Quinn could now clearly see the other man was Jory Bishop. His face was contorted in anger.

Ray stepped to the side, but Bishop put his hand on Ray's chest to stop him. The trooper then leaned into the older man's ear. Afterward, Bishop stepped back, and Ray walked out of the frame.

Bishop climbed into his car—a maroon Chevy Impala—and reversed out of his parking stall. Then he accelerated away.

"You need to see this," Quinn said.

"It's Jory Bishop."

He stared at her. "How'd you know?"

Marci's brow furrowed. "I just looked it up."

"Huh?"

"What are you talking about?" She pointed to her screen. "He's the owner of those LLCs—all six. I just confirmed it."

Quinn motioned her over. "Check this out."

They watched the video. When it was over, Marci leaned against the cubicle wall. "Bishop told us he joked with Ray. That didn't look like any joke to me."

"It looked threatening."

"Menacing."

"A better word," Quinn said.

"Thank you. I think I'll use it in my report." She walked to her desk and dropped into her chair. "When should we bring him in for another chat?"

"Not yet. He still might not be involved."

Marci's eyes narrowed. "For real? Look how often Bishop's name keeps coming up."

"Maybe it's circumstantial."

"How so?"

"Margaret Kelley's death happened at his business. Parker investigated it and said it was accidental."

"Parker." The way she muttered it sounded as if she were cursing.

"Anyway," Quinn continued, "the ME confirmed Margaret drowned after experiencing a heart attack. Then Ray goes there to return a wallet and has a run-in with a guy that's a bit abrupt—"

"A bit?"

Quinn waved her comment off. "Then Ray starts playing amateur detective and pokes around the man's life. He creates all these Bishop Easter eggs we keep uncovering."

"Which you think is somehow giving us confirmation bias?"

He shrugged. "Maybe. Do you want to drag a fellow officer in here and accuse him of having a hand in Ray's death?"

"If he did it, I wouldn't have any problem doing so."

"And if he did it, I'll be right there with you, but I want to make sure we've got him dead to rights before we do such a thing." Quinn shook his head. "Besides, I get the feeling Bishop is a smart one. I don't want to press him too early and lose our advantage. We might have already given too much away by meeting for coffee."

"We didn't know what we had then."

Quinn looked at the ceiling. "I'd like to learn more without spooking him."

"You talked with Hackworth and Senai, right?"

"Even that might have been risky. What if they're friends with him?"

"What do you think they would do? Advise him how to destroy evidence?" As soon as the words left her mouth, she shook her head. "Never mind."

Years prior, an off-duty patrol officer was accused of rape after meeting a woman at a bar. The two had gone to her apartment and had sex. That part of the story was not in question. What was argued was her consent. Several fellow patrolmen called or texted the accused officer with suggestions on how to reduce the possibility of evidence—cut his fingernails short, throw away his clothes, shower and scrub with a heavy loofah brush. When these calls and texts were discovered by the media, it made for a storm, and many reprimands followed. No one lost their job, but it cast a dark cloud over the department for some time.

Still staring at the ceiling, Quinn said, "We need someone who would give us the full scoop on the man and not worry about ratting him out."

"Like IA."

Quinn looked at her. "Like IA. Exactly."

***

Years prior, the Internal Affairs office was located in the Monroe Court Building. Back then, it was aptly named the Office of Professional Standards. Unfortunately for the department, decreeing a department with that name wasn't a good look, especially when trying to weed out unprofessional behavior. Officially, it was OPS, but every cop knew it as OoPS.

Now, the small Internal Affairs office was in the Gardner Building.

Quinn knocked on the open door, and Lieutenant Neil Culkin looked up from his desk.

"Detectives," he said. "What can I do for you?"

Culkin was a handsome man who recently turned fifty. He chose to wear a similar uniform every day—tan Dockers and a collared button-up shirt. Today, the shirt was blue. The rumor was that the lieutenant thought the look gave him an everyman appearance. He could have worn a Santa suit, and the entire department would still remember he was an Internal Affairs rat.

Quinn and Marci stepped into the office.

"We need a favor," Quinn said.

"A favor? Now, that's something I don't hear every day." He motioned them to the chairs in front of his desk. When he noticed the bruising around Marci's eye, he said, "What happened to your eye, Detective?"

"I got hit in class." Marci did not joke around with the IA lieutenant.

"So, not a use of force?"

She shook her head. "Definitely not. Class, sir."

"Okay, then." He turned his attention back to Quinn. "What's this about a favor?"

"We'd like you to contact your counterpart in the WSP. Ask them about one of their detectives—a Jory Bishop."

The lieutenant's face soured. "That's not how we do things, Detective, especially if this is some territorial pissing contest."

"It's not." Quinn explained the case they were working on. When he was done, he said, "That's why we want some additional insight on the man."

Culkin leaned back in his chair. He stroked his mustache with two fingers and a thumb. Quinn thought he looked like a villain in an old-time movie. Slowly, the lieutenant's head started to shake. Then he uttered, "No."

"Why not?" Quinn asked.

"Because I said so."

Quinn scooted to the edge of his chair. "We're investigating a murder."

"I understand, but I don't see how this helps."

"Jory Bishop might be involved. We want to know more about him without tipping our hand. We thought there might be some fraternal order of IA investigators—

that maybe you shared some info with each other."

Culkin flippantly waved a hand. "It doesn't work that way. Information comes into this division; it doesn't go out. If I ask a counterpart for a favor, then I'll owe him one. I don't want to be in that position."

Marci leaned forward. "The chief has told us we get any resource we need in this case."

Culkin frowned. "Not from me, you don't. Especially an interagency jump at the state level. You two are on your own."

Marci stood. "Last chance, Lieutenant. We'll make this request through the chief."

"Are you threatening me, Burkett? Your file is already big enough. I don't think it could handle another complaint."

Now, Quinn stood. "She's not threatening you, Lieutenant."

"You are, Delaney?" Culkin's smile lacked mirth. "Because if you are, I will relish the opportunity to bring you down a peg."

"Lieutenant," Quinn said, "we're asking nicely for your help."

Culkin pointed to the door. "And I responded nicely. No."

"Have it your way."

***

Melanie White hung up her phone. "He'll see you now."

Quinn turned to Marci. "Let me do the talking."

"Why?"

He cocked his head. "Trust me."

"Oh, right," she muttered. "Friend of the administration."

Quinn nodded once to Melanie then stepped around her desk to enter the chief's office.

Liam Dillon leaned over his desk. He shuffled a stack of papers together before tapping them straight. He then slipped them into an oversized envelope. "Detectives."

"Chief," they said in unison.

"I'm pressed for time." He set the envelope down and searched for something else on his desk. He lifted several documents but didn't seem to find what he was looking for. He absently said, "I've got a budget meeting with Hizzoner in ten minutes."

Neither detective said anything.

Dillon looked up. "In other words, make it fast."

Quinn said, "We need your help on Ray Christy's case."

The chief continued his search by flipping documents. "What's going on?"

"We believe we have a suspect."

"You believe?"

"It's complicated."

Dillon straightened then checked his watch. "Speed it up, Delaney."

Quinn quickly filled the chief in on what they knew of Jory Bishop and Ray Christy's connection to him. When the detective finished, the chief picked up his phone and pressed a single button.

"Melanie," he said, "call the mayor's office. Let him know I'm running a few minutes behind." Dillon then dropped into his chair and studied the two detectives. "You have no physical evidence linking this trooper to Ray's death, just the video of them talking in the west parking lot. That's nowhere near enough."

Quinn said, "But we know Ray poked into Jory Bishop's life before his death."

The chief lifted his hands. "You don't honestly think

that's enough for an arrest."

"No, sir. We just want a deeper look at the man."

Dillon rubbed his chin. "This might be a lot of nothing."

"It might be," Marci said. She glanced at Quinn before continuing. "That's why we went to Lieutenant Culkin. We wanted him to ask his WSP counterpart for an opinion on Bishop."

"What did he say?"

"He said no."

Dillon shifted his sitting position. "What are you looking for?"

Marci shrugged. "Background. Maybe his department thinks he's a turd. We have a few of those in our department."

"Careful, Burkett."

"I just meant not everyone is squeaky clean."

The chief shrugged noncommittally. "And maybe the guy is a super cop."

"Great," Quinn said, "that's fantastic. Let their IA supervisor tell us that. Let us hear some feedback like that, and we'll stop worrying about him. We only want a better picture of the guy. Maybe we've got it all wrong, and we're spinning our wheels by focusing on him. Regardless, we have a potential resource in our department who doesn't want to help solve Ray Christy's murder."

Dillon tapped his desk. "Point scored, Delaney. Anything else I should know?"

Marci thumbed toward her partner. "Culkin threatened Quinn with a file."

"What for?"

"Because he said we were going to come to you with this request."

Dillon eyed Quinn, and he shrugged in return. The

chief asked, "What about you, Burkett?"

Marci rolled her eyes. "He said my file was too big for another complaint."

"He's not wrong." The chief stood and picked up the oversized envelope. "I've got to go. I'll call Culkin on my way to the mayor's office. You'll get your help." He hurried past them.

***

Quinn dropped his keys just inside the front door of his apartment. He continued into his kitchen, where he set down his phone. He briefly eyed the refrigerator but decided he wasn't hungry.

He took off his badge and left it in the kitchen. Then he went into the bedroom, where he removed his gun and holster.

As he undressed, the loneliness Quinn felt the previous night returned. Maybe he should have stayed later at the office. He could always find something new to do. There was plenty of work left on other cases. Before Ray Christy's murder, Quinn had half a dozen open and active files. That didn't count the cold case he'd been assigned over a month ago. His work on that was uninspiring so far. Current cases demanded immediate attention, and Ray's superseded them.

Quinn hung up his suit jacket and pants. As he reached into the dresser for running shorts, he thought about Jory Bishop. There was something about the guy that bothered Quinn. It wasn't his arrogance. Plenty of guys in the department were cocky. If that type of behavior bothered him, he couldn't do his job.

No, there was something else.

Maybe it was Bishop's casual disregard for things. He didn't seem bothered by Margaret Kelley's death. He didn't seem upset by the disappearance of Kayla Reed.

Quinn stopped changing. He stood still with one leg in his running shorts. The other remained poised to go in.

Where had Kayla gone after she quit? She still hadn't returned his calls. He should attempt to contact her again in the morning. Marci had flagged her name in the system, but no one had located her yet. But did that mean anything? Maybe not. Most folks go through their lives without contact from law enforcement. If Kayla Reed just lived a normal, boring life, the Attempt to Locate would go unfulfilled.

Quinn put his second leg into the running shorts. A normal, boring life, he thought. So many people want more, but that leads them to trouble. It's what he'd been railing against the past couple of days.

No, his life wasn't normal.

It was safe.

Safe and boring.

Was it the safe that made it suffocating? Or the combination of the two? He shook the thought from his head. He didn't want to think that way tonight. He liked thinking about work.

Quinn's thoughts returned to Jory Bishop and the man's apparent lack of compassion. Quinn wouldn't expect Bishop to be concerned by Ray Christy's death, but he didn't even offer the slightest empathy for the department's loss.

Did that mean anything? Probably nothing. Emotional depth wasn't a requirement for innocence.

Quinn slipped on a t-shirt. He then reached into the closet for his running shoes. They sat next to a backpack that Quinn used for long hikes. He straightened without picking up the shoes. His eyes remained on the bag.

Joseph Bishop—they hadn't followed up with him after they found Jory Bishop.

He sat on the edge of his bed and began the slow process of going back through the case. His run would have to wait.

As thoughts of the Ray Christy murder investigation raced through his head, Quinn Delaney failed to realize that his life no longer felt safe and boring.

Chapter 21

The door buzzed, and Joseph Bishop entered the small room. He wore an orange jumpsuit courtesy of the Spokane County Jail. A deputy followed him inside, then closed the door and moved to a corner.

Quinn Delaney stood against the far wall.

Joseph scowled at the detective. "I remember you."

"I'm Detective Delaney."

"You're the asshole who got me thrown in here."

"You did that to yourself."

"I don't have to be here." Joseph turned to the deputy. "I don't have to be here!" He faced Quinn again and thumped his chest in emphasis. "I know my rights!"

"Take it easy, Joe. I've got a couple of quick questions."

Joseph's upper lip curled, and he gnawed on the lower. Quinn couldn't decide if it was something Joseph thought made him look tough or if it was a nervous tick. "Say what you want so I can get on with my life. I got shit to do."

The detective motioned toward the small metal table affixed to the concrete floor. "Want to sit?"

"No."

Delaney shrugged a single shoulder. "Fine. Where were you Monday night?"

"Back to this?" Joseph walked over to the small table and dropped onto a stool bolted to the floor. "I told you. I was sleeping off a drunk at a friend's house."

Quinn sat across from him. "What friend?"

"I don't know his name."

"That's not going to fly."

"It is what it is." Joseph defiantly looked away.

"You need to do better. A man was murdered Monday night in a home invasion robbery. A witness came forward with the name Joey Bishop."

Joseph's head whipped back to Quinn. "Yo, man, what the hell? I never let people call me that." His face purpled. "That's a baby's name."

"Do you know how many Joe Bishops there are in town?"

"How would I know?"

"There are a few."

Joseph threw his hands in the air. "Then why are you pushing up on me?"

"Do you know how many of those Joe Bishops have a record for robbery, burglary, and assault?" Quinn held up three fingers.

"What am I—a mind reader?"

Quinn lowered two fingers and pointed the remaining one at Joseph. "Just you—one Joe."

"It wasn't me."

"Then make me believe you didn't kill a man, then rob him."

Joseph violently shook his head. "For real. I got drunk and passed out at some dude's house. It was an after-party. I don't know his name."

"Where was it?"

"In Hillyard. Just behind that convenience store at Wellesley and Haven. No, Market. Those streets go opposite directions." Joseph's hands waved back and forth next to each other. "You know the store. It's a Chevron. They make the best burritos."

Quinn studied him. It was oddly specific if it was a lie and came very fast. Maybe Joseph had time to practice it.

"Do you have a car?"

Joseph smirked. "The last one I had, you fuckers took.

Bullshit suspended license law. The only thing I got now is my bike. Speaking of which, what happened to it after I got arrested?"

"They probably put it on property for safekeeping. You can get it back when you get out."

"Shit." Joseph looked at the ceiling.

"Was it stolen? Is that why you ran?"

Joseph's face hardened, and he brushed his nose with his thumb. "I plead the fifth."

"Ever hear of Ray Christy?"

"Is that the dude who got hisself killed?"

Quinn shrugged.

"Nope. Never heard of him. Listen, you've already got my fingerprints. If you need a sample of my blood, I'll give it to you. Believe what you want to believe about me, but I didn't kill this Ray guy. I've never killed nobody. I'll even take the lie detector test for it." As an afterthought, Joseph said, "But you can't ask me any other questions about nothin'. Got it?"

Quinn looked at the deputy standing in the corner.

"Time's up," the deputy said.

Joseph Bishop stood. "Yo, you know Yvette, right? My P.O.?"

"Yeah."

"Tell her I'm sorry for runnin' and fightin'. She didn't deserve that. She's tough but always fair. I kind of feel like I let her down."

"What about the cop you hit?"

Joe frowned. "The mean one with the rookie? Nah. Fuck that bitch."

***

When Quinn exited the jail, his phone buzzed. He pulled it from his pocket and checked the screen before answering.

"Hey, Marci. What's up?"

"Where are you at?"

"Heading back from—"

"I see you." She ended the call.

Quinn looked toward the Public Safety Building. Marci trotted toward him. She wore a black pantsuit with a red shirt. She carried a long coat in her hand.

"Let's go," she said. "I'm driving."

He jogged along with her toward the north parking lot. "Where are we going?"

"They found Kayla Reed."

"Who is they?"

"The County."

"Where is she?" Quinn asked.

"Up in Elk."

"What's she doing up there?"

"Rotting."

Quinn slowed to a walk. "She's dead?"

Marci turned and spun her arm like a windmill. "C'mon, Delaney! They're holding the body until we get there."

She hurried away.

***

Quinn sat in the passenger seat while Marci drove toward Elk, a town in northern Spokane County. From the Public Safety Building, he expected it to be a forty-five-minute drive.

He tended to do most of the driving whenever they were together. It wasn't based on chauvinism but rather his seniority. He liked to be in control, as he believed most cops did. But Marci was an excellent driver, and the courses all officers took ensured it.

Quinn asked, "How long have they been on scene?"

"A couple hours, I think."

He lifted his hands in frustration. "And we're just getting notified? I thought we flagged her name."

"We did, but they didn't identify her until a few minutes ago."

"How did they find her?"

"Some guy with his dog. You know how it is."

Quinn leaned his head back against his seat. "Margaret Kelley drowns. Then Kayla Reed is found dead. There's a lot of death stemming from that house on Fleming Street."

"Don't forget Ray Christy visited it."

"Yeah."

They drove in silence for a bit.

"So," Marci said.

"So?"

"It's definitely Jory Bishop."

The silence returned for another few miles before Marci glanced at him. "Are you trying to formulate an argument over there?"

"Pay attention to the road."

"Tell me what you're thinking."

"His cell phone," Quinn said.

"What about it?"

"Do we have enough to request a search warrant?"

"You think maybe we can track his location? Maybe see where he was recently? I like it."

Quinn shrugged. "I doubt it will matter."

"Mr. Positive."

"Think about it. No one saw a strange car in Ray's neighborhood that night. And the killer unscrewed a light bulb."

"Maybe it was left like that."

Quinn faced her. "Ray was retired military. His house

was impeccably clean. He was not a man to leave a light bulb partially screwed in. Let a defense attorney argue that point—not us."

"So, you're saying…?"

"The killer was careful. He entered Ray's house and beat him to death. There's no weapon for us to trace. Then he slipped out of the neighborhood."

Marci waggled a finger. "Only to show up at the Volunteer Services office."

"Dressed in a hooded sweatshirt and sunglasses. The guy parked his car away from the parking lot. God knows where."

"Are you getting to a point with all this cheerful optimism?"

Quinn ran the back of his hand along the edge of the passenger door. "My point is a killer like this guy won't be sloppy enough to carry a cell phone with him. He'd know it could be tracked. He would leave it behind somewhere."

"Why wouldn't he disable it so it couldn't be tracked?"

"Because he would want it tracked. He'd want it in a single location far from whatever crime he was about to commit."

Marci nodded. "That way, if we tried to use a warrant to prove he was at the scene of the crime, all we'd end up doing is proving he was where he said he was."

"Exactly. The guy thinks ahead. Like he's playing chess."

"You keep saying 'this guy' like he's some nebulous form in the shadows. It's Jory Bishop."

Quinn tapped on the passenger window with his knuckles. "What did killing Ray Christy get him?"

"Especially since the medical examiner said Margaret Kelley drowned. I read Parker's report. He did good work."

"That must hurt to admit."

She shrugged a single shoulder.

"What are we missing?"

"We can still pull the phone records, right?"

"If we think he's the guy."

"He's the guy," Marci said emphatically. "Why do you keep hedging?"

Quinn rolled his head around his shoulders. "Because it feels like we're rushing on this one."

"We've solved other cases fast before. What's wrong with doing it on this one?"

"Maybe I want to slow down and make sure we get it right because he's a cop."

She clicked her tongue against the back of her teeth. "He's a dick who might have killed a senior volunteer. Being a cop is secondary."

***

Marci pulled the car to the south side of the road and parked. They were on East Bridges Road in the small town of Elk. Several patrol cars were silent in front of them. All were marked except the last one. A forensic van stood at the front of the line. To their right was a densely forested area.

Quinn climbed from the passenger side and stretched.

Marci walked around the car to join him. The swelling around her eye was completely gone now. Only discoloration remained. She'd covered most of it with make-up, but if Quinn stared at her long enough, he could see the tell-tale signs. The painful black and purple were replaced with a sickly green and yellow.

She said, "Seems colder up here."

"It usually is."

"Glad I brought a coat."

Quinn shoved his hands into his pockets. "About that."

She smiled. "We needed to go in a hurry. You can wait in the car if you want."

They headed up the line of cars, then turned into a patch of trees where there was a cluster of uniformed personnel.

"Who are we looking for?" Quinn asked.

"Dunno. Dispatch got a ping on her name and contacted the supervisor on scene. Then they called me. I told them we were on the way and asked them to not remove the body until we got here."

Quinn stopped a deputy with silver hair. "Who's running the crime scene?"

"Chambers." The deputy pointed to a tall man wearing a ski coat over a suit jacket. "That's him."

Quinn and Marci moved up to a line of tape—the outer perimeter. They waited. If this was a crime scene in their department, they would have simply stepped under the tape and moved on, but they were guests. Etiquette dictated a certain behavior.

Another deputy soon noticed them and approached. Both Quinn and Marci pulled their suit jackets to the side to reveal their badges.

"We'd like to speak with Detective Chambers," Marci said.

The deputy shrugged. "Help yourself."

Quinn and Marci ducked under the tape and headed toward the next line of tape. Once again, they stopped. Just ahead, Detective Chambers stood over a body in a shallow grave. His head was bowed, his shoulders rolled forward, and his hands were stuffed into the pockets of his pants. He appeared lost in thought.

"Detective Chambers," Marci said.

The tall man straightened and turned their way. He

was in his early forties with light brown hair and dark, inquisitive eyes. "Are you the city detectives we've been expecting?" He jerked his head as an invitation to enter.

A deputy approached with a clipboard. Quinn and Marci provided their names for the crime scene log, then slipped under the tape.

"Tom Chambers," the detective said. He didn't bother looking at either of them or removing his hand from a pocket to shake.

Quinn and Marci introduced themselves, then the three detectives stared at the body for some time.

The woman was fully clothed and covered with dirt. Someone had brushed most of it off, but the body wouldn't fully be clean until it reached the medical examiner's office.

"A dog found her," Chambers said. "The owner lost track of it for several minutes. When he found it, the mutt had dug a hole deep enough to reveal a hand. Then he called us. The owner, not the dog." Chambers drolly said that last part.

Even though they just met, Quinn didn't take Chambers as a man prone to humor.

Quinn knelt next to the woman. The deep bruising on her face showed that she'd been assaulted. Ligature marks on her neck revealed she'd been strangled. "How'd you identify her?"

"Her driver's license was in her back pocket." Chambers removed a Ziploc baggy from his pocket and handed it to Quinn. "Do you know her?"

Quinn glanced at the driver's license, then handed it to Marci. He said, "Kayla's connected to a case we're working."

"How so?"

"She worked at a group home," Marci said. "A woman there drowned."

Chambers stepped back from the grave and faced his counterparts. His gaze lingered on Marci's eye. "Did this Kayla have something to do with the other woman's death?"

Marci shook her head. "We don't think so. The medical examiner ruled the old woman had a heart attack before drowning."

"So, her disappearance and the drowning are coincidental?"

"It would seem so," Marci said. She faced Quinn. "You want to bring him up to speed?"

Quinn eyed the county investigator. "Have you worked with a WSP detective named Jory Bishop?"

Chambers cocked his head as he thought. "I've never heard of him."

"Kayla Reed was his employee."

"Which means the trooper owned the group home?"

"That's right," Quinn said. "The story lays out like this."

While Quinn explained the Jory Bishop situation, Marci removed her cell phone and videotaped the body. Since it wasn't their crime scene, they wouldn't have immediate access to the investigation file. When Quinn finished explaining, Detective Chambers moved back toward the dead woman.

Chambers said, "Your murder investigation intersects with mine."

Quinn nodded. "We're not a hundred percent sold on Bishop being a suspect, but a number of circumstantial things point to him."

The county detective squatted near Kayla Reed.

"We need to cooperate," Marci said.

Detective Chambers looked up. "I understand. I'll work this case, but if you need anything, don't hesitate to ask. And I would expect similar cooperation."

"For sure," Quinn said.

"Good." Chambers stood and brushed dirt from his knees that wasn't there. "Now, if there's nothing further. We're going to move the body."

***

It was almost noon, and they were stuck in the lunch-hour traffic on North Division Street.

"Are you hungry?" Marci asked, "because I'm hungry."

"Take a right," Quinn said at Francis Avenue.

"What are you thinking? Not the Dairy Queen."

"I brought my lunch. It's back at the station."

She frowned. "How long is this brown-bagging thing going to go on?"

"As long as it takes." Quinn felt silly for his recent self-pity trip to Dick's Hamburgers.

"If you're not going to lunch with me, why'd you make me turn? I would have hit the Jimmy Johns near the station. You know that's my place."

"Let's go by Fleming Street."

"What for?"

"What's the caretaker's name?"

"Kayla Reed."

"No," Quinn said. "The one who still works there." He pulled out his notebook and flipped back several pages. "Elise Morrow."

"That sounds about right."

"It is right." He showed her his notepad. "See?"

"I'm driving. And why do you want to talk with her now? She wasn't motivated to talk with us previously."

"Let's show her the video of Kayla Reed's body. Maybe that'll loosen her tongue."

Chapter 22

"You're not coming in," Elise Morrow said.

Quinn and Marci stood outside the house on Fleming Street. The screen door was opened wide as Quinn had thought to knock on the actual door—one less barrier to get through. Unfortunately, it wasn't working out as he had planned.

His hand wrapped tighter around the aluminum door. He'd already spent a frustratingly long minute trying to explain the importance of Elise talking with them. Next to Quinn stood Marci. Her head was lowered as she worked her cell phone.

"Ma'am," Quinn said, "this is important."

"Not to me." Elise stepped back. "I don't need to speak with you."

"You need to hear what we have to say."

"No, I don't."

Marci slipped in front of Quinn and stood on the threshold.

"Hey!" Elise shouted. She lifted a hand to halt her. "You can't come inside."

But Marci didn't even try. Instead, she held her cell phone, so Elise could easily see it.

The caretaker's face blanched, and she covered her mouth. "Oh my God," she whispered. "Is that?"

"Kayla Reed." Marci nodded. "You knew her then?"

The caregiver stumbled back and caught herself on the back of a couch. Marci slipped her phone into her pocket, then stepped into the house. She held onto Elise to stop her from falling completely to the floor.

"It's okay," Marci said softly. "Why don't you sit down?"

Quinn entered the house and helped Marci escort the caretaker around the couch.

Marci sat next to her. "Would you like a glass of water?"

Elise shook her head.

"I'm sorry I had to show you that."

The caregiver looked away.

Quinn sat on a recliner opposite the two women.

Marci asked, "You knew each other?"

Elise looked back at Marci. It appeared as if she'd seen a ghost. "I'm sleeping in her room." She pointed toward the hallway. "In her bed." Tears welled in her eyes.

Marci said, "But you knew her before."

"I worked in a home over on Lindeke. Still do. Whenever Kayla took time off, I'd cover for her and vice versa." Elise shut her eyes, then shook her head. A tear rolled down her cheek. "That's what we do, what we did. We covered for each other."

"Did Kayla ever steal?"

Elise's eyes snapped open. She didn't seem angry— quite the opposite. She seemed hurt. "She stole something? What?"

"We think she might have taken a wallet—from Margaret Kelley."

The caregiver groaned. "It makes sense now."

"What does?"

Elise faced Marci. "Jory told me he had to fire Kayla, but he wouldn't tell me what for. I got the feeling it was for stealing. That's one thing he won't put up with. That's why he asked me to cover."

"He fired her?"

She shook her head. "He said she split before he ever

got the chance. Just bailed and never came back.”

“What day was that?” Quinn asked.

Elise eyed him but didn’t answer. She swallowed as her lips trembled.

“When we first met, you said she was fired the day before Margaret drowned. But Vera said she was here that morning.”

The caretaker looked down and nodded.

“So,” Marci said, “she was here the day Margaret drowned?”

“She left before,” Elise said, “but yeah, it was the same day.”

“Jory wasn’t really going to fire Kayla for stealing, was he?”

Elise nodded emphatically. “Oh, I believe that—one hundred percent. I think she quit before he had a chance to do it.”

“And then Margaret died.” Marci tilted her head. “Bad timing, eh?”

Elise shrugged.

Quinn hated coincidence. He felt the two events had to be tied in some way.

Marci asked, “Did Kayla take all of her things?”

“No. She left them.”

“Don’t you think that’s weird?”

“Not really. It’s happened to me before, and that’s what I figured happened to her. That maybe she went to stay with family or friends for a day. Like maybe something happened, and she blew a gasket and needed to go somewhere to cool off. You gotta understand. Living at this place full-time wears you down. You don’t get the weekends off—nights, either. The residents have full access to you. After a time, trust me, we all gotta get away to protect our sanity, but we don’t have enough vacation time for such a thing.”

Quinn pulled out his notebook. "If you already have another house to cover—the one on Lindeke, why are you sleeping here?"

"Because Jory wanted it."

"Why?"

"I mean, I get it." Elise briefly looked to the ceiling. "We can't afford to have another problem at this house. We're already on the state's radar with one death. If Jory loses the license for this place, they all go down."

Quinn and Marci glanced at each other. "Say that again," Quinn said.

"They all go down?" Elise said. "I don't understand how the licensing thing works, but supposedly if he loses the license to this house, he loses them all. Like a house of cards."

"So," Quinn said, "you and Jory are saying that you worked here the entire day that Margaret drowned just in case the state investigator asks?"

Elise looked down but didn't answer.

"Why doesn't he hire another caregiver for this house?"

Elise frowned. "If it were that easy, sure. But it's not like hiring someone to flip a burger. We've got to be trained and licensed just like the big facilities."

"What do you know about Jory?"

"He's my boss. Why do you ask?" The caregiver seemed concerned by the question.

Marci bent slightly closer to Elise. "What kind of person do you think he is?"

"He's been good to me. And he's always treated the residents well."

"What about Kayla?" Quinn asked.

Elise's eyes narrowed. "What are you implying?"

"I'm asking a question," he said. "How did Jory treat Kayla? Was he good to her like he is to you?"

"She wasn't the most dependable. I liked her, but she was flighty. Full of drama. She made for an interesting friend, but I wouldn't want her as my employee. Know what I'm saying? I'm sure that frustrated Jory. Firing her wouldn't have been hard had she stuck around. I'm sure he was relieved she didn't come back. But shit, how she ended up."

"How do you think he'll react?" Marci asked.

Elise shrugged.

"How's he been lately? When we met him, he seemed stressed."

"I'm not sure I should be talking about this."

"Talking about what?"

Elise stood. "Any of this." She pointed at Marci's hands which were now empty. "You show me a video—a horrible video—and now you're asking me about Jory. He couldn't be involved with anything like that. He's a nice person who does a hard job and owns a difficult business. He couldn't hurt anyone. Wouldn't hurt anyone. You've got the wrong guy."

Vera Drayton shuffled into the room then. "We have visitors." When her gaze fell upon Marci, her face lit up. "It's my new friend! Did you come back to say hello?"

Marci stood and greeted her. "I came to talk with Elise."

Vera hugged Marci, who politely returned the greeting.

"Would you like me to make us some coffee?" Vera waved at Quinn. "Your friend could join us if he wants. You, too, Elise. There are some cookies in the cabinet if Bob hasn't eaten them all."

Quinn stood. "Thank you for the invitation, but we need to go."

Marci faced Elise. "We appreciate your time. If you think of anything, I hope you'll call."

"There's nothing for me to call about."

Marci and Quinn headed for the door.

Vera followed them. "It doesn't have to be coffee. We could have tea. I don't like it myself, but we've got all sorts of flavors."

Marci patted the older woman's arm. "I'm sorry, Vera, but we really do have to go."

Quinn slipped by and headed for the car.

***

Lieutenant Neil Culkin dropped a yellow legal notepad onto Quinn's desk. Nothing was written on it.

Quinn's gaze left his computer and settled on the blank pad. He looked up at the smirking lieutenant.

"Where's your partner?"

"Getting a search warrant executed." Quinn had written the warrant for the jail security footage. Marci offered to get it signed. "What's with the notepad?"

"Those are my notes from the call with WSP's Office of Professional Standards. Thanks for going to the chief, by the way."

"We tried to warn you."

"You did. I won't forget that."

"That we warned you or that we went over your head?"

Culkin's smirk deepened. "Both."

"Is this your way of saying you didn't call?"

"Oh, I called. Like I'm going to put my head on the chief's chopping block to spite you."

Quinn picked up the notepad, but the lieutenant snatched it back.

"If you called WSP," Quinn asked, "why didn't you take notes?"

"Because there are protocols and privacy concerns.

Nothing can fall back on either side. You understand."

Quinn crossed his arms. "You sound like a bunch of spies."

"Play it how you like, Detective." Culkin pointed the notepad at Quinn. "They're watching your boy."

"For?"

"They can't figure out where he's getting his money. He owns these side businesses—these group homes. The money seems fishy, and they want to know how he got them."

Quinn's brow furrowed. "Did they come out and ask?"

"They did. They didn't like his answer."

"Which was?"

Culkin looked at his blank notepad. "Something with borrowing money, but their concerns are not our problem."

"There are two murdered individuals who might think differently."

The lieutenant cocked his head. "You've got a second murder now?"

"County does."

Culkin rolled his eyes. "Don't go case shopping, Delaney. It makes you look greedy. What I'm telling you is what WSP knows. They're watching Bishop. They can't figure out if he's working drugs or skimming money from somewhere. If he is, they haven't found it yet. And they've randomly drug-tested him."

"Randomly?"

Culkin shrugged. "He's come back clean both times. If they do it again, it'll wind up as a union claim of a hostile work environment."

"What you're saying is WSP thinks he smells dirty, but they can't find the origin of the stink."

The lieutenant held up the notepad and pointed at it. "Unofficially."

"Protocols and privacy concerns." Quinn turned back to his desk. "I got it."

***

An email alert popped up on Quinn's computer. It was from Donald Faust with the subject line: *More Bishop Properties.*

He opened it immediately. There was no greeting inside—just an attached file. Quinn double-clicked it. Listed in the file were six names along with the corresponding property addresses.

Bad Bishop, LLC
Bishop's Endgame, LLC
Bishop's Opening, LLC
Good Bishop, LLC
Fianchettoed Bishop, LLC
Horwitz Bishops, LLC

Quinn immediately sent the email to Marci.
"Hey," he said.
She looked over from her computer.
"I sent you an email with a list of LLCs. Do me a favor and verify that Jory Bishop is in each of those."
"What are you going to do?"
"Research."
Quinn called up Google. The first four sounded like names of movies or books, but the last two were so odd that he wanted to start with one of them. He entered 'fianchettoed bishop' into the field and pressed Enter.

Several of the results included 'chess terms.' Quinn selected one. It turned out that fianchetto was an Italian word and referred to moving a pawn to free up the bishop on the long diagonal. Quinn ran through the remaining terms and confirmed they were all chess related. He turned to Marci.

"Jory Bishop," she said. "He's in them all."

"The LLCs are all chess terms. Like the others."

"So how many does that make? This is six."

"There were six before so twelve. The guy owns twelve group homes. Well, I'm assuming this new batch is group homes." Quinn crossed his arms. "Geez."

"Geez?"

"You know what I mean."

"Yeah, grandma, I know what you mean. You're wondering where a guy like him gets that kind of money."

Quinn cocked his head. "Are we looking at it the wrong way?"

"How so?"

"It's like Kirby."

Marci's face soured. "Why are you bringing him up?"

"To make a point."

"Should I bring up your ex-wife?"

"If a valid point needed to be made, maybe."

She crossed her arms. "Can you make this one without bringing up an ex-boyfriend?"

Quinn thought about it. "No."

Marci's chin dropped to her chest. "Go on."

"You know that rental property he had?"

"Of course, I do."

"And how I was bothered that a young guy like him could afford one like it?"

She looked up and frowned. "Now you're bringing his age into the discussion?"

"I'm making a point."

"Make it quick."

"The point is this—I'm less worried about how a guy like Bishop gets his money now."

Marci pulled back. "Oh, I'm sure WSP's IA will be happy to hear that."

"Remember when the DEA went after that downtown restaurant operator?"

"Yeah."

"They investigated him for two years."

"At least."

Quinn continued. "How much money did they spend to do that? A lot. And they brought in the IRS and the FBI. All because some agents couldn't figure out how the guy made his money. The guy's record was impeccable—college graduate and a veteran—but they still went after him. Why? Because they couldn't wrap their heads around what an entrepreneur does. I'm not saying I'd understand it any better."

Marci tapped her desk as she thought. "That was the case with the big write-up in the paper, right? A couple years back."

"And do you remember what the guy got out of it? He had to agree to an improperly filled-out loan application. *One.*" Quinn held up a single finger. "Out of how many applications the guy filled out correctly? No jail time. No fines levied or paid. Just an admission that he filled out a document wrong so the feds could justify their time and treasure spent."

"To your point?"

Quinn fell back into his chair. "What if Bishop did everything right with the money?"

"What if he didn't?"

He waved her off. "Don't go down that rabbit hole until we find evidence of such. Otherwise, we might be doing exactly what the DEA, the FBI, and the IRS did."

"Yeah, okay." Marci rested an elbow on her desk. "And you needed to bring up Kirby to get to that point?"

"Maybe not, but it got me started."

"Got me started, too."

"Anyway, my thinking is this." Quinn rested his elbows on his knees. "Bishop isn't trying to disguise how he got the money. He doesn't care who knows. He isn't hiding his ownership in the properties. Every LLC we've found has Bishop's name prominently on it. Am I right? And you're not having any trouble finding he's the registered agent."

Marci's nose scrunched. "So now you're thinking he's not our guy?"

"I'm not saying that—no. What I am saying is we shouldn't be concerned about *how* he got the money. We should be concerned with what he's doing to *protect* the money."

Marci's eyes went toward the ceiling. "Ah."

"Right? Elise said if Bishop loses the license on the Fleming house, he loses them all. Is that because the Fleming house is the base for the house of cards? Or are the cards tied together in some weird matrix?"

Marci's eyes narrowed. "If you flick one out—doesn't matter which—the whole thing comes down."

Both detectives stared at their computer screens.

"Maybe you're on to something," Marci muttered.

Quinn stood and grabbed his jacket from the back of his chair. "Let's make another run at Bishop tomorrow."

"Now, you think we have enough?"

"I'd like to have more, but we can't wait around forever. You said that. From what this guy has shown, he's a chess player. Is he the type that pushes an advantage, or does he lay in wait?"

Now Marci stood. "I don't play chess."

"Don't like the strategy aspect?"

"I like strategy fine. There's just not enough punching in that game."

***

That night, Quinn sat at his computer in his apartment. He ate a piece of leftover meatloaf while he scrolled through one of the blogs he occasionally read. He'd skipped running earlier and instead decided to distract himself with the help of the internet.

His cell phone rang. The ID screen showed the caller to be Lieutenant Brand. Quinn thought about ignoring it. If he was being assigned another homicide, it would usually come through dispatch.

Usually.

He swallowed his bite then answered. "Delaney."

"Lieutenant Brand. Patrol found the video."

Quinn's mind immediately went to the parking lot footage outside the county jail. He'd written the warrant on it earlier in the day, and Marci got it executed. After they delivered the paperwork to Sergeant Truitt, all their bases were covered.

"Sir?"

Brand said, "I was back at the office on an unrelated homicide. Anyway, a patrol officer just brought it in and hand-delivered it to me. I've watched it. It shows a Dodge Challenger parking in a lot behind a used record store about a half a mile up Monroe."

"They had a camera on the back?"

"Whoever would want to steal old records is beyond me, but that seems to be a concern in our city. Anyway, a man in a hooded sweatshirt gets out of the car. He's not wearing sunglasses. I'm emailing you a picture of him now."

"Thank you for the call."

"Don't hang up, Delaney. Look at the picture. Tell me this is our guy."

Quinn removed the phone from his ear and opened the

email app on it. There was a new email from Lieutenant George Brand with no subject line. He tapped it, then opened the attached photograph.

"Is that our guy?" Brand asked. His voice sounded as if it were at the bottom of the well.

Quinn held the phone back to his ear. "Yeah. That's him."

"Fantastic," Brand said. "I'll update the chain of command."

Chapter 23

The two detectives stared at Quinn's computer screen as they watched the video footage a second time. A long shadow stretched across a large section of the little lot. A gray Dodge Challenger pulled into the darkened corner. There was no front license plate on the Challenger. The car sat in the shadow for five seconds—Quinn counted them—before the driver's door opened.

What was the driver doing during that time? Grabbing his gloves? Pulling out his cell phone to leave in the car, or would he have left it at home? Or was he contemplating the actions he was about to take?

A figure emerged from the car and stepped into the shadow. It was difficult to see the man—only a shape could be discerned. Had the driver stayed within that strip of darkness, this video might have been worthless.

But the man didn't stay there. Instead, he walked toward the alley and was illuminated by the light on the back of the building. He stopped and stared directly up at the camera. His face registered surprise then disappointment. His shoulders slumped slightly, and he looked about.

Jory Bishop wore a black hooded sweatshirt, blue jeans, and black boots. In his right hand appeared to be a pair of black gloves. Quinn assumed the sunglasses were in the pocket of the sweatshirt. He shook his head, walked toward the alley, then disappeared around the corner.

The time stamp on the video was 3:11 a.m.

"With the other video," Marci said, "we've got him dead-to-rights."

Quinn nodded but remained silent.

On the monitor, the video flickered, and the time jumped forward to 4:07.

Jory Bishop casually walked back into the lot. He climbed into his car and reversed into the alley behind the building.

"I couldn't see the back license plate," Quinn said.

"Doesn't matter. We can see his face."

"Still. I would have loved to prove that was his vehicle."

Marci smirked. "I would have loved a video of him entering Ray Christy's home, but that isn't going to happen either. We work with what we've got. What's wrong with you?"

"I want to make this stick."

"It will."

Quinn nodded. "Then let's bring him in."

***

Jory Bishop leaned back in his chair. He wore a lightweight jacket and a black t-shirt. His face was unshaven, but his hair was combed today. He still appeared tired. His thumb dropped into his empty holster, and a finger absently flicked the unbuttoned safety strap. "Why am I here?"

"We have some follow-up questions—" Quinn placed his hand on top of a manila folder "—to clarify a few things."

They were seated in Interview Room #2. A small metal table was between the men. Marci stood in the corner with her arms crossed.

"I'm not sure if I'm cool with this," Bishop said. "Am I free to go?"

Quinn nodded. "At this point, yes."

Bishop's chair fell forward with a thunk. "At this point?" He glanced at Marci then returned his attention to Quinn. "Maybe I should have my lawyer."

"Already admitting you've been put in check?"

Bishop frowned. "Huh?"

"Relax. We're just talking." Quinn pointed high up on the wall. "If this was official, that light bulb would be lit red, and we'd be recording."

Bishop shrugged. "So, we're just talking."

"That's right."

The trooper leaned back in his chair again. "If that's the case, then why'd you ask for my gun?"

"Protocol. Besides, we left ours outside to make you feel better."

Bishop pointed to Marci, who stood in the corner.

"It's two against one," he said.

"You're scared of me?" She smiled demurely. "I'm flattered."

Bishop turned to Quinn. "Does she need to be here?"

"Don't let her spook you."

"She's not—"

Quinn interrupted. "Can we get back to why we asked you here?"

Bishop picked at something imaginary on the wall. "I get what you're doing."

"We're not doing anything."

"Sure you are but go ahead and ask your questions." Bishop looked at Quinn again. "If I don't like them, I'm leaving."

"So you can avoid the checkmate?"

Bishop cocked his head. "Excuse me?"

"What got you into chess?" Quinn asked.

"How do you know—"

"Was it the last name?"

Bishop's lips briefly twisted before he answered. "My

dad taught me. He said with a name like ours, we better learn how to play, or we should get into the church. He drank too much and swore like a cop to be of much use for the Lord.”

“Are you any good?”

“At chess?” Bishop shrugged. “Better than my dad, I guess. Haven’t played since college. I sort of outgrew it. How about you?”

“I don’t play.”

Bishop eyed Marci.

“No,” she said.

Quinn turned the folder to open it so Bishop couldn’t see inside. He pulled out a sheet of paper then slid it across the table. “Tell me about those.”

Bishop’s chair dropped to the floor again, and he leaned over the paper. “There’s nothing illegal there. Go ahead and try to find something. Everything is so above board it’ll make your head spin—attorneys and accountants every which way you turn.”

“Twelve properties,” Quinn said. “How’s a guy build something like that?”

“By understanding money. That’s not illegal. If that’s what this is about—” Bishop waved his hand about “—then you’re going to be sorely disappointed, and I’m going to have a conversation with your supervisor.”

“What did you call them? Adult care facilities?”

“Adult residential care facilities. What about them?”

“And the state regulates them?”

“Seriously?” Bishop checked his watch then stood. “Listen. I’m on the clock. My team needs me.”

“Your supervisor knows you’re here.”

“Say what?” Bishop’s face reddened.

“Our boss talked with your boss. Everything’s fine.”

“You had no right.”

Quinn said, “Don’t overreact. Your sergeant thinks

you're helping us with a case. When you leave here, tell him whatever you want. We don't care."

"You had no right," he repeated.

"What's done is done," Quinn said. "Take a seat, and let's get through these questions. Then you can get on your way."

Bishop's brow furrowed as he considered his options. When he came to a decision, he glanced at Marci. "Don't just stand there." He sounded irritated. "Grab a chair or leave for all I care."

"I'm good," she said.

"Suit yourself. Your face is looking better, by the way."

Marci didn't respond. Now wasn't the time for verbal jousting.

Quinn pulled the list of properties back. "How's the licensing work? Each property has its own LLC, right? Does that mean you're working with twelve adult care facility licenses, too?"

"How's this important?"

"Humor me."

Bishop rubbed his chin before answering. "There's a single master license with the state." He waved his hand toward the piece of paper. "That one license covers the entity that leases the properties from the various LLCs."

"What's the entity that owns the business?"

"Bishop Enterprises."

Quinn ran his finger down the list to confirm that he hadn't heard of that business before. "Bishop Enterprises doesn't own any real estate; it leases the houses?"

"That's right."

"You're leasing from yourself," Quinn said. "It's a shell game."

"No, it's not." Bishop exaggeratedly rolled his eyes. "It's how money moves. Keep your interests separate, leverage the tax advantages of all entity types, and never commingle your real estate with your business."

"Why not mix the two?"

Bishop frowned. "What is this? A master's class in entrepreneurship?"

"We're just talking."

"I should charge you for it."

Quinn sat quietly.

"Yeah, whatever. Amateurs mix the concepts, but if you think long and strategically about it then you'll see a time when you may want to sell the business. Or maybe you'll need to sell the real estate to raise capital for further expansion because the business itself is far more profitable. It's about having options."

"Always have an out. Like chess."

"Like business."

Quinn again opened the folder in such a manner as to hide what was inside. He pulled another document from it. "Tell me about Kayla Reed." He slid the photo of her driver's license to Bishop.

"What about her?"

"She worked for you."

The trooper's eyes narrowed. "She quit."

"Did she actually do that?"

"The hell does that mean?"

Quinn shifted in his chair. "We heard she left and never came back."

"That's the same as quitting."

"Is it?"

Bishop smirked. "Have you ever owned a business? I didn't think so. People don't always call in and conveniently give notice. That would be nice, but this is real life. Sometimes they just stop showing up. You'll know this since you used to be in patrol—they still require you to do that before they let you be a detective, right? People's lives are messy. When you're their boss, you get pulled into that cluttered bullshit. Sometimes they stop showing up, and you gotta say 'good riddance' to them. Better to bring in someone new than to worry about where the old employee went."

Quinn nodded. "And that's how Elise Morrow came to the property?"

"Elise was already working at another property. She's helping on the Fleming house until I find a replacement. It's difficult to hire people to do that job. Required skills and such."

Quinn pointed at Kayla's picture. "Why do you think she quit?"

Bishop's gaze traveled up to the unlit bulb. When he looked at Quinn again, he shrugged. "Who knows? The young are prone to rash decisions."

"What day did she not show up?"

Bishop stared at him, and his eyes narrowed. He opened his mouth to speak but slowly closed it. He inhaled deeply then exhaled through his nose. "She came in last Thursday morning."

"Thursday?"

"That's correct."

"The day Margaret drowned?"

"Kayla came in that morning, then took off right after she found Margaret."

Quinn eyed Marci before asking, "Are you sure of that?

"No, but it's the only thing that makes sense. Margaret was the first person who died under her watch. She probably freaked out."

"But Vera Drayton discovered Margaret in the bathroom."

Bishop shrugged. "Vera reported it, but I think Kayla found her first."

"Then took off without notifying anyone?"

"What do you want me to say? She was weak. She saw a dead woman and quit. It's the only connection I can make. Unless she figured out that I was about to fire her and quit to avoid that."

"Why were you going to fire her?"

"Because she was terrible at her job."

Quinn turned slightly in his chair. "We were told you were going to fire her because you thought she was stealing."

Bishop glanced at Marci, then his eyes traveled up the wall to the darkened red bulb.

"Elise told us," Quinn said.

"I suspected Kayla of stealing," Bishop said, "but I never had any proof."

"Do you suspect her of stealing Margaret's wallet?"

"I won't speculate on that."

Quinn stared directly into Bishop's eyes. "Why won't you? Especially if you were about to fire her."

"Because I won't."

In the corner, Marci lowered her arms to clasp her hands. "A death in an adult care facility is normal, but a theft wouldn't look good."

Bishop eyed her. "Like I said, I won't speculate."

"Elise originally told us that Kayla left on Wednesday, then changed her tune to Thursday. Why would she do that?"

"I won't speculate on that either."

"You also told us Kayla left on Wednesday."

Bishop cocked his head. "I did?"

"At breakfast."

"I remember," Marci said. "You did."

"Must've had my days wrong. Kayla was there Thursday morning but took off early."

Quinn pulled another piece of paper from the folder. It

was a photograph of Kayla Reed lying in a shallow grave. He held it so Bishop couldn't see it. "We saw Kayla yesterday."

"Yeah?" Bishop said. "How's she doing?"

"Not so good." He placed the photograph in front of Bishop. The trooper studied it. "You don't seem upset by it."

Bishop shrugged. "I've seen dead people before."

"But she was your employee."

"So? She wasn't family. She wasn't even a friend." Bishop's gaze returned to the photo. "What happened to her?"

"Someone beat her and strangled her."

"Where was she found?"

"In Elk."

"Huh." Bishop slid the photograph back. "I hope you find whoever did that to her."

"Me, too," Quinn said. He tucked the Kayla photograph back into the folder. "Tell me about Ray Christy."

"This again?" Bishop looked toward the ceiling. "We've already been over this."

"You said you had a friendly conversation outside of jail."

"I said that?"

"You did, but we've seen the video footage. It didn't seem friendly at all."

Bishop chuckled. "Big deal. I told the old man to stay away from me and my businesses. What of it? That's not an arrestable offense."

Quinn's eyes narrowed. "You seem stressed out."

"Because of your question about the old man? Get the fuck out."

"Doesn't he look stressed out to you, Marci?"

She nodded. "Totally."

Bishop slid his chair back until it banged against the wall. He stood. "I've had about enough."

"It looks like you're not sleeping lately," Quinn said. "Like you've been burning the candle at both ends."

"Maybe he feels guilty about something," Marci added.

Bishop flicked his hand. "You don't know nothing. I don't feel guilty about shit."

"Then what is it?" Quinn motioned for the man to take his seat.

"I'm leaving."

"Then tell me why you look stressed all the time."

"It's the job."

Quinn smirked. "Don't feed us that. We do the same job. You gotta come up with something better than that."

Bishop shook his head. "It's a deal I'm working. Maybe you don't know what goes into all that, but that's what's eating me up." He tapped his chest. "I've got a lot riding on it."

"A deal?" Quinn extended his hand again—another invitation for Bishop to return to his seat.

The trooper eyed Quinn with suspicion.

"You don't have to tell us."

Marci scoffed. "Yeah. It's not like we've got the money to do anything about it."

Bishop ran his tongue over his upper teeth. He sat again and pulled the chair closer to the table. "I'm trying to sell my business."

"Not the real estate?" Quinn asked.

"Good for you," Bishop said. "You were paying attention."

"How's it going?"

"Not great." Bishop's index finger lightly drummed on the table. "At first, I thought we'd get there, but the group I'm dealing with—they're out of Seattle—they're pushing hard for the real estate, too. I'd love to dump just the business aspect of it because it's such a pain in the ass now. I thought there would be an economies of scale thing that would have come into play long ago, but I don't believe that's possible with these smaller homes. It feels like I'm getting eaten alive by the business. I'd like to keep the real estate and just collect the mailbox money. You know? The rent? Anyway, I've put twenty-year leases in place on all the homes. I thought I was being smart, but it's coming back to bite me. The buyers either want the real estate, or they want me to rewrite the leases to one-year terms. It's me on both sides of those contracts, so I can easily kill them, but still. The buyers have non-compete language in our deal, so if they move out, I'm stuck with residential properties. Maybe it's not so bad, but I'll have to spend money to reconvert the properties back to single-family homes."

Quinn nodded. "There's a lot of money on the table."

"It's all right," Bishop said. "If I agree to sell the real estate, it's life-changing money. Do I want to do that, though? That's giving up cash flow for money today. I don't know."

Quinn rested his hand on the manila folder. "Ray Christy's poking around must have been aggravating during this time."

"You think?"

"When did you find out that he discovered a list of your properties?"

Bishop rolled his lower lip down. "I have no idea what you're talking about."

Quinn removed the earlier list from the folder and slid it back to Bishop. "We got most of that list from a contact of Ray's. The old guy discovered you owned a bunch of group homes. You must have found him snooping around some of them. Am I right?"

Bishop shook his head. "Never saw him anywhere but the Fleming Street house and the parking lot outside the jail."

"Is that so?"

"I just said it was."

Quinn pulled the list of LLCs to him and pretended to study it. "Ray made a mistake, though."

"What was that?"

"He thought you murdered Margaret Kelley."

Bishop barked a single laugh. "She drowned. I told him that."

"So did Detective Parker. Seems Ray couldn't resist playing Ellery Queen."

Bishop's brow furrowed. "Playing what?"

"Nancy Drew," Marci said.

Bishop turned his head slightly. "What are you two babbling about?"

"Amateur sleuths," Quinn said. "Except in the TV shows, they're never murdered for their meddling."

Marci nodded. "That would sort of ruin the fun."

Bishop pointed at the folder. "I didn't have anything to do with Ray Christy's murder, and I didn't have anything to do with Kayla's either."

Quinn pulled out a small, white card from the manila folder. "I think it's time to read this." He flicked a switch in the wall, and the light bulb above them burned red.

Bishop reeled back. "The fuck?"

"You have the right to remain silent," Quinn said.

"What are you doing?"

"Anything you say can and will be used against you in a court of law."

Bishop stood abruptly. His chair skittered back and banged against the wall. "I'm not hanging around for this."

Quinn said, "Sit down."

"This is entrapment." Bishop moved toward the door, but Marci blocked his path. "Get out of the way, lady."

She dropped her height slightly as if preparing to jump one way or another. Her hands lifted into a defensive position.

Bishop's lip curled. "I'll blacken that other eye, bitch."

Now Quinn stood. "If you try, we'll arrest you for assaulting an officer. I'll remind you that you're being recorded."

The trooper looked back at Quinn, then his gaze went to the red light on the wall. His attention returned to Marci. "You got lucky."

She nodded. "I'm sure."

"Please sit, Mr. Bishop," Quinn said.

When the trooper took his seat, Quinn began the Miranda Warning over. "You have the right to remain silent."

Even though he'd read them uncountable times throughout his career, Quinn read every word as written. This was too important of a moment. When he finished, Quinn looked up. "Do you understand the rights I have just read to you?"

Bishop glared at him.

Quinn counted the seconds in his head. *One-thousand-one. One-thousand-two. One-thousand-three.* When he reached fifteen, he repeated, "Do you understand the rights—"

"Yes."

"With these rights in mind, do you wish to speak to me?"

Bishop's eyes narrowed, but he didn't answer immediately.

Quinn started counting again. *One-thousand-one. One-thou—*

Marci crossed her arms. "Check or checkmate?"

The trooper eyed her, then faced him. "You can't goad me into talking."

Quinn nodded but reread the last line of the card. "With these rights in mind, do you wish to speak to me?"

Bishop slapped the table. "Gimme a pen. I'll sign it. I want to see what you think you've got."

Quinn slid the card across the table along with a ballpoint pen.

"But when I say we're done, we're done, and you get my lawyer." Bishop scrawled his name across the bottom of the white card. When he finished, he flipped the pen onto the table and leaned back.

Quinn collected the ballpoint and the white card. "What kind of car do you drive?"

"My car? What's this got to do—"

"A Dodge Challenger," Quinn said. "Destroyer grey. I'm not a car guy, but that's a cool name for a color. I looked it up on the internet."

Bishop's eyes flicked to Marci then back to Quinn. "What's that got to do with anything?"

"Did you put Kayla Reed in the back of your car?"

"That's what you think?" Bishop laughed. "You're barking up the wrong tree, pal." He pulled a set of keys from his pocket and tossed them onto the table. "Test the car if you want. You'll get nothing." He fully faced Marci now. "Checkmate, my ass. You two are fishing." As an afterthought, he said, "I didn't do anything wrong, so why you're coming after me makes no sense."

Quinn eyed the car keys. He grabbed them and tossed them to Marci.

"You're really taking me up on the offer?" Bishop asked.

"Unless you don't want us to?"

"I don't care. Do what you want. It's in the west lot. If you think you'll find anything connected to Kayla in there, you're wrong."

Marci stepped from the room and closed the door behind her.

Quinn studied Bishop for a moment. "The way we figure it, Margaret Kelley drowned, and Kayla Reed panicked. Maybe she was short of cash which is why she took the woman's wallet."

Bishop rolled his eyes. "You're wrong. Give it a rest."

"We've submitted the wallet for fingerprints."

"Kayla lived in the same house as Margaret. That doesn't prove anything. Why aren't you trying to find her real killer?" Bishop's head canted. "Wait. Why *are* you investigating her murder? She was found in Elk. That's the county's jurisdiction." His eyes went to the door.

"Back to Ray Christy."

Bishop's brow furrowed. "I didn't have anything to do with that."

Quinn opened the manila folder and pulled out a photograph. He turned it upside down so only the white backing showed. "Whoever murdered Ray also stole his keys and ID badge. They didn't take his wallet or any money. We believe they took those items so they could break into the Monroe Court Building and gain access to the Volunteer Services office—a place where Ray Christy worked."

Bishop's eyes were drawn to the hidden picture.

Quinn flipped over the photograph of a hooded man in sunglasses. He pointed at the picture. "This man entered the building using Ray's ID card then entered the Volunteer Services' office."

"That's not me," Bishop said.

"Are you sure about that?"

"You bet, I'm sure." The trooper stood. "I'm done."

Quinn stood also. "Just a few more pictures."

"I'm leaving."

"You'll want to see these." Quinn removed three photographs. The first was of a destroyer grey Dodge Challenger pulling into the parking lot behind a used records store. The second was of a figure exiting the car. The third was a clear photograph of Jory Bishop wearing a hooded sweatshirt and looking up into the camera.

The trooper leaned over the table and stared at the three pictures.

"The record store had a recent break-in," Quinn said. "It was their third in eighteen months. Their insurance company suggested they put in a security camera before they paid out on the claim. They put it in three days before the day this footage was taken. You probably didn't even notice it when you pulled in that night. With how careful you'd been with everything else, you almost certainly scouted that location before. Or maybe you knew it existed for years and hung out there to do paperwork. But this look—" Quinn tapped the photo of Bishop staring into the lens "—shows how shocked you were to see a camera. But at that point, what choice did you have? You were there, and you were already seen."

"I parked there to meet a friend who lives in the neighborhood." Bishop sounded unconvincing.

"Which friend?"

The trooper's face darkened. "I'm not telling you, so you can go bother her."

"It's okay, Jory. I don't believe you."

"Well, fuck you, too."

Quinn tapped the photo of Bishop looking into the camera. "You pulled into the lot and stared into the camera. There was nothing you could do. The clock was ticking. Ray was dead, and you had no idea how quickly he'd be discovered. You had to get into the Volunteer Services' office."

"Why would I do any of what you're saying? It makes

no sense."

"Sure, it does. Ray kept a notebook just like any cop. Maybe it had entries about you in there. You had no way of knowing. There were also his printouts of the LLCs. Who knew what else he had? Well, you knew. Right? You beat an admission out of the old guy, didn't you?"

Bishop pointed at Quinn. "Say this to anyone, and I'll sue you."

"What else did you take from Ray?"

The trooper pushed the photographs away. "This is circumstantial. It can all be explained." He looked up. "You've got nothing."

The door to the interview room opened, and Marci stepped in. Two uniformed officers stood just outside. "The sunglasses were in there," she said. "I'll write up a search warrant to get them. What do you want to bet the hoodie is somewhere in his house?"

Bishop's gaze traveled around the room. He put his hand on the table as if to stabilize himself. "You're not going to find anything," he said.

"But we will find something. Won't we?" Quinn reached for the trooper's hand. "Jory Bishop, you're under arrest for the murder of Raymond Christy."

"I want my lawyer."

"You'll get a call at jail."

Bishop looked up at the red light on the wall. "I want my lawyer!"

Epilogue

Captain Ackerman draped his arm over Quinn's cubicle. "Nice work, big hitters. That's a huge one for the win column."

Quinn nodded. "Thank you, sir."

Marci pushed her chair back to better see the captain, but she didn't respond.

"How tight is the case?"

"It's thin," Quinn said. He stood now and put his hands in his pockets. "We've got a lot of circumstantial evidence. Nothing physical. No eyewitnesses."

Ackerman dropped his arm from the cubicle. "Nothing else?"

Now Marci stood and moved next to Quinn. "We searched Bishop's house and found the hoodie."

"It's a sweatshirt from Carhart," Quinn said. "They're a dime a dozen in this town. We've submitted it to the lab for testing, but we're betting he didn't wear it to Ray's house."

"What else were you hoping to find?"

Marci said, "Anything to tie him to Ray. Maybe Ray's keys or ID badge. Or Ray's notebook. We'd have been happy if we had found the printouts Ray got from his friend in the assessor's office."

Ackerman sighed. "But you got nothing. Can you get him to talk anymore?"

Quinn shook his head. "He lawyered up. And the longer he thinks about it, the more he's going to realize we're working with smoke and mirrors. If it goes to trial—"

"It'll go to trial," Ackerman said flatly. His face

hardened, and his jaw flexed. "He's not walking on this one."

Marci nodded. "And a guy like Bishop would never plea to it."

They all paused for a moment to let the reality of a plea deal settle on them.

"When it goes to trial," Quinn said, "we're going to need the prosecuting attorneys to spin one helluva story for the jurors. They're really going to have to connect the dots on this."

"Worry about what we can do. If the attorneys screw it up, it's on them. We've done our job. Are we forgetting anything?"

Quinn said, "We wrote a warrant for Bishop's phone records. Hopefully, we'll get a ping on his GPS that puts him at Ray's house or out with Kayla Reed's body. Either would be great, but we're not hopeful. It's our guess that he left the phone at home. He'd know it could be tracked."

"We do what we can. Speaking of the county, how are they coming with their case?"

Marci shrugged. "It's still early."

Ackerman considered both detectives. "Still, nice work. You guys did good."

As the captain walked away, Detective Andrew Parker approached. "Did Ackerman give you the big-hitter bullshit?"

Quinn shrugged a single shoulder. "I'll take it over the alternative."

"What about you, Burkett? You probably liked that sunshine up your skirt."

Marci frowned. "What's your problem, Parker?"

"Nothing. It's the luck of the rotation, I guess. I get the drowning victim, and you get the big-time homicide."

Quinn said, "We'd have been happy if you dealt with

the administration on this one. You could have taken all the heat.”

“Heat?” Parker scoffed. “They asked what you were doing. That’s part of your job. Quit being a couple of pussies.”

“That’s offensive,” Marci said.

“Oh, I’m sorry, Burkett.” Parker made a face. “I didn’t know you were on your period. Do you wanna call HR and lodge a complaint?”

“Parker, you got me all wrong. I handle my own complaints.” She acted as if she were about to throw a punch. Parker flinched backward, caught his foot on Quinn’s chair, and tumbled to the floor. He scrambled upright.

Marci chuckled as she sat at her desk.

Parker pointed at Quinn. “That woman ain’t right.”

***

Quinn and Marci climbed out of the unmarked patrol car. They parked at the furthest edge of the lot—not out of respect for friends or family but because there were no closer spaces available.

“He must have been a popular guy,” Marci said.

“You meet a few people along the way to seventy-two years.”

She glanced around. “I think this is different. Feels like it, at least.”

They walked toward the church. Several other latecomers joined them. Most of them were senior citizens. They smiled politely at the detectives but didn’t offer to speak. Quinn and Marci remained silent.

It wasn’t normal for them to attend a victim’s funeral, but as the chief pointed out several times, Ray Christy wasn’t a usual fatality. He’d been a member of the department. Besides, Chief Dillon had informed them he would speak at the service and asked if they would be in attendance. Since the memorial was on a Friday afternoon, it was hard not to say yes. They'd be paid for their time, and it looked good politically.

Inside the church's lobby, several attendees waited to sign the guest book. The detectives skipped it and headed for the main hall.

A large screen hung on the back wall above the dais. Ray Christy's picture was centered in it. Underneath it were the words *In Remembrance.*

There was a smattering of available places to sit.

"Let's stand," Quinn said. He moved to a position along the back wall.

Marci shuffled next to him. "Who else do we know from here?"

Quinn's gaze went to the front pews. Seated next to each other were Heidi and Pamela Christy. On the left of Heidi sat a teenager. Quinn guessed that to be her son. "Ray's family is up there."

"I meant from the department. Is that Brand and Ackerman near the family?" Marci pointed.

Quinn nodded. "Where's the chief?"

"He's on the other side. Sitting with a big guy."

"Who's he with?"

Marci shrugged. "No idea."

Quinn continued searching the crowd. There was an overwhelming amount of light blue shirts—the signature color of the volunteer program. Most of the wearers had gray hair. Some were extremely young—members of the explorers or co-op programs. Quinn couldn't see their faces to correctly ascertain their ages, but he was surprised to see so many young people here. They should have been in class at that time of day—either high school or college.

There were a handful of dark blue uniforms that sat among the volunteers. Quinn didn't know who they were and imagined them to be reserve officers.

"Nice to see you two."

Both Quinn and Marci turned to see Yvette Oliver. She wore a community corrections jacket, blue jeans, and black shoes. "Quite the turnout."

"You knew Ray Christy?" Quinn asked.

"He came into our shop all the time. He was friends with Cliff Beck, the head of COPS West." She pointed to the front. "He's sitting with the chief."

Quinn looked at the big man sitting next to Dillon. "Huh."

"You guys knew what Ray was like," Yvette said. "It's no secret why he's getting this kind of turnout. I'm going miss him popping in to say hello."

A well-dressed man walked onto the dais and moved toward the lectern. "Good morning," he said. His voice sounded loud and clear through the church's speaker system. "I'm Pastor Meese. Thank you for joining us this morning as we celebrate the life of Ray Christy."

As the pastor talked, Quinn scanned the crowd. He noticed Dixie Richter from the records department sitting with the other volunteers. A row behind her, Quinn saw the guy from the assessor's office. He struggled to remember the man's name. Donald something or other. It began with an F.

Fawcett, he thought, but that didn't seem right. He gave up and continued scanning.

There was a small cluster of uniformed SPD officers. He knew a few in the group. That was the problem with being in the detective's office for so long. More officers entered the department, and he no longer knew them all.

Quinn stepped forward and checked out those who stood along the back wall. Several other patrol officers were standing there with solemn looks on their faces. They probably took that position in the event they needed to leave quickly.

There were no detectives other than Quinn and Marci in attendance. Quinn wondered where Nash and Higgins were. They seemed to like Ray Christy.

"What are you doing?" Marci whispered.

"Nothing," he said and resumed his position.

Quinn stopped searching the crowd and paid attention to Pastor Meese. He was speaking about how long he'd known Ray and his wife, Audrey.

Faust—that was the guy from the assessor's office. Quinn was happy that he remembered the name. It would have bugged him if he couldn't have recalled it.

Marci leaned over and pulled him down so she could whisper in his ear. "Where's Sergeant Newman?"

Quinn straightened and searched the crowd. He couldn't imagine the sergeant not being there. Not only did he run the program, but he must have known the chief was going to be in attendance. The gaffe would most certainly be noticed.

As if on cue, Newman walked into the main hall and proceeded down the center aisle. He stopped near a pew full of younger volunteers. He motioned for them to scoot over. When they made room for him, he dropped into his seat.

"Now," Pastor Meese said, "the family has asked Chief Dillon of the Spokane Police Department to say a few words."

The chief stood, and all heads turned in his direction. He walked up to the dais and nodded his thanks to the pastor. When Dillon took his position behind the lectern, he pulled a notecard from his pocket.

The chief straightened and looked out at the crowd. "Ray Christy was my friend." His voice cracked. "More than that, he was a member of the Spokane Police Department. He was part of our family, and we take care of ours."

Quinn studied the mass of volunteers. They watched the chief speak with rapt attention. At that moment, Quinn felt shame.

Those volunteers, especially the seniors, cared far more about the department and its mission than he did about them. Considering the lack of officer presence in the church, Quinn had the feeling he wasn't the only one.

He eyed Marci. She appeared to be struggling with her emotions. Was she feeling the same thing?

Quinn's attention returned to the chief, but he didn't hear the man's words. Instead, he concentrated on Ray's family in the front row.

***

Quinn entered The Max and looked around. He found her sitting in a booth with her head bowed over a menu. A place setting and a menu were already waiting for him. He slid into the seat across from her.

"Sorry, I'm late, Babs."

Barbara shrugged. "No worries. Work?"

"Needed to run home and change. Didn't want to bring the office to our date."

"Is that what this is?" Barbara leaned back in her seat. "Because I'm seeing someone. I thought you knew that."

"It's not that kind of date." Although Quinn wished it could be.

"Then what is it?"

"A friend date," he said. "Don't you ever have those?"

"Not with my ex-husbands."

Quinn cast a sideways glance. "How many ex-husbands do you have?"

"Just you, and we don't do friend dates."

"We can start."

A server came over. He asked, "Can I grab you a drink, sir?"

Quinn shook his head. "Water's fine."

When the server walked away, Barbara pulled her glass of wine closer. "What's going on with you? I agreed to meet because it sounded like there might be something important to discuss."

"Like what?"

"I don't know. Maybe you met someone and are getting married."

"Is that what you're doing?" Quinn hoped he hid the disappointment on his face.

Barbara's brow furrowed. "What? No. I've just started seeing— It doesn't matter. This is why exes don't have friend dates."

"Why not?"

"It's weird."

"But I like you."

"I like you, too." Barbara's smile was kind but almost patronizing. It quickly disappeared. "But it's still weird."

"I don't understand why we can't make it work."

"Because we used to be in love—"

"I still love you."

Barbara frowned disapprovingly. "This is why."

Quinn looked down at the menu.

They sat quietly for several moments. Eventually, Barbara asked, "What's this really about, Quinn?"

"What are you having?"

When she didn't respond, he looked up and sighed. Quinn pushed his menu to the side. "Are you happy?"

"Relatively. Are you?"

"I guess."

She cocked her head. "Are you depressed?"

"No."

"Then what is it? Are you dying?"

He laughed. "No. I'm fine."

"Then tell me."

Quinn watched a couple enter the restaurant. They held the other's hand as they waited to be helped. He said, "I handled a case this week. The victim was seventy-two, retired military, married, three kids, grandkids—"

"You saying you want kids?"

"People liked him."

"People like you, too."

He shrugged.

"I mean it. Even during the divorce, you were nice. That means a lot. Are you going to tell me what this is about?" Barbara glanced around their table. "Why did you ask to meet for dinner?"

"I don't have any friends, Babs."

"Sure you do."

He shook his head.

"What about Mike?"

"Colleen was your friend. Mike and I only did things with you two."

"Okay." Barbara's eyes went up as she thought. "How about Steve?"

"He got married. We haven't hung out since before our divorce."

"I didn't know. You can still call him."

Quinn waved her off. "We weren't those types of friends."

"What about guys in the department?"

"No," he said. "The older I've gotten, the less in common I have with most of those guys."

"Then what about Marci?"

"She's cool, but if we did anything together, it would

send the gossip factory into overdrive."

"Is she seeing anyone? Maybe you two could go out? Like on a real date."

Quinn emphatically shook his head. "She's not seeing anyone, but that will never be us. We're partners, and even if we weren't, Marci's not my type."

"What's your type?"

He raised an eyebrow.

"I'm seeing someone. You want me to set you up?"

"No."

"Then what?"

Quinn leaned back in his seat. "I don't know. I guess my life feels safe and boring."

Barbara laughed. "Are you for real?"

He felt immediately embarrassed.

"You're a Major Crimes detective, Quinn. There's nothing boring or safe about your life."

"You don't understand."

She nodded. "Sure, I do. You've got the blues. Everybody gets them now and then."

He looked away.

"I know you, Quinn, and I'll tell you what you need."

"What's that, Babs?" He was slightly irritated that Barbara was talking to him in that way. "And if you say a woman—"

Her nose crinkled. "I'd never say that."

"Thank you."

"What you need is a vacation."

"I've taken a vacation."

"Oh, you have? When's the last time you've been away from Spokane for more than a day?"

He shrugged.

"New York, wasn't it? With that yoga instructor. What's her name?"

"Doesn't matter."

Barbara rested her elbows on the table. "That was two years ago, Quinn. Taking some days off and hanging out at home isn't getting away. You need a break—a real one. Get out of town. Just get away from all the death and sadness you see every day."

The server returned then. "Are you ready to order?"

"Are we going to have dinner?" Quinn asked.

"Yes," she said, "and we're going to plan your vacation."

"Going somewhere?" the server asked.

"Looks like it," Quinn said.

Did You Enjoy the Book?

Thank you for reading *The Only Death That Matters* and visiting the 509! I hope you enjoyed meeting some of the recurring characters. This is a continuing series with other characters occasionally stepping into the lead role. There are two parallel series to the 509 Crime Stories—the Flip-Flop Detective and the John Cutler mysteries. I hope you'll check them out.

I'm always grateful when a reader takes time out of their day to comment on one of my novels. If you do write a review, please email me, and let me know.

I'd love to say thanks!

About the Author

Colin Conway is the creator of the 509 Crime Stories, a series of novels set in Eastern Washington with revolving lead characters. They are standalone tales and can be read in any order.

He also created the Cozy Up series which pushes the envelope of the cozy genre. Libby Klein, author of the Poppy McAllister series, says *Cozy Up to Death* is "Not your grandma's cozy."

Colin co-authored the Charlie-316 series. The first novel in the series, *Charlie-316*, is a political/crime thriller that has been described as "riveting and compulsively readable," "the real deal," and "the ultimate ride-along."

He served in the U.S. Army and later was an officer of the Spokane Police Department. He has owned a laundromat, invested in a bar, and run a karate school. Besides writing crime fiction, he is a commercial real estate broker.

Colin lives with his beautiful girlfriend, three wonderful children, and a codependent Vizsla that rules their world.

Find out more about Colin at colinconway.com.